A GIFT OF ONYX

Also by Jocelyn Kettle

THE ATHELSONS

A
GIFT OF ONYX

by Jocelyn Kettle

G. P. Putnam's Sons
New York

Capy 2
Bm

A GIFT OF ONYX

I

THE nursery had been dry-scrubbed with sand in the morning. The draft was still seeking out its fine white particles and sketching delicate, frondlike patterns along the joins in the boards of the floor. The child watched, unconsciously absorbing this prosaic domestic detail, and long after she had ceased to recall the occasion for her grief with any clarity, a newly sand-scrubbed room would always lay a chill upon her as though it were damp from a washing.

But now the present anguish was enough. It held her in uncanny stillness, half kneeling, half crouching in the shadows, and yet the small white face told nothing. If there had been a trace of wonder about the brow, a puckering of the mouth, it would have been more natural. If there had been tears, so much the better.

"There! It's no use you grieving. Come and sit with me and be comfortable, do!" The woman in the high-backed chair, close to the fire, seemed to address her full attention to her sewing, but her eyes strayed continually across the room while she worked. She had been trying for upwards of an hour to find the right words to break the silence, but it was not easy. In the end she spoke out of desperation and sounded more impatient than she intended. She added more gently, "I fear you'll take a chill over there on such a cold night."

The only response was the slight hunching of a shoul-

1

der as the child warded off any interruption of her own thoughts. Annie sighed. No, the Lady Eugenie was not an easy nursling. Not that she was ill-tempered or ill-behaved—never. But she was a one who lived very much "in herself," as Annie would often confide to the house-keeper, Mistress Grigg. Perhaps it came of being an only child.

A simple countrywoman, one of a large family, and not given to flights of fancy, Annie nevertheless tried hard to understand her charge. She tried to reach her on a different level.

"Why, just look at the way your rug do flap its wings tonight," she said on a sudden inspiration. "If we opened the window, I declare it would be gone!" Eugenie was listening at last. She had turned her head slightly to glance at the blue-green silkiness of the Persian rug, which was usually one of her chief delights with its design of curious beasts and armored Eastern princes. By candlelight, on a windy night such as this, with its fringe beating like a caged bird and the figures rippling into life, it never failed to beguile her. She would sit on it and trace the wonders of the pattern with her fingers.

Still, she did not move. Her hands lay loose in her lap, the palms turned upward in a gesture of supplication to the adult world which she did not understand.

"I'll warm some milk," Annie said soothingly. "Get you ready for your bed, and sleep will be the best healer. What's said is said, And what's done is done. We learn to live with it in the morning."

Quiet words of human wisdom, they made some sense to the child. There was a movement, a faint rustle. Annie was quick to press her advantage. "I'll set a pan on the fire. There . . . come and see it doesn't boil over while I get your nightgown. We'll have you between the sheets before you know it."

Slowly, testing the strength of her cramped limbs, the child uncurled herself and stood up, leaning against the

2

wall for support. Called back to reality, she was aware of the cold and began to shiver uncontrollably.

"Yes, it is just as I supposed. You are half perished, poor lamb." Annie swept across the room. "Let me help you. Next thing we know you'll be ill and set the whole house in an uproar." She would have put her arm around the shaking shoulders, but Eugenie stepped away from her.

"I thank you, I am not cold . . . at least only a very little. The fire will soon warm me."

"Watch the milk then," Annie said. She knew better than to force any demonstrative behavior on this child and instead began to make a deliberate bustle about her tasks, humming a familiar nursery song while she turned down the bed, arranged the silk curtains around it, and poured water for washing from a silver ewer.

She was tying the last tapes on Eugenie's nightgown before she attempted to reopen the painful subject uppermost in both their minds.

"You'll be saying your prayers now."

"Yes."

"I fear you displeased your parents today. You'll have a word to say to God about that." Annie was a great believer in the efficacy of unloading a troubled spirit in prayer.

"Yes." It was firmly spoken, but the eyelids fluttered and were downcast.

"No need to take this too hard, though," Annie added, striving to get the balance right. "You are a pretty-behaved girl most of the time, and we are allowed a mistake when we are eight years old. I make no doubt your mother—" The brown eyes opened widely at her, searching, and Annie paused, and bit her lip. Devil take the Lady Madeleine Carle that she had not the motherliness in her to know the child must be fretting and come to smooth matters before she slept! "I make no doubt your mother and your father will have forgotten and forgiven by tomorrow," she concluded with more confidence than she felt.

Would it serve to comfort? Hardly. The child knew, as children always do, when there is doubt behind reassuring words. Annie, making officious adjustments to the lace nightcap over the shining pale-gold hair, felt her own inadequacy. She was not judge, and she dared not even be advocate.

"I will stay with you until you are asleep, sweeting."

Eugenie nodded compliantly. Mistress Grigg would have Annie's supper ready, but it was an easy thing to feign sleep.

Within ten minutes the nurse would be convinced, and with a further five she would be unburdening herself to a favored ear. She would have a deal to say on the subject of noble parents and the callous way in which they treated their offspring. She would say my Lord Carle and his lady should know better than to argue their differences where her innocent might overhear them, and indeed everyone else in the house for that matter. And, finally, Mistress Grigg proving as partial an audience as anyone could wish, she would list the dutiful qualities of her charge, exaggerate her accomplishments, and enact the scene she was least likely to play, where she presented herself in Lady Carle's boudoir and gave her a piece of her mind.

Through a chink in the bedcurtains Eugenie saw the clouds streaming across the face of the moon. A high wind blew around Carle House, and there was an illusion that the top floor—the nursery floor—was swaying. Eugenie liked the moonlight and the shapes it spun in the darkened room, and to please her, Annie would not cover the windows except in a frost. But tonight there was a sense of panic in the racing clouds, of flight rather than the chase for sport. She closed her eyes tightly and relived the terrible experiences of the afternoon. First there had been her father's voice, welcome confirmation

4

of his eagerly awaited arrival in London. He was in her mother's apartments, just below.

Eugenie could not resist creeping out to the head of the nursery stairs to press her face between the oak posts and wait for him to ask for her. Oh, he would surely ask for her! Annie was gone below to see the laundrywoman. How else should she know when he wanted to see her unless she listened? And then had come the dreadful realization that her father was angry. The familiar tones had an edge to them.

"And I say we will to Blowick this Christmastide." Only half the exchange reached her. Her mother's light, rapid manner of speaking did not carry, but the drift of the arguement was not beyond Eugenie's understanding.

They had spent last Christmas in London because her mother willed it so, and Lady Carle had dared to presume that once broken, the custom of the family keeping its festival at Blowick would not be reasserted. It was no secret that she detested Blowick Castle, remote on the Northumberland-Cumberland border. But here was her father back from his hunting lodge in Leicestershire and demanding why there were no preparations under way for the journey to Blowick.

"Devil take it, woman, do you think I would have ridden to London in such haste if I were not to escort you to Blowick? What do you mean you assumed I was merely joining you for Christmas? Why the deuce should you assume anything unless I have made my wishes clear? I wrote you Thursday I should be here today. Surely that indicated my purpose!"

Eugenie had gripped the stair rails ever more tightly. Hot tears filled her eyes. What was happening to the looked-for homecoming, the joyous time when her mother would not go out of an evening, but would sit with her father in the salon after dinner and she would be sent for and petted, and taken on her father's knee, and have her mother stroke her hair while asking her questions in French and Italian to show she had learned her lessons well.

"Lady, you are much above yourself to dare govern me." Her father was shouting. Eugenie had seen him displeased with servants but never so angry and never ... never with her mother. "You have your style of life, and I do not like it. I tolerate it just as long as it *does not cross mine*. The child is my heir—God knows she is the only one you are like to give me—and if I say our tenants look to see her at Christmastide, and me also, that is enough."

The door of the boudoir had been left ajar. Suddenly it was flung open, and she could see her father's tall figure, his mud-splattered boots planted astride in the doorway. "You will make ready to leave the day after tomorrow. Cancel your engagements and recall your invitations."

Now she could hear her mother's voice. *"Mon dieu!* You will make me a laughingstock in all of London."

"I care nothing for that. You should have considered my wishes before making arrangements."

"And if I do not choose to come to Blowick?" Her mother followed him to the threshold, and her appearance was strange with her hair halfway dressed and her wrap clutched indignantly over her hooped petticoats.

"Why, then I shall close this house about your ears, lady, and if you will not follow me, you shall beg your bread of your father. . . ."

It was at this point that Eugenie, trembling with fear and horror, had lost her footing on the stairs and tumbled down the nursery flight almost at their feet.

The shock took her breath away. When she looked up she saw her father's face dark with anger and her mother staring out of the deadly pallor of powder without the finish of rouge. Eugenie began to sob for fear, for the pain of her bruised ribs and throbbing knee, even —although she could not possibly have explained why—for the loss of the baby brother, whose coming had been surrounded with such importance, but who had died when she was three years old.

What followed was confused in her mind. Annie miraculously appeared and came running to pick her up. Her father could be heard sternly demanding what she was doing upon the stairs and whether she had broken any bones. And her mother looked angry, too, standing still and silent in the doorway. Eugenie clung to Annie like a raft in the storm.

"I f-fell down the stairs."

"Indeed you did!" Annie said. "And a nasty, steep flight it is, too. But no real harm's done, I think." She set Eugenie on her feet. "There . . . you can stand? Come with Annie then and we'll bathe your bruises."

"I should first like to know what she was doing upon the stairs," Lord Carle persisted. "Answer me, child, where were you going?"

Seeing her speechless, Annie made haste to explain her own errand to the laundry. "Very likely she was looking for me, my lord."

"And is she permitted to leave the nursery and wander about the house as she has a mind to?"

"Why, no, my lord, certainly she is not. But—"

"There are no buts. She did what she has been forbidden to do. Explain yourself, Eugenie."

In her fright the words would not shape themselves. She wanted to tell him that she had been waiting for him to come ever since breakfast, that it had seemed a long time since September when she last saw him, that she had worked him a cover for a footstool with his family motto in cross-stitch. . . .

"I heard you." She blurted out her answer and saw his scowl deepen. "I mean, I heard you talking to Mama and then. . . ." Her tongue faltered. Dimly and too late she realized that this admission had made matters worse. She looked at her mother. Now *her* eyes were hard also.

"You have the impertinence to stand there and tell me you were listening—*deliberately listening*—to a private conversation I was having with your mother?" His tone

7

cut her like a knife, and he stared at her with cold disfavor.

"Such conduct shows a want of proper feeling in you. I am shocked and distressed that you could do such a thing," her mother said. "Go to the nursery this instant and reflect how you have offended us."

Silently Annie led her away. Later there had come a tap at the door and the maid, who waited on the nursery, to say that Lord Carle sent word Eugenie was to be given no supper.

"Well, I'm taking nay notice of that," Annie told her crossly. "The child's had hurt enough for one day, and you may tell cook I shall be down to the kitchen myself to fetch her whatever she fancies."

But Eugenie, having heard her father's orders, declined to eat any supper. The least she could do was to obey him.

Her disgrace weighed very heavily upon her. "The child is my heir—God knows she is the only one you are like to give me." What did it mean? Of course she had understood for a long time that her father wished she had been a boy. *He* did not say so, but the servants at Blowick said it for him. It went hard with a man who had no son to follow him, they said. She had tried on this account to do everything to please him. Until today. For the first time in her life she had made him angry. He was angry with her mother, too. And that was strange because many gentlemen seemed to admire her mother and were always visiting her and bringing her pretty presents.

Of course if it were her mother's fault that she had no brothers, her father might well be angry about that. But Annie said it was God who sent children. Perhaps her father was upset because her mother did not like Blowick. It was his favorite place to live, but her mother was French and she said the climate of Northumberland did not suit her. She much preferred their house in London. For her own part Eugenie did not mind where

8

they lived—Blowick, London—it was all one if only they might be together. And she wept again before she fell asleep thinking how little chance there was of that now that she had fallen into such disgrace. Her mother might go away, too. She liked to go to France. She was always laughing and very kind when she was going to visit her parents, the grandparents Eugenie had never seen. Would they end by living in separate houses, far apart? It was a lonely thought.

The worst of these fears was never realized. Nevertheless, from about her eighth year Eugenie's family life set in a new routine.

Ranulf, Lord Carle, Earl of Blowick, was a man who liked the country. He liked to hunt and to shoot, liked to ride the borderland and drink deep of an evening in the company of gentlemen neighbors until he fell under the table. He loathed drawing rooms and the company of women. His wife, on the other hand, very much a woman of her native country and her time, admired what was fashionable and witty. She preferred flowers made of Sèvres porcelain to real blooms and considered a practiced gallant an indispensable furnishing for her boudoir.

The preoccupations of a large family might have blurred these differences of taste and temperament, but as it was, Lord and Lady Carle began deliberately to draw away from each other after the death of their son in 1705. The birth had been difficult, and Lady Carle was unable to bear more children. In putting the disappointments of the underoccupied nursery out of their minds, they were sometimes capable of forgetting its sole occupant, each seeking distractions which the other detested.

It became their custom to live apart for three-quarters of the year, Madeleine occupying the large house conveniently close to Hyde Park—where they kept a cow so that Eugenie could have an unlimited supply of fresh

9

milk. At the beginning of June, mother and daughter would journey to Blowick. Lady Carle would stay for a month to fulfill her obligations as hostess, while her husband entertained the county, and then, leaving Eugenie to spend the remainder of the summer in Northumberland, she would travel to France to visit her parents.

In autumn Lord Carle would escort his daughter to London, deposit the Michaelmas rents with his man of business and make all speed to his hunting lodge at Melton Mowbray. They would not see him again until late December, when he came to spend some two hundred guineas with his tailor and wager considerably more—a carefully judged tenth of his annual income—at White's.

Reluctantly persuaded to discontinue the customary family Christmas at Blowick, he would instead remain with his wife and daughter in London, grumbling a good deal about the fashionable company Lady Carle entertained at his expense and generally fretting after diversions more to his taste. By the end of January he would be gone, back to Blowick over the worst roads in the country at their most treacherous season.

During the years that followed Eugenie could not avoid overhearing many another angry and bitter exchange between her parents, but she never again made the error of confronting them with her knowledge. A solitary child, rarely enjoying the companionship of other children, she attained an early maturity of vision in human relationships and soon realized that circumstances had decreed her to be the last surviving interest which her parents could share. Because of this, she walked a delicate line between the two of them, striving to be all her father wished when she was at Blowick, ready to please her mother's whims in London.

Lady Carle, prodigiously well read in French, German and Italian literature, was in fact rather better educated than her husband. She took great care in the selection of

10

tutors for her daughter, and one might say that she was a woman who enjoyed maternity at one remove.

Eugenie studied diligently at first to please her mother and later to please herself. By the time she was seventeen her thought processes were cultured, her mind well furnished, her tastes intellectual and her conversation assured.

Somewhere along the way she had changed from a pretty child into a beautiful woman.

She had become a considerable heiress. Her father's estate was not entailed upon male issue, and Eugenie's fortune would include Blowick, a further two thousand acres in Leicestershire, a comparable property in Warwickshire, a house in Richmond and a forty percent financial interest in a Barbados sugar plantation owned by her Uncle William. Apart from minor bequests the only other legacy would be for Madeleine, a handsome annuity in the event of her widowhood and Carle House in London. These, too, would devolve upon Eugenie.

Small wonder that Lady Madeleine should make a cautious selection of guests for Eugenie's first ball or that she should prune her list and revise it and derive as much pleasure from her exclusions as she did from the contemplation of what a triumph the occasion would be. She had but one daughter to marry off and that one—the whispers behind fans had reached her—reputed to be exquisite and incalcuable rich. Eugenie might have a duke at least.

II

FLAMBEAUX are ablaze in the November dark. Lord and Lady Carle give a ball tonight to introduce their daughter to a rich and fashionable London acquaintance. Strays of the London streets have drifted up against the high iron railings, which close off the forecourt of Carle House from the thoroughfare, and await a free peep show. There will be linkboys and chairs and coaches; perhaps a coin to be earned by a strong fellow who can leap to the heads of a plunging team; perhaps a gem lost from its setting or a purse dropped by an impatient guest, who will walk the last few yards rather than wait in the line of vehicles.

The doors open, and four footmen unroll a red Turkey carpet down the damp stone steps. Their uniforms are of fine green cloth, heavily frogged with silver, their hair stiff with pomade and densely powdered. They pretend not to notice the crowd, affecting the superiority of their master's status, and their hauteur is far in excess of his own. A woman with fine sand for sale claims that they are all seven feet tall. Her sand has polished the floors of this very house, and she is an authority. Sighing with wonder, the crowd believes her. But in fact she exaggerates. Each man is exactly six feet in height, since Lady Carle will employ no liveried servant about the house who is either an inch above or below this mark.

Now chandeliers are being lighted. Brilliant rooms

12

take shape and hover an instant in a shimmer of gilt and crystal before the drapes are drawn. The cheated spectators whistle and jeer their disapproval.

Mercifully their clamor is inaudible on the second floor, where the apartments look toward Hyde Park and have double windows in the French manner.

"Enfin!" Lady Carle drew a long breath of satisfaction. "It is enough, I think. Stand up, *ma petite.*"

Eugenie obeyed thankfully. She had been seated before her mother's dressing table for what seemed like an eternity while her hair was pulled back from her forehead and brushed and underbrushed and dressed over a pad of lamb's wool to give it height. Then there had been the hot irons to persuade fragile curls to curve upon her cheeks and mold the long ringlets that lay over one shoulder. And Claudette would set a pin here, and her mother would not have it so. It must be moved, and yet after all it had been better where it was before and must be moved again. There had been some trials with a ribbon, but the effect was not pleasing. A velvet rose was too large, an enameled clip ridiculously small. Finally they would leave her head unadorned, save by their own skill.

Careful of the unaccustomed hooped skirt, Eugenie moved into the center of the room and slipped off the cotton wrapper that had covered her gown while her hair was dressed.

"Well, Auguste?" Madeleine invited an opinion from the gracefully disposed figure on the couch.

The Chevalier de Mulignac summoned the assistance of his eyeglass, and the fatigue of lifting this toy on its slender gold stick almost overcame him. There was an anxious silence. Madame Clothilde, who had made the gown, darted forward and twitched shimmering folds of ice-blue taffeta to a better display. "The petticoat," she said, "the finest Flanders lace, m'Lord, ruched with *silver* thread." Still the chevalier said nothing.

"And my Claudette," Madeleine prompted, "she has

the art with the hair, has she not? We have striven for an effect *jeune fille* . . . simple." There was a suggestion of deference in her tone, for although the chevalier was an old friend and one of her most devoted admirers, he was also a noted arbiter of fashion. Still there was no answer.

"Shall I turn around?" Eugenie asked politely.

The chevalier signified with a slight gesture of one fragile hand that this would be agreeable to him.

Lady Carle's small feet began to tap out the signal of her mounting impatience. "This toilette—" she began indignantly.

"Is incomplete." The chevalier yawned. *"Quelle oubli."*

"Why, sir, whatever can you mean? I have neglected nothing!" Nevertheless, Madeleine hastened across the room to view her daughter from where De Mulignac was sitting.

The chevalier shook his head wearily. The shortcomings of his fellow creatures consistently gave him pain. "You cannot see?"

"I cannot."

"No jewel."

Madeleine gasped at the revelation. "No jewel!" Her eyes repeated the horror to Madame Clothilde.

"The bosom," Madame echoed dolefully. "So bare!"

"Claudette, my jewel case. Bring it. *Vite, vite!*"

The jewel case was produced. The three women pored over it anxiously.

Eugenie watched the chevalier and, with a new adult awareness, thought what a tease he was and how her mother always came to the lure. He was enjoying her confusion now; the faintest curl about the corners of his mouth betrayed him. Then his eyes moved suddenly and met Eugenie's stare, and she thought that they were sharp eyes. Like a cat's. The lids were heavy and indolent, but it was a pose.

He nodded confidentially in Eugenie's direction. "It should be a sapphire," he said softly.

Madeleine heard him. "A sapphire? I never wear sapphires. I believe there may have been a turquoise in the collection Carle gave me when we were married." The chevalier shuddered. "No. Of course you are right. A turquoise would not do in any case."

"For Eugenie . . . so fair-skinned and this hair . . . pale gold and this gown. . . ." The chevalier spread his hands. The conclusion was inevitable. "Nothing, will do, save a pendant sapphire of the first water and a distinctive shape, set in silver."

Madeleine straightened up defiantly and shut the velvet-lined casket with a snap. "I have no such thing. There is a tassel of pearls, or there is nothing."

"Pearls, if they are well matched, will do very well." He allowed Madeleine time to reopen the box "When she is five-and-twenty."

"Oh, Auguste! You are impossible! I do not know how I have the tolerance for you." She rounded on him furiously. "Here we are with our first guests practically on the stairs, and you plague me for a necklace which you know cannot be produced. . . . Oh, God! I have the *mal de tête.* . . ."

"My dear Madeleine, calm yourself, I beseech you. Who said a jewel could not be obtained? It so happens that in the pocket of this coat—this coat by the way, do you not admire it?—I carry a silver chain with some trifling stone which may serve." The chevalier stood up, turning around before the long glass to admire his own magnificence, and then, having sought about in one pocket, finally produced from another a great pear-shaped sapphire. He swung the silver chain casually, and the stone twirled back the light from every candle in the room.

"Come here, child."

He fastened the clasp of the chain about her neck and then led Eugenie to the mirror.

"Now look at yourself and tell me what you think."

"The jewel is extremely fine, sir. Will you indeed let me borrow it?"

"Certainly not. I never lend jewels to beautiful women. There is no telling what use they will make of them. *Par exemple,* you might dazzle the eyes of some worthy man with this bauble and bring him to his knees. I will have no part in the seduction of a good man's senses. I will give you the sapphire and then what you do with it is your concern—not mine."

"But I cannot take such a gift. Why, it must be worth. . . ." Eugenie hesitated. She had, in truth, no idea what such a stone might cost.

"A thousand guineas or I do not know my own name." Madeleine descended on them in a swirl of coral brocade. "Auguste, you old fox! No wonder you questioned me so closely on the color of the gown I was having made up for Eugenie. You planned this all the time. Ah, but such an extravagance, such a generosity. The child is overwhelmed, and so am I." She patted Eugenie's hand reassuringly. "There, you do not know what to say do you, my love? Never mind. Say nothing. Auguste is very rich. He would drop the cost of it at a game of hazard in one night." She turned to her women. "Now all is well. Beseech you, send the page for Lord Carle. Claudette, some wine for the chevalier. Am I in need of a little more powder? I declare I am aglow. . . . Carriages will be here."

Shocked that her mother should casually dismiss such an expensive present, Eugenie hastened to make amends with more elaborate thanks.

"It is my pleasure to indulge you, child." The chevalier shrugged. "There is no more to be said."

But there was, and by Lord Carle. Striding into his wife's boudoir some minutes later, he noticed the jewel at once. When he knew its origin, he made his displeasure very plain.

"Whatever are you about, lady, to let De Mulignac spend his fortune on our daughter? If the child has no jewels of her own, you should have told me."

"You might have thought of it for yourself," she answered coolly. "Auguste did."

Eugenie looked from one parent to the other, thinking that without the least intention of doing so they had between them contrived to turn the gift from a pleasure to an embarrassment.

"Well, De Mulignac, I would not have you think me churlish," her father said after a discomforting pause. "You are uncommon generous." He turned to Eugenie, and she was relieved to see the dark scowl fade. "Very becoming, yes, the gown is very becoming. And I am thankful your mother has had the sense not to powder your hair." He darted a sidelong glance at his wife. "It is a pretty shade, and nature can seldom be improved upon in my view."

"Indeed, my lord, if that is your true opinion I wonder that you trouble to cultivate the land at Blowick or refine the stock upon it," Madeleine said sweetly.

It seemed to Eugenie that there was a sudden chill in the room, a cold current of thought. It wanted only that her father should cap what her mother had just said and they would be in the midst of one of those exchanges she so much dreaded, where the words were pointed and the implications wounding. She crossed the room, deliberately interposing herself and curtsied to her mother.

"There are but ten minutes of eight o'clock, Mama. Will you wish me to inspect the supper tables with you or shall we leave it to Ferne?"

She was aware that she risked a setdown, but efficient as Ferne was in his capacity as majordomo, her mother would hardly leave him the final word on the arrangement of the supper room.

Within seconds they were descending the stairs. On the ground floor the doors stood open to the main salon, where more than four hundred candles were already lighted in the big three-tiered chandeliers and the wall sconces. The supper room was on the left and the drawing room, with tables set out for cards, just beyond. They had only time to take in these arrangements at a glance and for Madeleine to make a nice adjustment of the decorative foliage and a better dispersal of the napery before Ferne was striking his long cane on the marble floor of the hall to warn them that the first chairs were being carried into the courtyard.

Musicians began to play, the voice of a footman called the names of guests, and there was the rap of Ferne's cane as he repeated them to Lord Carle. "Lord and Lady Aberlaune. . . . Mr. Jesmund Herries, Mistress Herries and Mistress Amalie. . . . Sir Horace and Lady Fitzwalters. . . . Monsieur le Duc de Caramborde et Madame la Duchesse. . . ."

Madeleine gave her hand graciously. Her manner implied that each guest in turn was the only one she had been longing to see "And may I present my daughter, Eugenie. . . ." "How do you do?" *"Enchanté."* . . . So many curtsies . . . hands raising her, eyes appraising her. . . . "Why, the child is exquisite!" . . . "An angel!" . . . "Ah, *vous avez de la chance*, Madeleine. *C'est une belle."* . . .

The ball commenced with the stately pavane (which was enjoying a fashionable revival that season). The knowledge that she must lead the dance partnered by her father had occasioned Eugenie many anxious moments. *Could* her father dance? It was a thing not readily imagined. And the pavane. True, the footwork was not intricate, but her dancing master had stressed the importance of a stylihh deportment. Such movements as there were wanted a fluid grace, and the attitudes must be held with a statuesque perfection. After all, she was to be pleasantly surprised. He danced well, and she was free to concentrate on her own performance, praying urgently that it was not entirely unsatisfactory to the many critical eyes which followed her through every figure.

It was just as she completed the final graceful honors of the dance that she perceived one observer more intense, more arresting than the others. She found herself looking directly into a pair of gray eyes, and their expression was disconcerting—a light, something akin to triumph. What could it mean? The man was unknown to her. He was tall, taller than most men, and yet *was* that the only reason she had distinguished him among so many?

Her father was speaking to her, and as he led her back to the alcove where her mother was sitting, she must look away from the stranger. Good manners demanded it.

"I shall give your mother a draft for fifteen hundred guineas tomorrow. You may spend it on such jewels and trinkets as you wish; only see you invest in good stones. Lanson will advise you well. Go to him. His reputation is sound."

"Father, you are very kind. Should I really spend so much?"

"Certainly. You are my daughter, my only child. Now you are grown it is fitting you should have baubles, as do other women of your estate."

They were forming sets for a country dance, and Auguste de Mulignac claimed her. He danced very prettily. His glissades put many a younger man to shame. Eugenie began to enjoy herself.

"Are you happy, little one? I see you have put everyone in a stare."

"They are staring at my sapphire."

"*Vraiment?* Then I should have kept it to wear as a fob with a coat of velvet. I dearly love to be stared at."

Eugenie laughed softly and permitted herself a discreet inspection of his lilac silks and elaborately dressed hair. "Why, sir, I cannot believe you ever lack attention. And is it not said, after all, that the only things a man can be sure of keeping are those he has given away?"

An expression of amused indulgence softened the chevalier's rouged mouth. "You are learning to be artful with words, *ma petite*, but your argument fails to move me. There is no philosophy in my soul, you see. I can imagine no circumstances in which a man can give something away and still possess it"—he frowned thoughtfully—"unless of course he gives it to his wife. Ah, yes, I see it now. Perhaps you are more subtle than I thought. Perhaps you are inviting me to offer for you?"

"Why, no, indeed not!" Eugenie peered anxiously into his face. His expression was entirely serious.

"You need not fear to own it," he said gently.

"But . . . but you have entirely mistook me," she began earnestly, then: "Oh! You are laughing at me. And you plague my mother in just the same way, so I should have known."

"Yes, I am the scourge of women. That is why none of them will marry me. It is sad, is it not? Will you take pity on me and relent?"

"I think it would put you in a great fright if I did," said Eugenie heartily.

De Mulignac was startled into a smile. "Your candor is irresistible, child, but it is not in the mode. Pray conceal it."

"Oh, yes, I will. I am only talking to you in this way because I have known you all my life."

"That is just the trouble with a long acquaintance. It encourages honesty." The music ended, and he bowed over her hand. "I see there is a positive crush of hopeful young men waiting to dance with you." Eugenie looked and felt a pang of disappointment that the tall young man with the singular eyes was nowhere to be seen. Could she have imagined him? No, ridiculous. But he had not been among the guests received at the doors of the salon. That meant he must have arrived late. And now it appeared that he had left early without even seeking to be presented.

The chevalier was bowing over her hand again. *"Merci, ma chère,"* and to her mother: "Madeleine, my felicitations. The child is delightful. Must I really surrender her to this *canaille*?" He glanced disparagingly over his shoulders.

"Oh, I say, sir! Not the thing." "Protest, sir!" "Have to call him out."

"Yes, Auguste, I am afraid you must," said Madeleine,

laughing. "These gentlemen have been waiting very patiently."

"Poor Eugenie! They will step on your feet and pay clumsy tributes to your eyes, and before the night is over, the one gaucherie will seem as tiresome as the other."

To some extent this prediction was fulfilled. But if the feet and sometimes the tongues of her partners were a little awkward, Eugenie was ready to forgive such trifling deficiencies. Her first ball and she had partners sufficient and to spare. The scented candles burned lower. As soon as one dance was ended, the musicians struck up with another. And still they came for her with outstretched hands, the Bartelmys and the Joshuas, the Williams and the Georges, making their studied bows and leading her through the maze of the sets. "Remember seeing you out driving with your mama." . . . "Believe you are acquainted with my sister, Sophie." . . . "Deuced glad to have the opportunity. . . ."

Since she had not sat out once, Eugenie welcomed the sight of her mother in conference with Ferne, followed by the announcement that supper was to be served. She would be thankful to rest for a while. And then privately Eugenie admitted another reason for her impatience to enter the supper room. Those who had been making use of the card tables would leave off their play and mingle with the dancers and it was just possible. . . .

She saw him across the room, by the fire. His attitude was relaxed, like a man in his own home. He leaned one elbow on the overmantel and thrust his other hand in the pocket of his brocade vest, oblivious to all around him and deep in apparently enjoyable conversation with an elderly gentleman, who laughed heartily and often.

Her first impression had not been mistaken. He was exceptionally tall and powerfully built. For a few moments she had the opportunity to observe him without drawing attention to herself. She saw that he was no disciple of fashion. His green velvet coat was unadorned, there was little lace about him, and his thick gold-brown hair, tied at the nape of his neck with a narrow ribbon, was left unpowdered. She guessed him to be a man who spent most of his time in the country and, like her father, made few concessions to formality. The man with him, though surely twice his age, was more the dandy, but he, too, had the same easy gestures and casual stance. What was it? A lack of self-consciousness? Yes, that was their quality. Such men were indifferent to what the world might say of them. They had no need to put on airs because they were exactly as they seemed to be.

"Eugenie, my dear! Wherever are your thoughts?" A reproachful rap from her mother's fan recalled her attention. "Come and sit down with me. Most of our guests are served, and Ferne is just bringing us some supper for ourselves at last." She looked more closely at her daughter. "You seem rather pale, my love. Have you over-fatigued yourself with the dancing?"

"Perhaps I have . . . just a little. I shall be better directly."

"A glass of wine will be the thing. And then after supper you may very properly sit out the first two dances. There are several ladies of our acquaintance waiting to talk with you." She patted Eugenie's hand in a conspiratorial way. "They are hopeful for their sons and anxious to look you over. Of course, some of them are looking above their means, but it does no harm to win approval."

"Yes, Mother. Just as you say."

They were joined by her father.

"Well, Eugenie, and how are you enjoying your first ball? Is it all a girl hopes of such affairs?"

"I thank you, yes, sir. Indeed it is."

"Two gentlemen here, anxious to be presented to you." She looked beyond her father and saw that the tall stranger and his companion had threaded their way through the crowd and were waiting to be introduced. "Now this is a valued friend of my boyhood, not seen alas for many a year, Madame, my wife, and my daughter —Sir Robert Hackthorne of Oxfordshire. And this young man is his godson—Athel Athelson from Lancashire."

Madeleine greeted them amiably, giving them each her hand, while Eugenie rose and performed the curtsy which her youth made proper.

Athel Athelson! The name had a fine sound to it. Eugenie lifted her chin and looked directly into his eyes. But the singular expression which had arrested her attention while she danced was no longer there. Now there was something brooding, even critical in his regard.

It seemed to Eugenie that her heart plunged. Seeing her more closely, he was disappointed. And yet what was that to her? A sharp stab of anger gave her strength. Deliberately she schooled her own expression into a bland mask and turned her attention to Sir Robert Hackthorne.

"Do you make a long stay in London, sir?"

"Regrettably, no. A fourteen-night is all my duties as a justice will allow. But young Athel will stay the month out, I daresay. We are lodged with my sister in St. James's Square, and she makes us very comfortable."

Lord Carle was in a jovial and expansive mood. "Indeed, old friend, it is short time enough to renew our acquaintance, but we must make the most of it. Before you leave tonight, I shall engage you to dine with us one day next week. Mr. Athelson, also."

The musicians had begun to play again in the salon, and the company was drifting away from the supper tables.

Madeleine stood up. "Eugenie, I think we must excuse ourselves. There is Lady Margaret Fitzwalters waiting to speak to us."

Much chastened, Eugenie was glad to be able to bow and turn away. She had displayed an unbecoming interest in this man, this Mr. Athelson, and had thought that he returned it. But after all, she was terribly mis-

23

taken. Given the opportunity, he had not addressed a single word to her, let alone solicited a dance. She hurried after her mother and for the next hour worked diligently at her obligations.

"The Dowager Countess of Fitch tells me you showed her a very pretty attention," Madeleine said approvingly. "I am so glad. Her elder grandson is a very pleasing young man and would be a most eligible *parti*. In your situation one need not be concerned with such matters, but she will leave him everything. Now go and talk to the little Caramborde. She tells me that she is in an interesting condition and will dance no more tonight."

The Duchesse de Caramborde, only a few months older than Eugenie herself and married to a man of fifty, was the daughter of a Polish count. She spoke no English and little French, and to entertain her was not an easy assignment. She had chosen to sit in the anteroom, well retired from the dancing. Eugenie drew up an adjacent chair and did her best to make conversation.

They had been engaged in a certain limited communication for several minutes when Eugenie became aware of the presence of Mr. Athelson, leaning in the negligent way which seemed to characterize him against one of the marble pillars of the arched doorway. She stopped speaking and turned a challenging look in his direction.

"May I join you?" There was a suggestion of boredom in his voice.

"If it would please you, sir." She kept her tone cool, the budding womanhood in her resenting his manner. "Madame la Duchesse de Caramborde, may I present Mr. Athel Athelson."

Her gestures were explanation enough, and the duchess nodded agreeably. Eugenie had an uneasy feeling that she was about to fall asleep. . . . Poor fatigued little soul with her pregnancy and the heat of the rooms. She would have been happier at home in her bed.

"The duchess speaks no English. You must address

her in French or, better still, Polish," Eugenie said, not without triumph.

"I have neither language. Nor do I have any talent for dancing, which is the only reason I did not engage you earlier."

Eugenie was disconcerted, not merely by the admission of such lack of accomplishment, but the way in which it was delivered, almost as though he were boasting. And reluctantly she was impressed.

"Madame la Duchesse is making her first visit to London." She must attempt at all costs to sustain a three-cornered conversation. Eugenie looked anxiously toward the salon, but her mother was nowhere in sight. What if the duchess should indeed go to sleep and she were to find herself *tête-à-tête* with this man who had such a discomposing effect upon her?

"Tell the duchess she favors an unwholesome city more than it deserves. . . ." Eugenie began translating, her eyes met his, inquiring the meaning he wished her to convey. "Tell her I had far rather she had stayed at home. . . . Go on, why do you hesitate? Tell her that she appears amiable enough and has pretty hands, but I had rather she was on the other side of the world than keeping us company here. . . . What is the matter? You do not put my words into her tongue. . . . Tell her that if she were otherwheres, I might draw one chair nearer to you, and then we should have no need to play this game because I could ask you the questions I long to ask and read the answers in your eyes."

"Wh-what questions?" It was a dangerous invitation, and she hastened to recall it. "No, do not tell me! I must address myself to Madame la Duchesse. . . . Madame, *permittez-moi.* . . ." She turned her head. The flowery compliment she passed on bore no relation to Mr. Athelson's words, but it contented their companion, who smiled and bowed.

"Do *you* like living in London, Lady Eugenie?"

25

The simplicity of the inquiry disarmed her. "Why, sir, London offers many diversions and abundant good company, to be sure. But when I am at Blowick with my father, I am well content."

"I am glad to hear that. My estate is extreme isolated. We see nothing of town life." Eugenie stared at him. "Well, come now, you guessed I intended to. . . . No, perhaps you did not. I have heard it said girls are knowing from the nursery these days, but perhaps not all of them. You must forgive me if I have been blunt, clumsy even. I am no practiced wooer I will own."

Eugenie listened to him with downcast eyes, overconscious now of the heavy, halting beat of her own heart. What was he saying to her? He talked so strangely it might well be she had misunderstood him.

Suddenly, to her infinite relief, her mother was by her side. And there was Mistress Herries and the Duc de Caramborde. They were talking, laughing, congratulating the duchess on the news which the duke had been unable to keep to himself. Mr. Athelson was standing up, was bowing, was turning away. He would go. She must have been mistaken. He would never ask . . . and Eugenie would never know that, as he glanced back and saw her with her lips half-parted and her wide eyes wondering after him, it was that look about her which would quicken his resolve just enough to seal the bargain of her life.

Lord Carle saw Britain as having a distinct and ineradicable line drawn across it from the estuary of the Mersey to a point just below the mouth of the Humber, and he was inclined to the view that any man born south of this line had already made his first serious mistake. Not without influence or friends in the southern counties he would occasionally own an exception that proved his rule—"A very decent fellow, *considering*"—but it was implicit that only remarkable resolution of character had withstood the corruption of environment. Lord Carle had his prejudices.

Strong persuasions, like strong winds, have always their leeside. Let him only know of a man that he be born and bred in the north, that he hold land in that part of the country and live upon it in preference to any other place on earth, and he would never be brought to admit that a man of that strain could have much fault in him. Such a man had judgment. Such a man walked in the path of rectitude. What is more he had a curious assortment of physical attributes such as "backbone," "stomach" and "bottom." Such a man was Athel Athelson.

Lord Carle was not acquainted with the Athelsons, but he knew them to be a Lancashire landholding family of no repute save that of long-continued existence in the same place. This Athel, whose father had died two years earlier, was already at the age of twenty-five in full possession of his property. As a suitor, he came better endowed than he knew.

Nevertheless, there were aspects of such a match that required careful consideration. Eugenie would inherit Blowick. Lord Carle loved every acre of Blowick. He knew his people by their given names, and their children, and whether it was little Katie or Jem, who had come first to the Hawkes' cottage at Long Side; he even knew the names of their dogs. It was a relationship that had its obligations, and a man did not put these off when he died.

He listened to Athel Athelson, and he understood that the younger man had the same feeling for *his* land and the people who lived on it. But was this a good thing? If he was already wed to his own property, he would have little care for that which came with a wife. Would he not—if given a free hand—milk Blowick to prosper Clere Athel? No, by God, that should not be!

This suitor, so prompt, presenting himself the very next day after the ball with Robert Hackthorne along to speak for him, had taken him by surprise. A proposal after one brief meeting! No finesse, of course, but what a

27

fine testimony to resolution and self-confidence. Naturally, the boy wanted Eugenie for her money. Lord Carle was too much of a realist to deplore this. Where there was wealth in a woman there would always be fortune hunters. At least Athelson had substance of his own and a worthy name to offer. And he was not a man who would gamble her money away, or spend it on idle show and bring himself to ruin.

Perhaps, if he and his man of law had wit enough, they could devise terms for a marriage contract that would bind the Athelsons to expectations and safeguard the interests both of his daughter and his land far beyond the probable term of his own life. He thought on these things, and then he sent for Eugenie.

"Come in, my child. Your mother has doubtless told you why I wished to talk with you."

"Yes, sir. I understand you have listened to Mr. Athelson's addresses."

What a fragile little creature she was. And yet well in command of herself. Lord Carle approved the stillness of her hands. There was none of that flutter about her which he so disliked in women.

"Aye, that I have. He is a fair set-up young man, I think. Not such a one as a girl would dread for a lover, eh? . . . eh?"

"No." It was softly spoken.

"You have a fancy for him?"

Now she blushed, slightly. "I thought him . . . handsome."

"He is . . . so he is . . . so he is!" Lord Carle was always at a loss in conversations with women, afraid of being too forceful and yet at the same time uncomfortably aware that such considerations often put him at a disadvantage. He tapped a thick forefinger on the table. The papers in front of him were covered with rough calculations of the marriage settlement which he had jotted down before Eugenie entered the room. He looked at them, shuffled them uneasily and finally turned them facedown. The girl had a presence like her mother, a damned, pervasive, feminine aura which could make reality—the essential monetary arrangements of a contract to wed—seem gross and brutal.

"Well, he is a north-countryman and his land is his own. Belikes his property is not elegant, but you can have money to spend on that. If I said his suit had my approval would you be disposed to favor it?"

She was slow to answer. "I will listen to what he has to say with pleasure, sir, if that is your wish."

"What answer is that, girl? God damn it, you know what he has to say, for I have just this instant been telling you."

She faced him determindedly across the table. "But I have scarcely spoken to Mr. Athelson. I would hear what he has to say from his own lips."

"So you shall, naturally enough. But a man such as this, a *north-country* man and proud, wants to know whether he will be favorably received."

Gently persistent she said, "I cannot know whether I wish to accept him before he tells me what is in his heart."

Lord Carle gave a cough of exasperation. In his heart, indeed. What fanciful stuff was this? Still . . . she was but a girl and it might be they all had their heads awhirl with romantic dreams at her age. The better reason for securing an early marriage, before she took to imagining herself in love with some landless adventurer with a pretty tongue.

"Very well," he said at last. "I will tell him that at least you are willing to hear him. But, mark me, although I give you your choice in the matter and will not force you to this marriage, I want you to think on it wisely. In the past week I have had inquiries made in many directions, and what I hear of Athelson pleases me. A plain, honest man may have no gift for words, but what other folks say of him will often prove eloquent enough. Look in him for what is steady and strong and may be relied upon. Do not require fine phrases of him. . . ." He smiled slightly. "I doubt he is a poet!"

Lord Carle was wrong. Athel Athelson did have something of poetry in him when he spoke of his land. And Eugenie listened and fell into first love, watching the way his face blazed with pride when he talked of the earth enriched by careful husbandry, of his tenants who had worked the same fields since the days of the Danish kings. He drew a plan for her which showed Clere Athel, set on the coast of North Lancashire, with a pine forest curving like an arm about its shoulder landward, and before it the pale-silver sand and the sea. He told her how the Athelsons were said to be of Viking descent and that the people of the village still sang "Isil's Song," which described the raiding of an Anglo-Saxon settlement by the Norse warrior Aethel and his men, who stayed to intermarry and plant the next harvest.

Eugenie was charmed by the legend and everything that Athel told her of his home. Isolated it might be, but it sounded idyllic, an innocent retreat in a knowing world.

"You may laugh at this," he said. "I am a father to my people, not a master. We are not rich in Clere Athel, but we are happy. We go our own way, an old way." Eugenie did not laugh.

Listening to Athel, she saw again that expression in his eyes, which had compelled her while she danced the pavane. It was a mystery to her, strange and forceful. She hoped and believed it was love.

Madeleine, Lady Carle did not approve of the match. She did not believe Athel Athelson would be a considerate husband to her daughter, and she said so many times.

"I cannot understand how you can be so stupid, Eugenie. The man has nothing in the world to recommend him save a good figure and a handsome face. Does he have any talent to the conversation? No, he does not. Does he have a fine house or amiable connections or a style of life to make you comfortable? No, he has none of these—nor ever will have unless you buy them for him. The man is nothing but a graceless country squire, come to town to carry off a rich bride, and there is your father handing you to him without the smallest care for what your life will be like when you are buried over your ears in the marshes of Lancashire." With scarcely a pause for breath she ran on. "To think that a girl with your fortune might have chosen any eligible man in the country. . . . Why, even had you been toad-ugly plenty of suitors would still have come a-calling. . . . But there you sit, with your fortune doubled in your beauty, and tell me you will accept this first offer. Well, I declare I must be much at fault not to have taught you better wisdom in your own interests. My friends will never have done laughing at me."

Eugenie bent her head dutifully over the tapestry she was working. "But you always said that with my fortune I might marry where I pleased, and Mr. Athelson pleases me." She knotted a thread with care. "He pleases my father, too, does he not?"

"First and foremost he will always please himself," Madeleine snapped back angrily. "I tell you, I know the kind of man he is. He is too much like"—she had been about to say "your father," the strength of her feelings almost overcoming her sense of propriety, but amended—"like other countrymen of one's acquaintance. They had rather have the company of their land steward, or even their dogs, than their wife! Now, if you would take my advice, you would marry a Frenchman."

"Someone like Monsieur le Chevalier de Mulignac?"

For a moment Madeleine's eyes flared at the suspected impertinence, but Eugenie continued to keep her own gaze demurely lowered to her work, so perhaps the inquiry was innocently made.

"Why, no. I daresay a man of Auguste's temperament would not make a good husband either," Madeleine spoke carelessly. "Perhaps, if one had caught him young

31

. . . before he became too set in his ways. As it is, one may amuse oneself with such a man. . . . The husband I would choose for you would be young. He would be well connected, and his fortune just one part smaller than your own. He would show his nature to you in open adoration of your charms, be continuously at your side in any gathering, plague you with small attentions. . . ."

Her mother continued to describe the paragon she envisaged. Eugenie was no longer listening. A carefully controlled smile touched the corners of her mouth, while she reflected that she might find the greater part of such qualities in a well-bred lapdog. *The man I want,* she thought, *must have his own way, and if I love him, I will make it mine.*

Three months later Madeleine was still complaining not only of the terrible *mésalliance* her daughter was making, but also of the plans to celebrate the event.

"What! Married at Blowick! How can you think of such a scheme, my lord? Surely you will wish to entertain our friends here in London?"

Lord Carle was in no mood to be crossed. He had been called away from his own land in the precious month of March, had wasted valuable time on a visit to Clere Athel and was now returned to London to make such final arrangements as were necessary, and as always Madeleine would argue with him.

"Not a doubt it will be better if the marriage takes place here." Madeleine set her mouth firmly.

"And I say we will to Blowick," Lord Carle roared. "Our tenants there expect it. I've no mind to waste money on entertaining a host of folks in London when I don't care two groats if I never see any of them again."

Madeleine's temper could be fully as fiery as his own. "Well, I declare, my lord, you astonish me. This is your only child and your heir, and not content with giving her into the grasp of this . . . this nobody . . . this Lancashire farmer . . . you will have them wed without a penny spent to make some occasion of it."

"Great heavens above, woman! Have I not given fifteen thousand pounds with the girl in settlement? And will I not give another three thousand a year out of income over the next five years? And shall she not have, in addition to that, *fifty* thousand in trust from which she can draw the interest for her personal needs? And shall she not on my death have an inheritance better nor another hundred thousand? If that is not spending money on her, I should like to know what is!"

Madeleine had no difficulty in waving away these considerable sums. "Such money is on paper. It is not *seen* to be spent. A girl such as Eugenie, being given in marriage to one whose fortune does not match her own, should be wed with the ceremony which must impress her husband with her worth. And our friends."

"Well, let me tell you, the friends you speak of are more yours than mine. And as for young Athel, he knows Eugenie's worth right enough, and he'll not need show to make him treat her right." Lord Carle smiled bleakly at the notion. "While you've had your mind on such fripperies as entertaining, my man of business and Eugenie's trustees and I have had our heads together. The Athelsons get thirty thousand pounds of her fortune and out of that must make improvements to their house as I have directed will make it fitting to receive her. One hundred and fifty thousand more they will never get their hands on in my lifetime or hers. It will pass to such heirs as Athel Athelson gets by her, when both she and I have done with it, and not one minute sooner. . . . Yes, I fancy they will treat her right!" He rubbed his hands in satisfaction at the prospect. "Moreover, if she predeceases me or if she gets no child, all promises are void, and the money is mine to bequeath where I wish. Oh, yes, they will have a *very* tender care of her, that I can assure you!"

But although disagreements continually erupted about her, Eugenie was not troubled by them. Her thoughts were daydreams and her dreams were her own.

The few letters she received from Athel Athelson were

33

brief and to the point. They talked of what he was doing to his house and what was happening on his land. But that he should want her to know these things and should take the trouble to write pleased her well enough. She read them through many times and sought for hidden meanings in his most casual turn of phrase. Why did he choose just that word? Did it say merely what it said, or more?

She stood long hours while Madame Clothilde wreathed her with Chinese silks and taffetas and pinned lace. She drove with her mother to the houses of merchant jewelers and in their salons, barred like vaults, chose fine stones such as her father wished and ordered them "in a simple setting—for the country." For the chemises, the robes, the stockings, the fans, the tiny high-heeled shoes, the velvet cloaks with fur-trimmed hoods, the powder and the scents, she left the selection entirely to her mother. The bridal chests came, wood-fragrant, and were packed with her clothes, lawn and linen for her personal household use, and the silver —each piece separately wrapped and engraved with the letter *A*.

She was to be married at the end of May. In April the girl Hannah Merries, who was to be her personal maid, was fetched down from Blowick to accustom herself to the ways of her young mistress.

Hannah was a farmer's daughter. She had never traveled ten miles from her home before, but neither the long journey by carrier from Northumberland nor the sights and noise of the London streets deterred her. Arrived at Carle House, with a new pair of satin ribbons on her chip-straw bonnet to give her confidence and her luggage tied up in a plaid shawl bundle, she at once established herself as an important member of Eugenie's future household.

Even Madeleine was approving. "Well, I left it to Carle to choose someone suitable and I must say he appears to have shown a very nice judgment," she confided to Claudette. "Of course you will have to teach her *everything*. She will know nothing about hair or how to look after the child's wardrobe. But she seems to have her wits about her, and I daresay if one is going to live in the country, then it is best to have a country-bred girl, who has learned to contrive in such conditions. An experienced maid, accustomed to service in fashionable circles, would likely not have settled in Lancashire."

She spoke with less enthusiasm to Eugenie. "You must not make a confidante of this girl, as I do Claudette. I permit Claudette liberties because she is sophisticated enough not to take advantage of them. But your Hannah is of a class slightly above that normally entering service."

"Yes, she is the daughter of Tom Merries, who farms at Bether Rise."

"Really?" Madeleine yawned. "You were not previously acquainted with her, I trust?"

"I have seen her hanging washing when I rode past the farm and we gave each other good-day."

Madeleine frowned. "You will both do your best to forget it. It is important to set the right tone in one's relationship with a servant. Perhaps you had better call her Merries."

But Eugenie called her Hannah. Hannah was twenty, a handsome young woman with sturdy good spirits and strong resolution of character. Eugenie at once ordered muslin caps for her, with frills two inches deeper then Claudette's, a quantity of beige and brown taffeta dresses and six sets of fine lawn undergarments, which secured her a degree of devotion sufficient for a lifetime.

At last every detail of the bridal preparation was concluded. There had been one final dispute between Lord and Lady Carle concerning the distribution of *livrées de noces*, the knots of ribbons to be worn about the arms of friends and acquaintances.

35

Lady Carle would have it that such a custom was gone out of fashion.

"Why, in France only the peasants give out ribbons. You will make us ridiculous, my lord."

"I don't give a fig for what they do in France, madam, or among *your* London acquaintance. I say there shall be ribbon favors, and there's an end of the matter."

His wife gave a short, derisive laugh. "Tell me next that you will allow guests to wrestle for the bride's garters at the end of the wedding!"

"Certainly. It is an old northcountry custom. Folks expect a bit of horseplay at a marrying."

Madeleine was almost speechless with indignation. But not quite.

Nevertheless, Lord Carle had his way and pleased his neighbors by leading the frolic that followed on the sealing of the marriage contract.

Eugenie did her best to take the merriment in good part and not to show her dismay when Athel himself joined in.

"There, there"—her father patted her shoulder heavily, being by that time somewhat in his cups—"a bride in a blush is a pretty thing, m'dear."

"She'll blush more before the night's over." It was one of her father's closest friends who spoke, and some of the women joined in the laughter.

Gone two o'clock in the morning, she faced Athel alone across the formidable expanse of Blowick's principal guest rooms. Hannah attended her and left, and Athel bundled the last unruly merrymakers out of the room and bolted the door, saying, "They've had all the jest they're getting out of us for one day. Let them find their fun elsewheres."

Clamorous protests continued outside for a few minutes and then faded along the stone passageway. The west wing was quiet and still.

Madeleine had hinted delicately at the requirements

36

of the marriage bed, and Eugenie was conscious of a small fluttering of apprehension. But only that Athel should be pleased with her and that she should seem desirable as a wife. She was not afraid. Where love flourished, there would be gentle hands, tenderness, patience and understanding. Believing this, in all simplicity she moved toward him, seeking the comfort of his arms after the long excitement of the day.

Athel's response was immediate. She was scooped up, flung onto the bed and possessed as though she were a wanton.

It was a measure of her faith in him that she attributed the violence of his lovemaking to the wine and forgave him in her heart, even while she cried out in pain. Then he fell instantly to sleep while she, raking the dark with puzzling woman's eyes, wondered over this manifestation of love and life and tried to reconcile it with her dreams, thinking over her mother's worldly-wise advice: "A man has no wit of a maid's feelings. He takes what he wants when he wants it."

By dawnlight she saw his face against her naked shoulder. He nuzzled her softly, stirring in his sleep. So boyish. So innocent. Yet he was strong. He would be her protector throughout her life and would father her children. *Whatever he does shall always seem right to me,* Eugenie resolved. Then she, too, slept.

They lingered on at Blowick for a week of celebration. But Athel was impatient to get back to his land. While the medieval grandeur of Blowick impressed him, he was not at ease, and although at the last moment Eugenie's parents were reluctant to part with her, Athel overbore even Madeleine's voluble protests and took his bride home at the end of May.

The turnpike system was not come to Lancashire in 1720. They traveled over roads rutted four feet across in places and nearly as deep. Exceptional early summer rains added to the hazards of the journey.

37

Athel urged the coachman forward. "What matters a splash of mud on the paintwork, or your high-shined boots? I want to be in my own house, man!"

There were two new wheels needed and a crippled horse put down before they drove into Clere Athel.

III

THE home to which Athel brought Eugenie was a stone-built manor house, principally of the fourteenth century. A modest wing, added in the reign of Henry VIII, had robbed its elevation of symmetry and supplied a handsome paneled dining hall in the process. Now a second wing would provide those improvements to the accommodation which Lord Carle thought necessary for his daughter's comfort. The work ought to be completed before autumn, and the new building had been sited to counterbalance the Tudor gable end. The fact that its design in no way harmonized with what had gone before did not trouble the master of the house in the slightest degree.

It troubled him far more that his father-in-law had insisted on such an extravagance out of the marriage portion. He would have preferred to spend the money on costly drainage for the low-lying land on the edge of the old salt marsh. It was beginning to be said that the treacherous "mosses" of Lancashire were reclaimable, and when Athel thought of that land lying spare, he was greedy for it. But experiments were costly. He found it in his heart to wish that Eugenie came with fewer conditions attached to her.

Nevertheless, she came with great wealth, and Lord Carle was in a position to call the tune. If he said his daughter must have her own apartments. a bedchamber of her own and a boudoir and an adjoining room for her maid and a salon and the like, well, so be it. Only it seemed a waste. The long room above the porch had done for his father and mother in their time and many another couple before them.

He brought Eugenie home in the late afternoon in a fine sifting rain. The first hay cut had been taken off the parkland, and he felt proud of its neat appearance, the fine timber, the oak and the beech, the blossoming chestnuts and the ancient yews. She was a pretty bride, so dainty in her silks and her velvet traveling cloak, and he had taken her by the hand and presented her to the servants with a flourish.

"My wife. Your new mistress, the Lady Eugenie."

Twenty servants, bowing and curtsying. Almost as many as they had at Carle House—well, almost. Of course, they did not all serve indoors, but tricked out smartly for the occasion, they looked as if they did.

Then he had sent Eugenie above stairs with Mistress Murchitt, the housekeeper, to conduct her.

"See my wife has everything that she requires." He had a certain proprietorial pride in saying "my wife." And to Eugenie: "Make yourself comfortable, my love. I must needs see how things stand after my absence. Until suppertime." He bowed over her hand and was gone.

Eugenie and Hannah followed Mistress Murchitt up the worn oak stairs, which had been polished to a finish like glass. Unhappily this impression of housewifely efficiency did not carry beyond the landing.

The room into which they were led was stark, damp and none too clean.

There was a great bed. A great, dark, looming bed of a style that had gone out of use two centuries ago. It

39

dominated the room, and there was little else in the way of furnishings—a high-backed chair and a footstool set in front of the empty hearth, a table with a washbowl, and another furnished with candles. There was nothing to suggest the accommodation of a woman.

Eugenie hesitated for a moment on the threshold of her husband's bedchamber, gathering her determination to meet its comfortless atmosphere. This was a man's room, she told herself. Athel had succeeded to it five years ago. Before that his father had occupied it alone for eleven years after the death of Athel's mother.

"The two doors at the far end?"

"A closet on the right, a small room as can be used for dressing . . . m'lady." The title came awkwardly to Mistress Murchitt's tongue. There had been no lords and ladies among the Athelsons in living memory. The men had an old way and called the master Athel Athelson when they spoke to him. And the wife of the master was "Ma'am," which they said did for old Queen Anne in her day, God rest her. So, like enough, it did for an Athelson bride. But this one was a lord's daughter, and they must give her a title. The housekeeper eyed her new mistress covertly. She was disposed to respect her but not yet to like her.

"Hannah?"

Mistress Murchitt found herself unceremoniously bundled out of the way by my lady's maid. She would have to watch that one! The girl had a bold, sure look.

Hannah was already striding across the room. She opened first one door and then the other.

"Well, the closet's a closet." She returned to stand before Eugenie. Her hands were planted on her hips, and she looked past her mistress to the housekeeper. "As for the dressing room—you can call it that if you will. There's naught in it but cobwebs. Hardly what you're accustomed to, my lady."

Eugenie sighed and slipped off her cloak. "Mistress

40

Murchitt"—her smile and her voice were gentle—"I wonder if you could discover a chair and some item of furniture which might serve as a dressing table?"

"There's space enough for a hanging cupboard, as well," Hannah added. "And if you will just send up a maid with a broom and duster. . . ."

Mistress Murchitt prepared for battle. "The room *has* been cleaned—"

"Not recently," Hannah cut in in her reasonable but uncompromising manner. "Never mind, you have much to see after in a house this size and"—she glanced about significantly at the crumbling plaster—"this age. Just send a maid, and I'll look to my lad's quarters from now on."

"Of course," Mistress Murchitt began plaintively, "with the building work going on to supply the new rooms it has been difficult to keep dust out."

"I am sure it has. The maid, if you please. . . . And if you could arrange for her to bring some cans of hot water, my lady might take a bath before supper."

The mention of supper cut short any further discussion. The housekeeper recollected that she had only four main courses and two puddings to offer. If her new mistress was so fancy in her ways, would this be sufficient? Better to see cook at once.

"I have put your bridal linen on the bed," she spoke directly to Eugenie. "The other chests have been stored in the empty room, next down the passage. Them's still locked, of course." There was a suggestion of disapproval. Nothing was ever locked in Athel Athelson's house.

Eugenie said, "Tomorrow you and I will sort the remainder of the linen and the silver which I have brought. You shall tell me of any other needs in the household, and I will supply what is wanted."

This was encouraging at least. Mistress Murchitt conceded that there might be compensations in the coming of Lady Eugenie. Heaven alone knew what problems she had to keep the hangings refurbished and the tableware in any serviceable shape.

When she had curtsied and left them, Hannah was at Eugenie's side in an instant.

"You must be exhausted. . . . Let me take your cloak. Do you sit in this chair and put your feet up."

"No, no, Hannah. I am not such a frail creature as you think." Eugenie went over and opened one of the windows. There were four mullioned casements. They were small, and the room was ill-lit for its size. But the moist scent that arose, of growing things and well-fed earth, was satisfying. "It *is* a pleasant place." She spoke with an emphasis, almost a passion. "One could be happy here, if only—"

"If only the bedrooms were habitable!"

Eugenie laughed. "London has made you soft in your tastes, Hannah. There are parts of Blowick Castle harsh enough to freeze the marrow in your bones. Anyway, we must not begin with grumbles. When the new wing is finished, we shall be very comfortable."

A tap on the door heralded a maid and a manservant with cans of hot water. A copper bath was produced from the closet.

Hannah put the maid to work cleaning up the dressing room and dismissed the man with orders that he should return when Eugenie was at supper and lay a fire.

Half an hour later, bathed and dressed in pale-pink silk, Eugenie made her way downstairs in search of her husband.

The hall was deserted, its stone pillars and low, vaulted ceiling now swallowed up in the late dusk, the only light from a lantern on the newel-post at the foot of the stairs. Eugenie moved forward uncertainly in the gloom. There was an archway just ahead of her and she was relieved to see the glow of candles in a passage beyond. The house was so eerily still it might almost have been uninhabited.

Would it be better to return to the bedroom and wait until supper was announced? No, that was stupid. Hannah was unpacking, and she would only be in the way. She would not retreat; she would go forward.

There were many doors along the passage. She hesitated, considering whether to tap on one of them and ask her direction. And then suddenly, joyfully, she saw that one of them was not quite closed and the welcome brightness of a fire within.

A silence suggested that the room was unoccupied. She pushed the door open and saw that it was a library. For several seconds she stood perfectly still on the threshold of this pleasant discovery. The room was quite large, even handsome, fitted with shelves from the floor to within a foot or so of the ceiling.

"Well, are you coming in?" The voice was slightly amused, slightly impatient, and Eugenie turned to look with some confusion at the man who had half risen behind the desk where he was working.

"I ask your pardon for disturbing you, sir. I am looking for my husband."

A short laugh answered her. "You're not likely to find him in *here*. Books ain't *his* score."

"Perhaps you would be kind enough to tell me where he is then."

"I daresay he's looking at the lower pasture. Little Rip broke its banks this morning, and the long meadow's flooded."

"Oh! Is that a serious matter?"

"It has happened before in a wet season, and I imagine it will again. Of course, I set the men on at first light to dig drainage channels, but Athel's sure to say we've taken the wrong line."

Eugenie noted the use of her husband's first name. She must be speaking to a member of the family, but who could he be?

Reading the thought, he said, "I suppose I had best

introduce myself. My name is Giles, and I am Athel's brother." And then sharply, "You look surprised—hasn't Athel spoken of me?"

"Why, yes, naturally he told me that he had two brothers, but I thought. . . . I mean, I did not know that you lived *here*. . . ." She was disconcerted by his expression, which warned that for some reason she was on dangerous ground. Had she implied a criticism? "I thought . . . Oxfordshire."

"It is Humphrey who lives in Oxfordshire. He is married to Robert Hackthorne's daughter."

"Yes, I met Sir Robert in London."

Giles merely nodded and changed the subject with a peremptory "I wish you will be seated and then I may sit also."

Really, his manner was quite rude, Eugenie thought, and this was not in the least what she had imagined of the first evening she would spend in her new home. In the circumstances, however, it seemed the sensible course to make the best of things.

"Yes, of course, I am sorry. And I will share the fire if I am not in the way."

"Not in the least. I left the door open to guide you here. Close it now, please, or else we shall have the dogs in. I don't let 'em in here since one of the damned puppies ate Gower. He was just making a start on Herrick when I caught him."

"Naturally one would not wish to see Herrick mauled." Eugenie shut the door as she was commanded. "On the other hand, I would defend a dog who ate Gower. It is just possible that this is the only way in which he can be digested." She had taken a high-backed tapestry chair by the hearth and was warming her chilled hands so that she did not notice the look Giles turned on her.

"So!" he said softly. "You have your opinions. I had hoped no less."

"You had hoped?"

"Did you not wonder where your books were? I made

44

sure that as soon as you had washed off the dust of your journey, you would come in search of your books." He gestured to the shelves behind her. "Great boxes of books! By God, it did my heart good to see those arrive. 'Ho-ho,' I said to myself, 'my new sister-in-law is not all ribbon and lace. At least she reads.'"

"You have my books in here." Eugenie rose in astonishment and crossed the room to examine the titles. It was on her mind to ask him how he came to open packages that had her name upon them, but when she saw how lovingly and tastefully the books had been arranged, first by category and then by language, she could not bring herself to complain.

"They will be best in here." There was perhaps just a trace of eagerness for her approval in this one respect. "The maids have my instructions not to handle them. I tell them to dust only so far as the wing of a goose will reach along the top edge of each volume. For the rest, I treat the bindings myself and I have a special care for the calf and the vellums, which keeps them in good condition."

She turned to look at him, puzzled. "You have a great love of books. That is not usual in the young men of my acquaintance. Do you study on a particular subject?"

He leaned back in his chair, and the keenness had gone out of him. "Aye, lady, that I do. I study on life itself." There was a weariness in his tone which arrested her attention, and for the first time since she had come into the room she made a direct examination of his face, seeing him not as a stranger or as an adjunct of Athel, but as a man a little older than herself, perhaps three-and-twenty, who was not out in the world as one would expect, but apparently living on his brother's bounty, who so far as she could remember was unmarried, and who appeared to have no career in hand or in prospect. What was it about him? There was something she could not give a name to. The quality of his expression was stillness; the planes of his face were smooth and strong.

Odd how little he resembled his brother. Where were Athel's regular features and burnished good looks? Giles had black hair, and his eyes were dark, intensely dark now, without even the light of interest. He knew he was being observed, and whatever spark of sympathy had leaped between them a moment ago was gone.

Nor was it to be recaptured since sounds of bustle in the corridor and the barking of dogs heralded Athel's arrival.

"I know where she will be," he was saying as he flung open the door of the library and—"There you are! Giles has her safe enough. Mistress Murchitt here in a flurry." He jerked his head. "Went to fetch you to supper and could not find you." He stood surveying them, filling the doorway, bringing the scent of the open air and the almost tangible atmosphere of his vigor into the room. "Well, you two are met and are spared introductions. Come to table, then. Eugenie, if you are one part as famished as I am, we will do justice to every dish cook has contrived, and devil help Giles if he lingers!"

"I'll follow you directly," Giles said.

"Nonsense, you'll come this minute, else the soup will get cold. Come on, man, she has to know, you can't hide behind that desk forever. Here, let me hand you your crutches."

"I can reach them myself, thank you." Giles' voice was tight with resentment and frustration, which Athel did not appear to notice.

"Here we are, up we get. Are you steady?" His interference made Giles more awkward than he was, so that he stumbled slightly in getting himself around the desk.

Eugenie watched, appalled. So this was the quality she had being trying to define. The quality was pain. Her eyes were compelled toward the space where Giles' right leg should have been and then raised with reluctance to meet his look of malicious relish in her discomfort. Living with this brother-in-law was not going to be easy.

Later, when they were alone, she reproached Athel for not having warned her about Giles.

"I might have said something unforgivable when I talked to him."

"Truth is I never thought to mention it. Tragic, but it's all in the past now. We were staying with the Hackthornes in Oxfordshire, and Giles tried to reach some cherries on a branch that hung out over the millrace. Damned silly thing to do. The branch snapped and he fell in. Got caught in the wheel."

"How terrible!"

"Yes," Athel said slowly. "I often wonder whether I did the right thing to pull him out. His leg was mangled, and they had to take it off at the top of the thigh and then. . . . Well, the thing is I didn't realize at the time but he . . . no, that's not a thing to tell a woman. I remember he kept saying, 'Why didn't you let me die? Why didn't you let me die?' He was only seventeen, and of course the accident ruined his life before it had even begun. He was going in for the law. Got a good head on him, Giles. Just as well. Got precious little else now."

"Poor Giles. How bitter he must be. Can nothing more be done for him?"

But the conversation was taking place in bed, and Athel, having other preoccupations, was not disposed to prolong it.

"No, what is there? He will live out his days here with me. I don't grudge him his keep, and indeed, he proves useful to me checking on Haldane's accounts and the like."

The compassion which this story had aroused in Eugenie helped her in the days that followed.

Athel was often out from first light until dusk, taking only a short break for dinner at noon and making his best meal at suppertime in the same way that his tenants and laborers did. The care of the land was his obsession. Nothing took precedence. It was not enough for him to give instructions; he must see them carried out. Each

47

morning his steward, Thomas Haldane, would call for him, and they made the round of the estate together. In the afternoons he took his dogs hunting in the woods or his warren, or dragged his carp pond, or enjoyed any one of the half dozen activities which constituted recreation in the life of a country gentleman of abundant energy and no pretensions.

This routine meant that she must often find herself alone with Giles. She soon discovered why Mistress Murchitt and her maids went to such extraordinary lengths to avoid an encounter with him. He had moods, black hours, when his sardonic humor flayed anyone who came within reach of him. Eugenie was at first shocked and later indignant to find herself a favored target. Sometimes it would seem as though her very existence provoked him. Yet if she avoided him, he sought her out, sent for her on the slimmest pretext —even pursued her to the farthest corner of the house when she would not come to him. And always, it seemed, to fight with her. Only she would not engage in the war he declared. Some angry reply would rise to her lips, and she would bite it back, remembering what he had suffered and what the moment of a youthful folly had cost him.

In the meantime she applied herself to the task of trying to run her new home. There were some successes. Mistress Murchitt, who had wanted only the presence of a resident mistress to give her authority among the rest of the servants, at once began to show herself more efficient in the discharge of her duties. Damp rooms were aired; dirt chased from obscure corners of the old manor house; hangings and curtains were renewed. The table at Clere Athel had never been sparse. The land provided in abundance. But prompted to a little show of imagination, the cook produced undreamed-of dishes, and Athel was less inclined to break his fast off bread and cheese in a field.

Rejoicing inwardly at this small triumph, Eugenie redoubled her efforts. However Athel might scowl over the conditions her father had made for their marriage, he must surely think them worthwhile if his home was more welcoming and she always receptive to his ardor. And so her days were filled with duties, and each evening she would employ taffeta and laces, scents and jewels to beguile him.

She had been six weeks a bride when Athel announced his intention of entertaining several gentlemen of the neighboring countryside to an afternoon's coursing with hounds.

"We'll put up hares as long as its light . . . say, until half after eight. Then we'll take supper. It will be proper for you to receive. But since there will be no other women of the party, you'll not join us at table."

If Eugenie was disappointed, she took care not to show it. She had yet to enjoy the role of hostess. Clere Athel was too isolated for uninvited callers to pay their respects. Still, Athel had promised her that they would have guests to supper directly after harvest, and as he made much of this concession, she was more than content.

In preparation for Athel's friends no trouble must be spared. Eugenie had the maids polishing the oak in the dining hall until it gleamed like the day it was finished, and there was such an array of dishes that Heskettson, the steward, vowed that eight men could never touch the quarter of it.

"We'll be eatin' it up for days, lady, mark my words! They'll be drinkin' far more nor they'll chew. I know Athel Athelson's friends, and with respect to your presence, there's something about a coursin' brings out a thirst and the worst in 'em." He looked her over kindly. He was a bachelor and disliked women in the general way, but she was young and trusting and it was plain to see that she adored Athel. He added out of the kindness of his heart, "If I were you, I'd say 'How d'ye do' and then go to my bed and lock my door."

It seemed very odd advice to Eugenie. What, lock her door against her own husband, and he perhaps wanting her to see after the needs of his guests? Such a thing was not to be thought of. Besides, if the gentlemen were drinking deep, who would make sure that the candles were extinguished and the fire left safe when they went to their beds? A manservant might doze if the hour was very late—anything might happen. And so she resolved to pass the night in reading and writing letters, keeping vigil until daybreak if necessary.

The gentlemen, when they arrived, were a good deal merrier from their day's sport than she had anticipated. Leather flasks had gone hand to hand while they worked the dogs, and bets had been pledged in the strong, home-brewed barley wine of the north. It was not easy to summon up the confidence to go forward and give them welcome. For Athel's sake she concealed her distaste for the rough jests and the smears of blood on their clothes and coaxed them to the supper table. Perhaps when they had eaten, they would be less rowdy.

Giles, who disliked making an entrance, was already sitting in his place at Athel's right hand. The men greeted him boisterously, chaffing him for a greedy knave, who had declined to join them in their sport simply in order to be first at the food.

He answered them in good spirit, and it was clear that the company provided a welcome change in the monotony of his life. Seeing this, Eugenie was pleased for him and also in some measure relieved. If Giles were enjoying himself, he would stay with them, and as he drank sparingly, there would at least be one sober head.

She remained a minute or two longer, fussing over the arrangements of the cold table and then, catching Athel's eye, was thankful to wish them good appetite and good-night.

It was just past ten o'clock, and Hannah, looking sleepy, was waiting to help her undress. They kept early, country hours as a rule, and it had been a long day. Eugenie confided her intention of waiting up until the party was over, but she firmly declined Hannah's offer to keep watch with her.

"No, no. Why should you? I may sleep as late as I please tomorrow. You look tired. Only help me with these hooks, and then you can go to your bed."

"I will do no such thing. I will brush out your hair as I always do. Which robe will you wear?"

"The blue velvet. Then I am presentable if I have to go downstairs for any reason. Leave my nightcap. I'll not put that on until I retire."

The long-case clock on the landing was striking midnight. Eugenie rose stiffly from the little table, where she had been writing letters for the past hour. The summer night had a chill in it. A pity that she had not let Hannah build a fire. She was growing very tired. The bustle and preparations had been more exhausting than she realized.

Resolutely she took up a book. But at least it would be more comfortable to sit on the bed and draw the quilt around her. . . . The clock was striking again. Eugenie awoke with a start. How many strokes? She couldn't tell. The candle beside her was guttering in its socket. She leaped up and lit a new one from it. It burned meanly at first, and the dark edges of the room closed in upon her. Even the bed was sinister. This was the first time she had awakened in it without Athel's head against her shoulder, and she was suddenly, shudderingly aware of all the Athelsons who had died in it. A feeling of desolation swept over her, and she wanted above everything to see Athel, at least to hear the sound of his voice, and to be assured that she was not alone with the creaking sounds of the house at night.

Shielding the flame of her candle carefully from the draft, she opened the door and crept across the landing to look at the clock. Just after three. Could Athel and his friends still be up? Perhaps they were playing at cards. For her own peace of mind she must find out.

She had forgotten to put on her slippers, and the oak boards were cold to her feet as she went downstairs. The stone flags of the hall were worse, and she hurried into the passage beyond. A roar of laughter told her that indeed the party was still in progress.

Eugenie hesitated. It would be disastrous to be discovered in her night attire stealing about the house in search of her husband. Yet neither could there be any rest until she had assured herself at least that Giles was still with them. Or that Athel was not *very* drunk.

A supply of candles had been left ready in the passage. She snuffed those that were burned down and lit fresh ones. She could hear their voices more clearly now, and as she turned the corner, she realized that the doors of the dining hall were not quite closed.

Quickly she drew back behind a stone pillar. Now if she could just distinguish Athel speaking. . . .

"Devil take it! Look at Charlie. I'm gelded if he ain't face down in the gravy!"

"Ugh! The feller's disgusting. Put him behind . . . screen . . . out of—out of m-my sight. Makes me want to retch."

"Well, don't retch over me!"

Good heavens, Eugenie thought, they were in a very bad condition. And where was Athel?

"Beats me," a voice was saying, "beats me how Athel can sit there drinking claret when he's got a bride in his bed. Now if I had a bride in *my* bed, I'd be covering her like a shaky bet on a faro table, damme if I wouldn't."

"Yes, old Athel's done all right for himself. Lovely girl and a fortune with her—what more can a man ask?"

"Oh, I don't know." Athel spoke slowly and his voice was slurred. "There's something more."

"Good God, man, what? You're hard to please."

Eugenie had been about to turn away. She wanted to

turn away, but she could not. Scarcely breathing, she waited for his answer.

"Well," Athel said, "a woman like my Eugenie makes a good wife. You get children by such a woman if she's healthy and she runs your house as you wish. But damn it all"—he laughed—"damn it all, a well-bred girl with thin flanks and fastidious ways don't put any fire into a man."

They greeted that with a roar of approval.

"By heaven, he's right you know *By heaven*, he is!"

"Give me," Athel said dreamily, "a country wench with a strong animal smell on her, great breasts and sturdy thighs—"

"Aye, you've a one like that, I've seen her!"

"My Sal," Athel said with satisfaction. "I give you a toast—to my bonny Sally with the laughing mouth, who never washes but on Sunday and has no other thought in her head than to content me!"

Eugenie closed her eyes tightly, listening. Then she opened them, and the silent, hot tears of humiliation ran down her cheeks. She began to grope her way back along the corridor. But something was wrong. There was more light than there should have been. The library door was open, and Giles was leaning against the doorpost.

For an instant she stared up at him through her tears. "Did you hear?"

The clamor of the toast was in the background.

"I did." His pale face was expressionless, watching her weep. And then: "Well, you shouldn't have been listening, should you? Go to your bed and pay no mind to what men say in their cups."

His lack of sympathy gave her strength, and she answered, with a sudden ferocity. "I shall never forgive him. I shall never forget!"

"That's the spirit," Giles said mildly.

IV

HANNAH, taking in a cup of hot chocolate for her mistress an hour later than usual, was surprised to find her already awake and seated before her mirror.

"My lady! Why did you not ring your bell? I had thought you would still be sleeping." She looked at Eugenie, and it seemed doubtful that she had slept at all. There was something different about her expression this morning. "You are not ill?"

"I thank you, I am perfectly well. . . . Where is my husband?"

Hannah smiled thinly. "Gone off to Upstrand to see his friends on their way, and none of them sitting very straight in the saddle, I can tell you! Heskettson told me he found them where they fell in the dining hall. He woke Master Giles and together they persuaded them out under the pump in the yard. Not much else to be done with them, seemingly. Not much breakfast called for neither!"

"Has Heskettson put the maids to work on the dining hall?"

"He has. And Master Giles told him to lay dinner for the two of you in the morning room. Master's not expected back till late."

Eugenie was brushing her hair. Her eyes meeting Hannah's in the mirror gave nothing away.

"I have been thinking," she said after a pause, "that we may as well move into the new wing today."

the mind in a woman. You are governed from the womb."

"You do not really believe that, for if you did, you would not try to challenge me in argument. Come, let us play at cards."

"I should loathe above everything to play at cards." He scowled at her, and then abruptly his face cleared. "I will play you a game of chess, though."

"A man's game! I don't know how to play."

"Then I will teach you. Since you are grown so cumbersome and cannot get about, it will help you to fill your time of waiting."

"Your motives are, of course, quite disinterested. Are you sure I have the intellect to grasp the rules?"

"I shall explain them to you in simple words," Giles said sweetly, "as though to a very little child."

There was a long tradition that on Christmas Eve the children of the village were given presents from the manor. They would come in a long, straggling, laughing line up to the house and then, in the hall hung with yew and mistletoe and holly, would each one be introduced by name and receive a small toy, a few pieces of marchpane in a twist of paper, an apple dipped in boiled sugar. Mothers would accompany them and in their turn receive a gift of game or maybe, in a prosperous year, a length of good woolen cloth. It had been the custom for the mistress of the house to dispense this goodwill, but following the death of his mother, Athel had taken over the small ceremony. Now he relinquished it with obvious pleasure to Eugenie.

"Much more the thing for a woman to do it. You'll know what to say to 'em. I ain't a hand at talking to children—and as for their mothers! Well, I may tell you I've run clean out of patience in the past. They stand there and have the devilish nerve to expect compliments on their offspring, when every year there's one more! I tell them straightly the land don't grow in proportion to their families, and there's a limit to the number of mouths we can feed from it."

"Perhaps you should tell their husbands," Eugenie suggested.

"Never fear. I do that, too."

"Where do we get the toys? Is there a toy seller in Upstrand?"

"There's usually a peddler there on market day has cup and ball. I buy from him. Then old Josiah Thatcher in the cottage next the church, he carves wooden animals. I buy all he can make in a year. They like them. Cook looks after the sweetmeats."

"I believe I shall enjoy the occasion."

"Well, it's possible," Athel conceded. "It's a good way for you to get to know our people. But make them stand back when they talk to you. They're a healthy lot in the general run of things—healthier than most, I'm proud to say—but it would never do to risk taking some childish ailment in your condition."

It was fun to make preparations. Eugenie saw to it that an enormous fire was built early in the day and kept stacked to drive the chill from the hall. She added one or two touches of her own and paid the expenses of them from *her* purse, lest Athel should not approve. The game would be given to the mothers in new osier baskets instead of being hung from a length of stick. She added ribbons for the girls and cotton neckerchiefs for the boys and directed that pasties and cordial should be served.

"Bless my soul," said Mistress Murchitt, when she was told of these arrangements, "you're making quite a party of it. I doubt if the master would approve. Once you begin giving them this and that, it has to be kept up in future years, you know, and it costs good money."

Eugenie laughed. "I intend to keep it up. And no need to look so grim, I can afford it."

The housekeeper was still doubtful. "It isn't you I'm

thinking on, my lady, begging your pardon. It is those as come after."

Eugenie was taken aback for a moment. But she was learning that in Clere Athel everyone took the long view of time. There was so much that was constant in the history of these people on this land that they had developed a singular awareness of mortality. The land would always be here, they seemed to say, but every man's tenure of it was limited. Innumerable tomorrows would follow yesterdays beyond the counting.

There was a great curiosity in the village to see Eugenie at close quarters. They had seen her drive or ride through the village. They saw her in church on Sundays and she had attended the ram wrestle after harvest. But few of them had actually had the opportunity of speaking to her. Servants up at the house said she was fine in her ways and that the new wing was furnished like a royal palace. They said she was one who spoke her mind. No fault in her for that. Folk in Clere Athel liked plain speaking. There were no hasty judgments, however. It remained to be seen whether she would produce the male heir—the qualification required in an Athelson bride above any other.

The first children of the village began to arrive directly after dinner. Athel was gone for the day to give the neighboring Mablethorpes the greetings of the season and not due back until suppertime, but Giles condescended to be present, to assist with introductions.

In fact, his help was little needed. Proud mothers were not slow to shepherd their families forward, and Eugenie, conscious of the small fluttering movements of the child she was carrying, looked with a wonder and a sharpened interest into every little face upturned to hers. Her hands would keep reaching out to cup the rounded delicacy of their chins, to caress the fine silken hair, close-molded to small heads, and the women understood. They looked her up and down and whispered

61

among themselves that she was slight for childbearing, yet carrying high, which was a good sign. Five months gone, was she? Some said six. They had it on cook's authority. The end of March.

The pasties and cordials were appreciated after the walk through the parkland on a cold afternoon. Gifts were distributed, and someone observing that a fine snow was beginning to fall, a general move was made to get the children home, before it "weathered worse."

But even as they were turning to gather up cloaks and hoods, there was a sudden stir of late arrivals at the door. Voices were raised. Heskettson was inclined to deny admittance. Eugenie moved forward from her position by the fireplace to tell him he must do no such thing, to let them come. Why were the women deliberately barring her way? There were cries of "Shame!" "For shame! Go home!". . . . Why? Bewildered, Eugenie turned to look for Giles. He was already swinging himself forward . . . past her . . . and the women let him through and then closed their ranks again. . . . "For the love of heaven, Sal! What the devil are you at?" Giles said, and at once the mystery was cleared. This was Sally Bowden, Athel's mistress. And she *had a child*.

"Giles!" Eugenie's clear voice cut across the argumentative murmurs. "Let the woman in."

"Leave this to me. You don't understand."

"There is a child with the woman. *No* child shall be denied here, this day."

The mothers, who had tried to intervene, drew back. There was compassion in their eyes. The pathway that opened up in their midst heightened the sense of drama in the confrontation, and Eugenie stared at Sally Bowden. It was easy to see what had attracted Athel. The woman had a bold mouth, a cascade of dark hair over one shoulder and a pretty plumpness that became her.

"Pray come forward," Eugenie said to her, and the woman, somewhat hampered by the child who clung and

62

hid behind her skirts, made her way slowly across the hall until she stood within touching distance.

Although it crossed Eugenie's mind that the other woman might only have come to challenge or to mock, she banished the thought instantly when she looked into the brilliant dark eyes. There was anger there, but hurt also, and the kind of defiance, which is the front of fear. It had cost this woman a good deal to brave the disapproval of the assembled lawful motherhood of the village.

Eugenie took up some of the spare gifts which still lay on the table beside her. "Will the child come to me?"

Sally Bowden disentangled the clinging hands with an effort and dragged forward a small boy of perhaps five or six years.

Eugenie lowered herself carefully until she was on a level with the child's face. *This*, every yearning instinct was telling her, *is Athel's child*. Anxiously she sought her husband's features.

The shock was so great that it almost overcame her. The fair hair was scant, wispy and lusterless on the misshapen head, and the eyes which met hers were Athel's eyes, yet clear, blank, devoid of that light which is the natural human response to inquiry. She knew instantly that in this child the mind had never kindled as it ought.

The boy stretched out his hands slowly for the gifts that she held, and she gave them to him. Then she stood up.

Sally Bowden said with an abrupt desperation, "I wouldn't have brought him, only he saw the other children setting off, jostling and merry. I can't tell what he understands. He knew they were going somewheres, and of a sudden I couldn't bear to deny him."

A feeling of nausea and faintness assailed Eugenie. The soft sensations of her own child moving had ceased, and instead, there was fear inside her. She fought it down with an effort and said, "You did right. It behooves

63

us to have a special care of such a child, lest we injure feelings we do not fully comprehend."

The hall seemed to be misting before her eyes. She forced herself to look at the boy again and then at Sally Bowden. *This woman,* she thought, *is desired by my husband and I am not, but there is no triumph in her coming here today. She has come for love of the child.*

Aloud, Eugenie said simply, "God must have thought well of you to entrust one of these eternal innocents to your care."

A slight inclination of her head took in the assembled women and indicated that the ceremony of the gifts was at an end. "And now if you will excuse me, I will wish you all good-night and joy in the festival of Christmas."

She crossed the hall slowly, climbed the stairs heavily, and the whisper of her silk skirts was the only sound in the hush she left behind her.

Athel had suggested that she might ask her mother to be with her when the child was born. This thoughtfulness touched her. Athel had been showing a deal of consideration since Christmas, and Eugenie wondered if Giles had a hand in it. Perhaps he had related Sally Bowden's visit with her son on Christmas Eve. Did the same fear run in Athel's mind as in hers? Did he wonder if he was capable of getting a normal child?

Unthinkable, of course, that she should ask him, that they could share the burden of this thought. For if there were ever talk of Sally Bowden between them, both his pride and hers must be sacrificed.

The short days of January and February seemed unbearably long to her. She suffered from a frequent sickness, and though her belly grew, her arms had lost their roundness and her cheeks were hollow so that she had the look of death upon her. She saw it in the mirror, and Hannah saw it, and the expression of her maid's face frightened her even more than her own.

Madeleine came at the end of the second week in

March and, within an hour of her arrival, aroused the resentment of every member of the household staff.

Eugenie was beyond knowing or caring. What went on downstairs or in the village had ceased to exist for her. There was Hannah, and there was Madeleine—suddenly wonderfully reassuring. There was a physician brought over from Upstrand and a midwife from the village. They came and went like phantoms, leaning over her, making her struggle upright to take broth, raising her pillows and lowering them, brushing her hair and bathing her. On the twenty-first of March, the first day of spring, she gave birth to a son: an exuberant, struggling, fist-clenching infant who was the very image of Athel. Eugenie looked into his eyes and knew beyond doubt that there was intelligence there. She thanked God and slept.

"And now," said her mother on the afternoon of the second day, "you will be pleased to know that I have found you a wet nurse. There, sit up and take this bouillon. I had cook make it to my own recipe, and there is a good red wine in it to give you strength."

"A wet nurse?" Eugenie was languid, her thoughts slow. "Yes, I remember Hannah told me there were two other babes due in the village. But I thought I might feed him myself."

"*Mon dieu!* You are grown quite rustic. What a notion. Besides," Madeleine added hastily, "you have not the constitution to suckle such a lusty child. Half the time you would leave him hungry and he would be fretful."

Eugenie wanted to dispute this, to tell her mother that she had seen cook's daughter feeding her baby by the kitchen fire and that the woman had laughed when she asked if it was difficult, saying it was the most natural thing in the world. But Athel would never forgive her if his son was not nourished as he ought to be, and she was still too weary to argue. Perhaps her mother was right.

Madeleine saw that she had surrendered and made things as easy for her as she could. "You will approve the girl, I know. She worked in your dairy until her time came, and dairy girls are always cleaner than most. Her name is Edith."

Eugenie nodded. "I remember her." She closed her eyes.

"I understand what you are feeling, child." Madeleine surprised herself with her own words. "It is not easy to surrender him to the breast of a stranger. You must think that what you do is for the best. He will prosper, and you will be able to return all the sooner to your management of the household. A woman who is feeding is careless in everything else, and soon finds her husband displeased." Eugenie's eyes opened questioningly at that. "Yes, indeed. Men are unaccountable creatures. They want children, but they are always jealous of the attention a woman gives to them. We will expel your milk and give you an infusion of dandelion to discourage a further flow. In no time you will be in your usual good looks."

Eugenie slept again, and when she awoke, Athel was in the room. He had just straightened up from an examination of the empty cradle beside her bed.

"Do not be alarmed, the wet nurse has him. My mother has put them in Hannah's room for the time being." Athel's face registered an almost foolish degree of relief. "What is the matter," she teased, "did you think the fairies had stolen him?"

"Don't joke of such a thing!"

"Oh, Athel!" She regarded him with an almost tender amusement. "Are you pleased with your son?"

"Indeed I am. He is a fine boy. All Clere Athel rejoices with us. My people send their respects to you and look forward to May Day, when I have undertaken you will both be present."

"Why, yes, if the day is fair, I think we may safely take him out by the first of May."

A slight frown creased Athel's forehead. "You're not intending to mollycoddle the lad, I hope. A boy should be raised hard."

66

"I'm sure you are right. But while he is yet an infant, we must have a certain care of him."

"Oh, aye"—hastily—"you shall rule his nursery days and I'll not interfere. . . . Er, you, er, don't consider he is inclined to be delicate, do you. . . . I mean to say, does he have the cough or aught like that?"

"The cough!" Eugenie laughed. "You talk as though he were a horse. No, of course he does not have 'the cough.' He is as healthy a babe as we could wish. Nevertheless, I think we will not dandle him in the north wind until he is in his second year."

Athel nodded. "The trick is to get more like him and then we shan't be worrying. I'll just go and take a look at him now, before I ride into Upstrand." He patted her hand approvingly. "Damned if I haven't a good mind to bring you back some trifle for a gift."

"You are exceedingly kind, sir." She could permit herself the indulgence of a mild irony since it would pass unnoticed.

"No more than you merit, madam, while you give me sons."

Madeleine, entering the room just after her son-in-law had left it, found Eugenie somewhere between laughter and tears.

"My child, what is this? Pray compose yourself." Her expression sharpened with comprehension. "That husband of yours, he has the clumsiness! He has said something to upset you."

Eugenie dabbed her eyes in a determined way and shook her head vehemently. "No, not the least in the world. It is a weakness came over me, nothing more."

"Ah, you may play that game with others, but not with me. I see that all is not bliss in your marriage." She sighed heavily. "I shall not say 'I told you so.' A man like that is not sensitive, not *sympathique* to the feelings of a woman—one should not have the expectation of it. Is there more I do not know, which you would like to tell me?"

Again Eugenie shook her head. "Indeed, you are mistaken." Pride would not let her admit otherwise. "Athel has just said he will bring me a gift from Upstrand. I am very happy, truly!"

Madeleine said, "Well, if you will have it so we will talk another way . . . we will make, how one says, the pretense, like when you were a child. Let us suppose that a woman is not the object of her husband's entire affection, that he does not care for her content—what does she do?"

Eugenie's eyes were suddenly attentive. "I do not know. What does she do?"

"Why . . . she lives a life." Madeleine shrugged, gracefully explicit. "It is only what we all do." She saw that Eugenie did not comprehend. "Look, it is this way. One might be blissfully happy, what is that? Is there a guarantee of permanence? Doesn't the beloved die, the beauty fade, the fortune change? It is not always the hand which is dealt that decides the winner. What matters more is how the game is played. One must play with spirit and strength, and then with just a little luck the cards may be turned to advantage." She tilted her head, her eyes narrowing thoughtfully on her daughter. "Now you have more than a little luck. You have a fortune. With that you can buy dignity and—most precious—independence."

"But happiness—"

"Is where you find it. When you find it, take it!" She smiled. "What I say may sound cynical to you. You are young and have your dreams still. When they fail you, remember my words. Be strong." She clenched her fists expressively. "Live your life with courage and vigor." She had said enough. Eugenie was frowning over her words, and her mouth was not happy. It quivered a little. Nevertheless, she had heard. "In a few days, when you are stronger, I must go to Blowick. I have written your father that you are safely delivered, and he will not think it reasonable that I should delay here longer than necessary. Heavens knows, your servants will be glad to be rid of me! They think I am a very shrew. I have done my best to set your nursery up as I think will be most convenient for you, and if you take my advice, you will build a new kitchen on at the rear of this wing. I have told Athel so, and I will speak to your father for the money. There can be no objection if he pays."

"What did Athel say?"

"He did not disapprove. Why should he, if we enhance his property at our expense? You may build anything you please, I think."

"Except a willow cabin at his gate," Eugenie spoke absently, hardly aware that she had voiced the thought.

"A willow cabin? *Now* I do not understand you. Who should want such a thing? Perhaps you *do* have a trace of fever. . . ."

"It was just a line from Shakespeare ran through my head."

"Oh, Shakespeare," said Madeleine dismissively. She thought he was nowhere beside Racine.

V

SPRING enters with a bashful sweetness in many counties, but it comes to Lancashire in quite another character—reluctant, teasing and fitful. On this account Athel liked May. It was his favorite month. *There* was all the promise of the growing year stirring the land. Hope without the disillusionment of a wet summer to flatten the grain in the fields. The chance of late frosts out of mind.

On May Day the tenants and villagers of Clere Athel might dance if they had a mind to do so. Athel would clap his hands in rhythm to the plaiting of the ribbons around the pole. He would tickle the children under their chins and give them sugar drops, slap a good plowman on the shoulder and maybe pinch the broad breasts of a wife there they swelled above the lace of a Sunday-best corset.

His firstborn son, Athel, was presented to the people on a May Day.

Eugenie, still hampered by her baby but with the wet-nurse to help, attended the festivities.

"Take a ribbon with me!" Athel had said. But four rounds were as much as she could manage, because she was still weak. Then he had seized Hannah about the waist to replace her, which was a pretty courtesty.

It was two o'clock of the afternoon—when the child had had chance to digest his feed—that the ceremony of presentation was performed and became the focus of the feast. The inhabitants of Clere Athel had been looking forward to that moment. They worked hard. Or rather they were hard-driven, since few men strive on another man's land unless they are directed and encouraged toward a collective achievement. Now they played because this was Athel Athelson's personal harvest. The child would one day possess their farmhouses and their cottages, and every inch of the ground on which they reared their own offspring. When the dancing was done, they gathered for the spit-roast pork and the syllabub and the ale with old apples afloat in the froth and thought themselves mighty lucky to have a master who knew how to celebrate if the time was right. Now they watched as he led his wife forward.

In the stillness the rustle of Eugenie's skirts across the grass was the only sound before Athel Athelson spoke.

"This is my male child!"

Eugenie drew back the delicate lace shawl so that all might see her son's face and sturdy limbs. He was awake, and wondering eyes gazed back at the people he would govern in his manhood.

"Ah!" The crowd expressed its satisfaction collectively in a long sigh.

Athel nodded slowly. "You may see that he is strong—a strong lad to whom you will one day give the same duty you have given to me and my fathers before me." He paused briefly. The men of Clere Athel had a deep feeling for their customs, liked them to be used ceremoniously. It was important to choose the right words. In the assurance of what they saw as the proper order of things going on forever lay the secret of their obedience. Athel understood this very well and, wanting to lay the right foundation for his heir, searched out such phrases as in all probability his own father had used twenty-six years earlier. "I shall raise my son in our long traditions and you shall help me. Together we will teach him to know our land. He will neither trap nor net hares out of season. He will not shoot wild duck while it nests. Such venison as we have in our woods will be cosseted against a time of need." The men murmured their approval, and there was a smattering of cheers from the boldest. Yes, that was what they wanted to hear. Athel continued, pleased to have still the better promises in his pocket. "He will learn from me to abide by our rules with regard to the succession and reassignment of tenancies. No man who works his land as he ought need ever fear to have it taken from him or his heirs and in a bad season or in sickness and trouble. You may expect, as always, to receive such support as a reasonable man would deem it reasonable to give." Now there were cheers and smiles on every side. God bless the master for the thoughtful man he was and a true son of his own father. No need to dread any boy *he* raised . . . and they forgot what their history taught them, that no man can promise for his heirs.

Eugenie's arm was growing numb under the weight of the child, but young Athel continued quiet and con-

71

tented, for which she was profoundly thankful. Her husband—pray God he did not go on talking much longer—would certainly have been angry if his son wailed on such an occasion. She glanced around for the nurse, but the woman was nowhere in sight. It was then that she saw Sal Bowden, standing on the edge of the crowd, and suddenly Eugenie had a feeling that the afternoon breeze was cooling, a growing sense that she was apart from the people she was with and the place she was in. She resisted, with difficulty, a ridiculous urge to run away from them all with her child: To carry him where? To Blowick, to her father? To London, to her mother? Either notion was laughable. Sal Bowden. . . . bonny as any man could wish with red ribbons slotted in her brazenly uncovered hair. . . . Mistress Sally saw no one but Athel.

She found, with relief, that Athel had come to the end of his speech. Eugenie bent her head graciously under the tilted brim of her wide straw hat and folded the babe back into his shawl as she turned away.

"Shall I take him now, m'lady?" The nurse at last. Eugenie relinquished her burden not without relief.

"He will need changing before he sleeps."

"*Yes*, my lady." Something in her mistress' look made the good woman bob two curtsies instead of one and take an extra care with her words. "The trap is waiting, as you ordered, and I will take him back to the nursery at once."

"I believe I will come with you. I am more fatigued than I had anticipated."

Athel heard her. "Oh, no! You will surely not leave now. There is to be more dancing. We shall become very lively as the ale flows. And later the men will sing our old songs around a fire in the dusk."

"How charming." Eugenie's smile was almost absentminded. "I should like to stay, but we must look to the future and I must guard my health."

Athel frowned and then relaxed, as she knew he would. Of course, of course. There must be no mishaps.

There must be future sons to guard the succession of his family and his name.

"Well, if you feel it is the better thing to do. . . ."

The last sight of him she had, as she was helped into the trap, he was already wending his way through his villagers toward the place where Sally Bowden was standing waiting.

The lad guiding the pony was overcareful. They made a slow leave-taking of the festivities.

"Pretty and pale as a briar rose, she be!" A man's voice.

"A great, fine child," said a woman in the press about them. "And I wonder at it when there's nowt on m'lady but the last pickin's of a chicken. I doubt she'll survive another."

We shall see about that, Eugenie thought, *we shall see*. . . .

August fulfilled what May had promised to the people of Clere Athel that year. There was a good heart in the grain and a good heart in the men who harvested it under high, clear skies. Freed from the anxieties of less reliable seasons, they scythed the fields with long, graceful strokes and sang while they worked. The sun brought out the pagan in them. They blessed Freya because she spun no clouds, and they left strange symbols in the empty fields, reassigning the earth to elemental deities, now that the gift of the harvest had been taken.

Eugenie ordered the cradle carried out into the park and rocked it with her foot, while she sewed beneath the shade of the chestnut tree. For the time being her life had contracted about the child, and in a mood of drowsy summer contentment she was able to forget Sally Bowden in her cottage beyond the gates of the park.

Athel did not always hurry away directly after his dinner. It gave him pleasure to watch his son learn to kick, to recognize the crow of recognition when Eugenie bent over the cradle. Mother and child—they made a pretty scene. He would stretch out beside them for half an hour, while the bees droned on the clover heads.

73

But both he and Giles sensed Eugenie's withdrawal, her preoccupation bordering on impatience when they disturbed her, and for the most part they left her in her own world.

The turn of the year brought visitors. Lord and Lady Carle came on their way to Blowick and admired their grandchild. The Mablethorpes and the Wenderbys and the Blundells, among neighboring families, paid their respects.

By February Eugenie knew herself to be pregnant again, and in the summer of 1722 there was a second son, Thurstan, to occupy the cradle beneath the chestnut tree. This time the birth had been easy, and the routine of the nursery was already well established.

Athel marked the occasion by giving her his mother's jewels.

Eugenie opened the box with the reverent care which she felt to be expected of her and found some rubies in an extremely ugly setting, an emerald and a number of gold clasps worked to old designs.

"Never had much time for folderols, my mother. The rubies were part of her dower, I believe, but I daresay they are out of the fashion now. You may have them reset, if you've a mind." He added carelessly, "I'll pay the cost, of course."

If Eugenie was offended to be paid in some material way for the production of offspring, she took care not to show it.

"You are very generous, sir."

"Not at all. I mean, two sons in two years . . . that's *very* well done."

Sometimes she would look in wonder at the man she had married. His physical beauty could still enchant her. The grace of him. The powerful shoulders and lean length of leg, his fine skin with the ruddy surge of life beneath it and the clear, bold eyes. She knew from observing him that he was not unfeeling, that he was not uncaring for her and his sons, and yet there was a part of him which she could never touch. She was his property, his family; he could even be jealous of her as he would the possession of a favorite chair. But she could never stir his senses in the vibrant way which instinct told her to crave.

There had been a night when she sent Hannah away early and left her hair unbound, brushing it until it gleamed in the candlelight.

Athel came to her room as she had thought he would. He stopped in the doorway, pulling up sharply like a startled horse.

"I beg your pardon, madam, I see you have not completed your preparations for bed."

"I have. I think I will not trouble to braid my hair tonight."

He had stared at her uncomprehending, shocked even. "You look like a wanton with your hair all about the place." The brush strokes slowly ceased. "No decent woman goes to bed in that fashion." He sounded discomforted, and his brows drew together, giving him a sulky, boyish expression. "My mother never in her life went to bed without arranging her hair."

"Indeed?" Eugenie said coolly. "Can you be sure of that?"

"I will come to you another night, when you are more yourself. . . . Perhaps the fatigue of the day. . . ." He left the rest unsaid. Eugenie understood. A wife, to Athel, had her place. And that place was apparently to get children in an orderly, even a formal fashion, with a pair of broad satin ribbons tied under her chin and an expression of bland resignation in her eyes. She had tried to be something other than that to him. She would not try again.

There was a space of nearly two years between Thurstan and Dickon. Dickon was the biggest baby she had born yet, and she was mightily proud of him, cherubic in his wreaths of infant fat about wrists and ankles and his head a halo of golden hair as soon as he was dried.

Eugenie looked at him and lingered over him and adored him.

"Your quiver," Giles told Eugenie in a dampening tone, "is quite full. I should stop getting sons if I were you. There is no land for them, you know. They will have to make their own way in a hard world."

"Not my sons! You forget I am a rich woman. Dickon shall have Blowick." To the child: "Shall you not, my precious?"

"Blowick will be for Thurstan," Giles pointed out.

Eugenie frowned at him. "Blowick will be for whomever I please."

"A wife's possessions are for her husband to dispose, in the proper order of his sons." Giles scowled. He knew perfectly well that it was not so with Eugenie's fortune. Her father had made extraordinary provisions for the handling of her inheritance by trustees, and Giles resented this governance almost as much as his brother did. Eugenie smiled slightly. There was no need to point out that these same trustees were empowered to release capital and assign some property as they judged fitting, or to drive home the point that since they were her guardians and her father willed it so, they would indulge her inclinations before those of any other.

"We will see when the time comes."

"You may not live to see," Giles said harshly. "Athel will have the management of all your wealth should you predecease him. And if you go on bearing children at your present rate, you make that more than likely." He turned away from her with an angry hunch of his shoulders.

"So!" Eugenie said softly, watching his profile minted against the metallic brilliance of a September sky. "You are concerned for me. . . . Go on now, confess you would be sorry to lose me! Who else would sit across the chessboard from you on a winter's evening? Who else would tolerate your caprices and ill humor as I do, and lend an ear to your spleenish attacks upon Congreve?"

76

"Woman, you are a she-devil in any mythology, and I would see you spitted like a sparrow before I would admit your company was precious to me!"

Eugenie seldom went about in the village unless she went with her husband upon some special occasion like the Maying or the harvest sports. Nevertheless, over the years, she grew to know the people by their names and learn their pursuits and something of their aspirations and their anxieties.

It was Hannah who taught her. Athel would sometimes mention the state of the land or the prices his people were getting in the market. But it was Hannah who made known the names of the villagers to her mistress and unconsciously helped build up a legend around Eugenie.

It came about in this way. Hannah had the acquaintance of Mistress Warrener, whose husband held tenancy of the largest farm on the estate. Nothing happened in Clere Athel which could long escape the attentions of this good, amiable, gossipy creature, and so it chanced that Eugenie, half-listening, would learn that the boys were swimming in Little Rip on warm summer evenings. Under the willows they would brag and duck each other, and some of the girls were shameless enough to watch them. . . . Haldane's youngest daughter was no better than she ought to be. There were those who said they had seen her taking a tumble, but time would tell the truth of it . . . Bertwold Cleper, who had never given his wife anything but the back of his hand for the past twenty years, had bought her a new cap at Beacon Cross Fair. When the other women looked her way, she shook the ribbons on it, and was begrudged, and envied, and didn't care.

Mistress Cleper, driving a pair of geese up to the house, was both startled and gratified when her ladyship said, "I think that is a new cap you have on. It is surely very fine." . . . And Susan Haldane was astonished by

Eugenie's intervention when her father and Athel Athelson between them were for dashing her hopes of a prompt marriage to Ned Tiddy.

"It's not a good match," Athel said. "A Haldane should have better than a cotter's son and him not man yet, scarce sixteen."

"Man enough to get her out of shape, I think," said Eugenie, who had eyed the girl in church on Sunday. "Best have a word with the lad before you make a ruling known."

Such remarks were overheard and repeated to the village, and so it began to be said that the Lady Eugenie did not miss much, that she might keep herself to herself, but that was no reason for underestimating her, and they accorded her a measure of respect which effort would never have won her. They did not love her greatly, for her ways were strange to them, and her reserve led them to say she was cold. But she was among them, and her presence was something to be reckoned with.

It would sometimes amuse her to reflect that a small part of the respect which the villagers seemed to award her was due to the Chevalier de Mulignac.

Her mother had lately suffered an unpleasant encounter with a highwayman known as Twice-Hung Jack. This was no ordinary "gentleman of the road," content to take the purse of gold, which prudent travelers kept ready to offer almost by way of toll when they were waylaid, but a brutal villain wanted for murder, as well as robbery. Most highwaymen were reluctant to kill, since they were then pursued by the law with greater determination, and the increased price on their heads made betrayal by their associates almost inevitable. Jack Swainson had shot and fatally injured a man early in his career, however, and since then it had been his custom to point out to terrified travelers that he had nothing to lose since he *could not be hung twice*. Hence the name by which he had become known.

Madeleine herself suffered no injury at his hands, although she was the poorer by several hundred guineas and a considerable quantity of jewelry when he left her. But her coachman, of long service, had tried to defend her, was shot full in the chest and died with his head in her lap by the roadside.

With this fresh in her mind, she declined—not unreasonably—to make her annual journey to Blowick unless her husband came himself to escort her.

Lord Carle refused to do anything of the kind. He wrote back scathingly of her demand for a gentleman's protection when she might bring any number of able-bodied servants with her and told her roundly to stop "dithering like a knocking-kneed old beldame," but to come at once. "I have half the county invited to a midsummer's ball and if you are not here to receive my guests you shall lack a half year's allowance."

This unendearing communication had thrown his wife into such a pique that she pressed De Mulignac to accompany her on the road to Northumberland. And as a further defiance she broke her journey at Clere Athel.

"For, after all," she reasoned aloud to Eugenie on her unexpected arrival, "I have a right to see my own daughter, I think. And it is all very well for Carle to talk of servants being a protection, but how many of them know how to use a firearm?"

Eugenie could find it in her heart to wish that her mother had visited her because she wanted to, rather than to spite her father, but nevertheless, she was glad of the diversion of company and bustled about to make them as comfortable as possible at such short notice.

Athel, none too pleased, tried to be gracious. "Well, I imagine you will like to have your mama's company. It is only a few days she will be stopping, I conclude?"

"A week," Eugenie said. "She says they will stay until Tuesday."

Athel looked happier. "Then we must offer them

some entertainment. Perhaps I can invite some of our neighbors to join us on Saturday evening. You would like to make a what-d'ye-call-it?"

"A soiree?"

"Yes, certainly." Athel was magnanimous. "And with cards."

"A little music, do you suppose?" Eugenie hesitated, not wishing to press him too far. "Might we fetch a player or two from Upstrand and offer dancing also?"

Athel frowned. "It is possible. It is not to be habit, mind you, not a regular thing. But upon this occasion—yes, I do not see why not."

Eugenie set about her arrangements with a will. The evening must be quite perfect. And Athel invited the Mablethorpes, the Hindleys, the Shaws, and a connection of the Seftons.

Clere Athel was already acquainted with Madeleine, Lady Carle. It had been astonished by her at first meeting but had now digested her. It had never seen anything like the Chevalier de Mulignac. Imagine a man, its people said, with his face painted and powdered and his hair curled. Add to that such a froth of laces and a rustling of silk, as never was witnessed, and sprinkle liberally with glinting stones. Put velvet breeches on him and set his well-formed legs on dainty-buckled, high-heeled shoes. It was so much against nature for a man to pretty himself in this fashion. Could he be real?

The chevalier, it must be owned, was not in the least discomforted by their stares. His prancing, careful walk took him down the village street to inspect the inn. He had even gone into their taproom and, keeping his handkerchief of scented cambric to his nose, ordered a draft of wine from the wood. His mincing manner and the indolent eyes with which he surveyed them as though they had been merely part of the scenery did not command their affection.

"*Ma chère* Eugenie." He tried not to wrinkle his top lip at the meat he was served, come suppertime. "You have

80

chosen to live in a place of curious customs. Do you realize that some coarse fellow *spat* in my presence today?"

"Folks spit around these parts when and where they feel inclined," Athel said bluntly. "A plain man don't quibble with nature."

"It must, then," replied De Mulignac, "be an unpleasant experience to live out life as a plain man."

The soiree on the Saturday evening was an elegant affair. Everyone said so afterwards. What happened in the small hours was to be disregarded. They ate an excellent supper—thirty separate dishes with garnish and sauces and brandied butters for the puddings. Even the fruit was soaked in liqueur.

The cards, of course, continued long after the dancers had tired. Youngsters were put to bed in the largest guest rooms—six girls in one and four boys in another. And a footman stationed on a chair between the two, warned to keep awake and see there was no commerce between them throughout the night.

The interest resolved on one card table. There was De Mulignac, Mablethorpe, Harvey Shaw and Warren Hindley. Hindley was a cocksure young man, had been to London and thought he knew it all. The play was deeper than he was accustomed to, but he would not admit it.

De Mulignac won consistently.

"By heaven tha' has luck," Mablethorpe said. He pushed away his cards ruefully. "I'll leave you. I know what I can afford to lose and I'm done for this evening."

Harvey Shaw followed him.

"Well"—Warren Hindley looked at De Mulignac defiantly—"I'll sit in another hand or two. I've dropped a quarter of my patrimony in your pocket, and you'll not walk away with that!"

"You ought not to be playing for your patrimony." De Mulignac's voice was gentle. "You are leaning on your luck, and that is a mistake."

But the heat of the room and the wine and the excitement of the play had gone to Hindley's head. "You mean to tell me you don't count on your luck, sir?"

"No, I do not. One should rely on one's skill. That is the only way to play at cards."

"And you are saying I have no skill?" Hindley's voice rose indignantly. "Then I tell you that if I do not have a winning set of cards in the next hand you deal, you are a cheat!"

De Mulignac stared at him coolly through his quizzing glass and dealt another hand of cards. Hindley lost again.

"On my life, I say you palm them!"

De Mulignac lifted the goblet set at his elbow, drank it and set it down with great deliberation. "If you say that, it will indeed be on your life. And your life will be extreme short. . . . Go to bed and I will like have forgotten it in the morning."

"The devil I will! You have my money!"

"Athelson," De Mulignac said wearily, "I do wish you will take this fellow to bed. He is overyoung to be at the tables, and I fear he has made a fool of himself. If you allow him to stay here much longer, it will be necessary for me to call him out."

"Come along, Hindley. Time you was in your bed." Athel took his arm.

"I ain't afraid. You don't think I'll run from a poxy Frenchman with that needle at his side." He tweaked De Mulignac's dress sword. "I daresay you've done some fine embroidery with it!"

"Gentlemen, I beseech you!" Eugenie said. "We will not take to heart what was surely intended as a jest. . . ." Her voice faltered, for she could see that none of the men was listening to her. Hindley had gone too far.

"You have insulted a guest in my house with the wildest and most unfounded of accusations, Hindley." Athel's face was grave. "You lost your temper because you lost your money. You'd best apologize at once."

"I'll do nothing of the kind. I say he cheated." Hindley

82

looked around at the men who had gathered about the table, seeking support. But there was no one, not even his own brother, watching in horrified wonder, who would countenance the allegation.

"If you genuinely believe *that*, you are mistaken. I have watched the whole game," Athel pursued relentlessly, and the rest of the spectators nodded their agreement.

Hindley's brother said, "For God's sake apologize. Cliff would say you must do so if he were here."

But Clifford Hindley, whose young wife had been brought to bed on the eve of the party, was not there to advise his younger brother.

"Perdition to Cliff!" Hindley shouted. "And to you—if you'll not back me up. I ain't afraid to face this fellow with his rouged mouth and his toy sword."

De Mulignac pushed back his chair with a sigh, stood up and shook out the folds of his taffeta coat skirts. He took snuff with stylish, careful movements. "As you wish, then. I imagine it will be light at five o'clock. If a half hour after that will suit you for a meeting, sir?"

"Why delay the extra half hour?" Hindley challenged pugnaciously.

"I never duel without first examining the ground," De Mulignac answered coldly.

There was a silence, and it was clear that they were all impressed by the professional tone of this remark. The truth was that there had never been a duel fought in Clere Athel within living memory.

Now that it was inevitable, now that there could be no going back, the faces of the men had taken on a different expression, something keen, anticipatory, relishing the sport that lay ahead. Eugenie saw this, and it disgusted her. Already they were assessing the contestants. Did they consider that Hindley was twenty-four, that he was taller, broader and would have a longer reach. And did they fix De Mulignac's age correctly? He would never see fifty again and was of a slight, graceful build. He might have greater experience and skill. Would that counterbalance the quicker reactions and the strength of the younger man?

Giles looked at her across the room, touched Athel's elbow and indicated the women, who had drawn instinctively together by the fire.

"There are matters must be discussed," Athel said. He bowed. "Madame, the hour is late. Will you be kind enough to escort the ladies to their rooms?"

They went reluctantly with many exclamations and questions. At last they were ushered to their beds, however, and Eugenie was left alone with her mother in the drafty corridor at the head of the stairs.

"You look unhappy, *ma petite*. No use to bother yourself. Men will play these games, and one cannot stop them."

"Games! But what if one of them is killed?"

Madeleine shook her head. "It is not possible. Auguste exercises every day with his Italian fencing master. He has met five men in the duel to my certain knowledge, but he will not kill this foolish boy. He will merely make him appear ridiculous."

Eugenie said, "I have known De Mulignac the whole of my life. Of course I do not want him to be hurt . . . but how can you be sure he will spare Warren Hindley?"

"I understand the man. If such an accusation had been made in a public place—say a club or a coffeehouse—that would have been different. But here, *en famille*, he can afford to be generous." She patted her daughter's arm reassuringly. "I have only ever known him kill two men. The one dishonored his sister, and the other talked about it." She waved an expressive hand. "What can be expected in such circumstances? Now let us get some sleep. It will be settled one way or another when we wake in the morning."

Eugenie doubted if she would sleep very well. She walked slowly to her room and found Hannah in a flutter of excitement. It seemed the whole household, indeed the entire village, had already got the scent of the scandal. There had been footmen waiting on the card tables, and it was natural that they would have spread such a startling piece of news.

"Oh, my lady, is it really true? Will the gentlemen meet tomorrow?"

"I believe so." Eugenie sank wearily into a chair and kicked off her satin slippers.

"Nick, the innkeeper, is already accepting stake money, they say, and everyone is for putting whatever we can afford on young Master Hindley."

Eugenie sat forward, suddenly alert. "What do you say, girl? The servants are betting on Hindley?"

"Why, yes—some of them as much as a quarter's wages. Well, they've seen the French gentleman and don't fancy him for a fighter."

"They are mistaken. Madame, my mother, tells me that De Mulignac has a great skill with the épée. They will certainly lose their money. Go at once and warn Heskett-son."

"But, my lady—"

"Don't argue. Go. Tell them I say Monsieur le Chevalier will win, and they should lose no time in getting the best odds they can."

Word of the duel had spread beyond the boundaries of Clere Athel by dawn. It was said afterward that people came from as far as Beacon Cross and even Wyre Rise to see it. Athel had chosen a piece of level ground, near the home farm and discreetly out of sight of the house.

Haldane's brother, Josiah, who had a cottage with a likely view, collected thirteen shillings from spectators, and there was many a bird startled out of the dawn choir by men who had no business to be up trees or crawling under hedges at that hour of the morning.

The manor had its money on De Mulignac and outfaced the taunts of the rest of the villagers, who sneered at what they considered to be misplaced loyalty, while Nick Throsling, perched in the fork of a chestnut tree, chortled so gleefully in anticipation of his winnings that he damn near fell out of it and, as it was, dislodged a sizable branch, which missed Athel by inches.

The chevalier, arriving on the field in puce smallclothes and a gray velvet coat with a shawl about his shoulders, shivered expressively in the misty morning air, giving the general impression of being more fitted for the next world than the one he was in. But stripped to his elegant shirt and breeches and testing the flexibility of his blade, he became a different man. Beside him Hindley seemed not so much powerful as clumsy.

The duel began, and it was at once apparent that De Mulignac was more than proficient with a sword, he was superb. The north-countrymen who watched him, and were more used to settle their differences with their fists, had never seen anything like him. He could have forced Hindley's submission a dozen times but stood back and gave him leave to go on. Hindley lunged. De Mulignac made a compound riposte. Lunge. Parry in *quarte*. It was clear that the younger man was aiming for the upper left part of the body, intent on doing his opponent serious injury. The gentlemen, who thought they knew how to use an épée, saw the *passato sotto*, the *remise*, the *croisée*, employed with such grace and speed as they had never imagined. The Frenchman did not merely duel with his adversary. He danced with him, tricked him and finally dizzied him to the point where he was actually facing in entirely the wrong direction.

"Un coup de maître," announced the chevalier and impaled Hindley's left buttock, neatly, efficiently and where it would be most painful without doing any lasting harm.

It was a triumph. Hindley went home lying facedown on a hay-filled cart and never again visited Clere Athel. And the manor house servants having joyfully collected their winnings from the grumbling innkeeper were blissfully unaware that he watered their beer for the next twelvemonth to balance the score.

Athel was visiting Eugenie before Dickon was out of swaddling bands. "What? Here again so soon, sir?" It had become her custom to speak to him in this manner, cool but good-humored. And he would answer in a like way, "Aye, madam. I leave it to your judgment, but if you do not find my visit unwelcome, I will spend the night with you."

She did not refuse him. Soon her sons would be taken from her. When they were eight years old, Athel would choose a tutor, and from thenceforward they must have the company of men. Already he said, "Don't allow young Athel to cling to your petticoats. . . . If he is in fear of me, it is for good reason. I do not beat him without cause." . . . "Send Thurstan to the stables directly. They say he has not sat a pony yet, and it is high time he learned to ride." And Thurstan was not six years old. Even Dickon would soon be tagging after his father through the muck and the stubble of the fields, and she must speed him with willing hands, watch him stagger and fall and turn her face away from his pitiful wails while other people raised him and rough voices told him to "be a man" and "stop his noise."

Eugenie, now twenty-eight, looked into the bleak years ahead and longed for the companionship of a daughter.

Once more she was with child. She had prayed and within a twelvemonth was acknowledging the fact to herself with secret delight. Surely after three boys would come a girl. She carried this hopeful burden with infinite care, eating wisely, exercising gently.

Athel was in London when she went into a premature labor. For the first time in living memory Clere Athel's boundary was in dispute. The broad sweep of the forest which stood at its back had defied encroachment for centuries until a new neighbor complained that its girth had spread over years and proceeded to fell several acres of pines.

Such action could not be allowed to pass unchallenged,

87

and Athel, when he heard of it, accepted Giles' advice that it was a nice legal point, got out his maps which clearly stated that the pinewoods belonged to Clere Athel and made for his man of law in London with all possible speed.

The journey was at least ten days there and ten days back in the winter. Taking advice and paying such complimentary calls as an occasional visit to the city demanded, he must be gone the best part of a month.

"You'll not take to your bed before I return?"

"I think not."

"Well, you have Hannah to care for you."

He was scarcely gone before a swirling curtain of mist began to descend over Clere Athel. It blew in off the sea, catching in the tops of the trees and wreathing in the eaves of houses. The marsh offered it a home, and it lay there for another day, gathering strength until it finally unrolled a clammy oblivion over the whole of that part of the coast of Lancashire. Folks said there had never been such a fog.

Eugenie's labor started at ten o'clock at night. By the middle of next morning Hannah's concern had translated into something approaching panic. There was still no baby, and what was more sinister, the spasms were weakening.

"I don't seem to be making much progress, do I?" Lying in her silk-canopied bed, Eugenie drifted in and out of exhausted sleep. Perhaps this was as simple and easy a way to die as any, a surrender of the struggle. Weariness obliterated fear. "I am going to die." Eugenie framed the words and did not know that she had spoken them aloud.

"You are not," Hannah answered her with great determination. "Willie Thrush has ridden to Upstrand for the physician, and in the meantime you'll try again now you've rested."

"It was never like this before. Thurstan and Dickon

88

were so easy." The effort of conversation had focused her mind, dragged her back to reality.

"Well, it's my belief this babe's coming into the world feet first, there's the hardship of it."

Eugenie could still find the strength to say teasingly, "And you a maiden!"

"I could send for Mother Chaffer, if you would have more faith in her."

"That old witch? You'll do no such thing! Clere Athel people prefer to contrive in any circumstance rather than suffer Mother Chaffer's ministrations!" In the final extremity she would be called because it was generally admitted that she had "a tidy way with death"—but not until then.

The suggestion had just such an effect as Hannah hoped for. "Come, let Mistress Murchitt hold your hands. Grip her hard, and I'll see what can be done. I've helped my own mother a time or two, and it maybe I learned something."

They knew throughout the house that Eugenie was struggling for her life. It was soon known in the village and on the farms, and there was a waiting and a watching and a listening with the children hushed for the sound of hooves. They came at four o'clock in the afternoon. Willie Thrush had had a hard task to find Upstrand, let alone the physician, and they were too late. The daughter Eugenie had longed for was stillborn.

A mild fever was merciful. It confused her mind just enough to take the edge off her pain, the desperate disappointment of the lost child, the anguished self-reproach because she had not been quicker to recognize that the onset of *this* labor was different. Could the physician have saved the baby if she had sent for him earlier? She would always wonder. She had been overconfident after Dickon's birth. Had thought herself a veritable "earth mother," whose body could disgorge life without apparent depletion. But this time she had needed help, and the weather detained it. She would always wonder who or what to blame and often, in lonely hours, would find none other but herself.

Six weeks were all that was needed to bring her to rights. Six weeks after nearly nine months of the carrying and the care. It seemed indecent.

Giles found it hard to climb the stairs. His room was on the ground floor next to the library. But he had written her a sympathetic note. She felt he understood, although the note was formal and to the point:

"I am sorry beyond words for the loss of the child. Although she never drew breath in this world, I saw her buried in the family vault, and since you were fevered and not able to give her a name, I called her Adela, Beatrice, Caroline, which were the first three I found under an alphabetical list of current Christian names in one of the books in our library. I hope this meets with your approval. Be well soon and content yourself in the three fine sons you have given to your husband. . . . Your affectionate brother, Giles."

There would be no other child, the physician said. He shook his head and said there must be no more pregnancies. So there would be no daughter. No companion to the years that lay ahead. Eugenie thought through a great many years and wondered bitterly how she would spend them.

Athel came home and said the proper things to her, but it was plain that he considered one more child neither here nor there. And a daughter would have needed a dower.

He had other matters on his mind. He wanted a governor for the boys, and it was hard to find the right man.

It was Eugenie's wish that her sons should go to Eton when they were of an age to do so, but although he would allow her her way with Thurston and Dickon, young Athel must stay on the land. A first-rate tutor might provide all the book learning needed for a man to administer Clere Athel.

"Humphrey and Jennie was in London. They presented their compliments to you."

"That was very civil of them. Pray return mine when you next write."

Athel and Eugenie were alone in the small room off the salon which they called the cabinet. Its atmosphere was intimate, as Eugenie had designed, with the walls covered in crimson damask and a soft glimmer of gilt furniture.

"I daresay they may visit us in the spring."

"That will be charming. I have often wondered that your brother never came to see us before. He must surely know Giles would welcome company since he cannot get about."

"Ah, well, as to that, I ain't so sure. . . ." Athel hesitated. "The truth is they'd be more like to stay away on account of Giles."

Eugenie stared at him in astonishment. "Whatever can you mean?"

For once Athel looked uneasy. "You never hear Giles speak much of Humphrey, do you?"

"No, now you mention it, I don't. . . . Do you mean there is some ill feeling between them?"

"Wouldn't put it so strong as that. A little resentment, perhaps, on Giles' part—that might be natural." He crossed the room and poured himself a glass of claret and was in no hurry to go on. Eugenie wondered with a touch of exasperation whether he intended to leave her with half a tale. It would be quite like him if he had changed his mind about telling her.

"Come and sit down, sir, do. You make a mystery, and really I had better know the whole if your brother and his wife are to be our guests."

He obliged her reluctantly. "Well, it's just a family to-do, bygone these many years and Giles will surely have put it out of his head . . . or will he? Devilish hard to know what Giles feels about anything. He don't say much to me. And then again I'm wondering how he'll behave.

Might be sweet as morning milk, might be downright rude."

Eugenie did her best to follow this line of thought but could make no sense of it and said so.

"I am just telling you, ain't I, though? Giles was to have married Jennie Hackthorne himself. They were betrothed from nursery days, and then after his accident, when he was ill for months and not thought likely to live, it seems she transferred her affections to Humphrey." He frowned irritably. "One shouldn't blame her for that, I suppose. She was always a lively, giddy sort of girl. Devilish pretty, too. Couldn't have borne with the quiet, retired life Giles has to live."

"But to have married his brother!"

Athel looked vaguely uncomfortable. "Aye, that must have been disagreeable from Giles' point of view. But as you know, Robert Hackthorne is godfather to all of us. He and *my* father were lifelong friends and determined on a match for Jennie with one of us."

"And she had a fortune, of course," Eugenie said dryly.

"Of course. That was not to be discounted."

Their eyes met and held for a moment. It was Eugenie who looked away first.

Athel continued: "There is a good reason for their coming. Apart from the very proper wish to pay their respects to you, it is possible they may be able to put us in the way of a likely governor for the boys. A cousin of Jennie's on her mother's side."

He had Eugenie's most complete attention at once. "Indeed! What are his qualifications?"

"Oh, a sound academic background, I promise you. Lately a scholar of Trinity College at Cambridge, and they do say he would have had a fellowship but for some trifling personal difference with the master. I told them to bring him to visit when they come and let us take a look at him."

"I beg you will make no hasty decisions. We must be sure we have the right man for such a post."

"Rest easy, madam. *My* assessment of him will be as careful as you could wish."

His slight emphasis was not lost on her.

"So!" she said after a pause. "We shall be a large party . . . and not an easy one, I think. They will bring their children?"

"The three older ones, the girls, yes. The boy is too young."

"Then we must make the children the center of attention. It will help to smooth over any awkwardness if the children are present."

Unexpectedly, Athel took her hand and raised it to his lips. "Madam, you are all finesse." And then: "Be so good as to go now and break the news to Giles. It will come better from you . . . a woman's touch."

"You cannot mean this minute!"

"Indeed, I do. Better he should be prepared." He rose and stretched languidly. "I have to go out. I have to see Shaw about those heifers he wants to sell."

"At this hour of night?"

He was already striding toward the door and did not trouble to answer her. Eugenie followed him to the hall, watched him swing his cloak about his shoulders. The crash of the heavy oak door and he was gone. Gone to Shaw or to Sally Bowden? No matter. Reluctantly she braced herself and turned down the passage to the library.

Giles was in a deep chair by the fire. He was reading and he looked up at her as though the disturbance were unwelcome.

"I heard the door . . . I suppose Athel has gone out and you come to me as the last resort of the lonely." His tone was light, and his lips curled in a suggestion of humor. But as always Eugenie looked directly into his eyes and

93

saw that they were dark and flat in color, which was not a happy sign. Perhaps he had more pain than usual to-night. The omens were not good, and she damned Athel for having committed her to the task before her.

"Shall I come in, whatever my motive?"

"Please do." He made her a slight, mocking bow, where he sat. "I have the best chair. Will you be content with second-best?"

"Yes," she said simply. "I think I am grown accus-tomed to that." His expression was suddenly sharply attentive. "I mean," she added, "that this is your province." Why was it she wondered that Giles had al-ways this power to draw from her a self-revelation, a deeper meaning than she intended? "Athel," she said bluntly, "has had a letter from your brother Humphrey." There it was out. He had tricked her, confused her . . . and where was that feminine tact that Athel placed re-liance on?

"So?"

"He and Jennie are coming to stay with us." She fal-tered. "I collect you have not seen them for some time." Giles said nothing. He kept his face turned away from her, staring into the fire and let her struggle on, her tone unnaturally bright. "It will be quite a family party, will it not? I wonder if they will bring their children. . . . I imagine so, if the weather is not inclement. Little Athel and Thurstan will delight to have company in the nur-sery. . . ." Her voice died away. She was suffering for him, and she could not show it.

"I know exactly what is in your mind," he said at last. "Athel has told you everything, of course, and you are thinking to yourself, 'Hey-day, here we go again! Poor old Giles has another sore on his soul. Better apply the poultice of induced confidence!' And if that doesn't work, you'll physic me another way. . . . Your cool voice will be like a hand on my forehead. You will take my emotional pulse with your careful questions and then you will blame my condition on the hour of day or the

94

day of the week—anything." He leaned toward her with a sudden intensity. "Do you want to know about my Jennie? Do you want to know that she has a tangle of red-brown curls, that she has dimples in her cheeks, and her eyes are as blue as the haze on a distant hill?"

"I understand," Eugenie put in tartly, "that you have a very high opinion of what you lost."

"Oh, I have! I have! There was never a one like my Jennie"—he laughed harshly—"never a one to be so quick to exchange brothers."

"Yet you would not have wed her when you knew the extent of your injuries." It was a bold assault. "Your pride would not have allowed it."

He stared at her. "She might have waited until I told her so myself."

"That is hurt vanity speaking. I know him. He is *my* adversary. He has nothing to do with common sense."

"Yes." He looked at her doubtfully and then added in a quieter tone, "I suppose that is why I tell you what I would not admit to anyone else."

Silence lay between them again, but it was the silence of understanding.

"So," Eugenie said, "Jennie and Humphrey will come, and you will sulk and be difficult."

"I shall be no such thing. I shall be scrupulously polite and gracious upon every occasion."

"How refreshing. Perhaps I can persuade them to live with us."

Giles chuckled. "No fear of that. Humphrey has political ambitions, and he and Robert Hackthorne have spent too much time and trouble upon their Oxfordshire neighbors. They'd never allow that to go to waste."

"Will Humphrey enter Parliament then?"

"No, his ambitions don't lie that way. I gather he sees himself more as a manipulator of other men's public lives. Politics don't interest me, so I ain't too bright at understanding them. But Athel says a man may make a career in shaping county affairs from behind the

95

scenes—fitting other men's backsides into parliamentary seats."

Eugenie frowned, trying to comprehend. "Deuced odd pursuit for a gentleman."

Giles smiled on her warmly. "Precisely what I said to Athel—deuced odd!"

It was clear that condemning Humphrey had cheered him for the time being, but Eugenie suspected that when she left him, his thoughts would return to Jennie.

Spring brought the promised visit. The party, arriving a day earlier than anticipated, caught Eugenie at a disadvantage in a gray wool smock and a dormeuse over her hair. She had been supervising the finishing touches to the guest rooms, and Athel had taken Giles into Upstrand to visit his tailor.

Jennifer looked her up and down and graciously assured her that they never had the least notion of any formality when they visited Clere Athel.

"Do not put yourself about on our account, my dear. I daresay I shall not trouble to unlock my jewel case while I am here. So *refreshing* to be *simple* in the country."

Shown into the salon, she professed herself amiably surprised at the changes a "truly housewifely woman" could make, and when Eugenie, escorted her to her apartments, she traced imaginery dust off a side table with one elegantly gloved finger and wondered whether it would be too much to ask for just a little *really hot* water brought up.

"Naturally you will want to bathe before supper," Eugenie said shortly. "You must be extreme dusty from the roads."

"Can the children be bathed too, do you think?"

"The nursery servants will attend to it."

At last she had asked after Giles, and Eugenie, unaccountably anxious for him, was glad that she did so.

"Giles has gone into Upstrand." She would not reveal that he had gone to collect a dark-green velvet coat, hastily ordered and needing a last fitting. This finery was for Jennie's benefit. Giles took no interest in his appearance in the general way.

"Really? I had no idea he was able to make such jaunts." Was there a trace of condescension?

"Oh, yes," Eugenie lied defensively. "He makes nothing of a drive and can get about as well as any man."

It was not true, of course. He would be tired and suffering from the jolt of the carriage. The effort of standing for his tailor would have given him cramp in his good hip.

"Poor Giles. So brave." Jennie sighed. "I suppose you know—"

"Athel told me."

The other woman's eyes misted. She really did have a very lovely face, and the sight of her must reawaken feelings in any man who had loved her. Only she was grown a trifle matronly in the figure, a plump woman squeezed into too-tight lacings and Eugenie hoped that Giles would notice that.

In the hall before dinner Athel and Humphrey had at once fallen on the topic of the land.

"You are too lenient," Humphrey was saying when Eugenie joined them. "If they don't pay their rents, you should turn them off."

"Odd sentiments to come from one of our stock." Athel frowned. "You know as well as I do that these folks have been here all the centuries. Can't turn off families who settled this land as long ago as ours did."

"Yes, you can. An estate must show a profit. Otherwise, how can you build up capital for reinvestment? I tell you plainly, Athel, it is a concern to me that you are not more realistic in matters of business."

"How interesting," Giles observed to no one in particular, "that when a man advises you to be realistic, it always transpires that he is urging you to be unscrupulous."

It was at this moment that Jennie had chosen to make an entrance. There was just the right haste through the door, just the perfectly judged hesitation. Her eyes found Giles, and she hurried to him across the salon.

"No—no! Don't get up, my dear. . . . See I will bring this footstool close beside you. . . . And Athel!" She held out her hand as she sank in a graceful billowing of silk at Giles' feet, and her wide eyes turned from one brother-in-law to the other. "So lovely," she murmured, "to be here with my dear, dear family!"

Athel did what was expected of him, bowing over her and murmuring apologies for having been absent when she arrived.

"Oh, pray do not trouble yourself for that. Your sweet wife showed us the most solicitous care." She gave a pretty trill of laughter. "We caught her with her maids and her dusters, did we not, Humphrey? But I see she is quite transformed now." She considered Eugenie's dress of amber-rose velvet and did not overlook the heavy rope of beautifully graded pearls that went with it. "Such a becoming shade—how wise of you to choose something that lends a little warmth to your pallor, my dear."

Eugenie glanced at Giles, but his expression was unreadable and in a minute or two she moved toward the fire and endeavored to draw the sixth member of the party into conversation.

Master Walter Corby, lately disappointed in his expectations of a college fellowship, was a young man of normally animated personality, now somewhat subdued by the ill turn of his fortunes. His answers to Eugenie's questions displayed scholarship, and she thought he must be sure to fill the role of tutor to their satisfaction. Yet it was clear that he had hoped for better things than schooling three young boys on an isolated country estate, and she wondered what had persuaded him to offer for the post.

She did not find herself drawn to him, despite his disarmingly good manners. There was a furtive restlessness in his eyes which belied the quiet speech. He has the look of a man at war within himself, she thought, and wished she dare share this impression with Athel. Athel would say it was the wildest imagination, a woman's whim. Perhaps he would be right.

"We have brought Eugenie a present," Jennie was saying. The announcement drew them together, while a servant was dispatched to fetch the gift and returned with a small lidded basket.

"There we are. . . . Out you come, my precious. I have christened her Mignon. Isn't she the prettiest toy? I have one myself at home, and I assure you there is no lady with any pretence to fashion will be seen without her lapdog these days. I vow I wept to leave my Belle, when we came here. Humphrey said the coach would make her sick, else I had brought her."

Eugenie took the white silken bundle gingerly. She had never owned a dog in her life. The little body was incredibly small under its long coat, perfectly containable in one hand. She felt the rapid beating of the heart. The creature was shivering with fear.

"Poor thing, it flutters like a bird on my hand. . . . No, Athel, do not prod her so, you are frightening her!"

"Take care my dogs don't see it, or they'll eat it!" Athel roared with laughter, and the dog crouched back against Eugenie's arm with a snarling display of teeth no bigger than pins.

"Why, see, she has some spirit, sir! Pray have a care of yourself. You will be bit."

The men laughed louder than ever at that.

"Jennie, this was a kind thought. I believe I shall have much pleasure in her."

Jennie yawned prettily. "Make nothing of it. As I tell you, every other woman has one already. I was plagued to decide between a fan and a dog, but it seemed to me this novelty might please you." She considered there had been attention enough shown to Eugenie and turned abruptly to Athel. "Do we go to supper now, my dear? You will permit me to make myself at home here and say that I am ravenous." And then to Giles. "I shall sit next to you. I intend to give you every second of my attention while we are here." She had thus adroitly displaced Eugenie as hostess and contrived to imply a neglect on her part of the comfort of guests.

Eugenie hastened to make amends. But on that and every other evening she would ruefully own to herself that she was never a match for Jennie. The visit grew to seem a lengthy one. It was only a matter of three weeks, yet in that time Jennie's children proved petulant and disagreeable in the nursery, and her servants caused discord in the kitchen.

Humphrey had continually irritated Athel with his criticisms of the way in which the estate was run.

"If you are slack with the tenants, they'll cheat you. It is in human nature to take advantage of a weak master."

"Not my people," Athel answered stoutly. "My men don't like to fail. If I give them the edge of my tongue, they'll make double the effort next season. And anyway, what is it to you if they don't come about?"

Humphrey declined to answer that directly. But he had gone on to say that in Oxfordshire landowners were already enclosing common land and putting it to the plow.

"Not on Robert Hackthorne's property, I'll be bound. I've talked to our godfather often enough, and he's not a man to take the land off his folks. I'll warrant you don't find him sympathetic to these notions of yours."

That had struck home. "My father-in-law is not a young man. It would be harder for him to change." Humphrey's face flushed.

"Well, what goes on in Oxfordshire is far more your business than what goes on here," Athel said bluntly. "And you don't need to give me that same nonsense again about my interests being yours, because they ain't. If my pockets was blasted, I wouldn't look to you for help, and I daresay you'd know better than to come to me in like condition. You'd get short shrift if you did."

Humphrey was painfully persistent, however, shaking his head and regretting that his brother would not see beyond the boundaries of Clere Athel.

"You forget my political interests. How you conduct yourself here must always influence my career. . . . Perhaps it might surprise you to know that Robert Walpole calls me by my given name. . . ."

That had been a dreadful occasion. Giles rocked with silent laughter, and Athel's mouth fairly dropped open with astonishment.

"Humphrey, you're a fool and you always was. It's nothing to me if German George himself drinks out of the same cup as you, and I'm astonished you should seek to impress us with such talk."

They went, at last, and Eugenie's only regret at seeing them go was lest Giles should miss Jennie's attentions. He had enjoyed a good measure of them.

"Good riddance," Athel said when they waved them down the drive.

"All very fine for you," Giles grumbled, "but who will offer to cut up my meat for me at supper now?"

"Yes, it seemed to me that you'd had about enough of Jennie. I damned near pointed out to her that it was a leg you lost and not an arm!"

The brothers looked at one another and began to laugh. They laughed so much that it became necessary for them to take a seat on the mounting block to recover their breath.

Eugenie listened to them with exasperated affection. She had no part in their merriment which was of a peculiarly male variety. They began to take turns in mimicking Humphrey, striving boyishly to outdo each other, and she left them to their enjoyment and went indoors.

Mistress Murchitt was waiting for her. The extra company had depleted the household stores. There was venison hung but nothing much else until the hares, she said.

101

Suddenly Eugenie came to a decision. "Tell the master. He will be glad of an excuse to take his dogs out after game. And make a list of what you want fetched from Upstrand next market day. I shall not be here. I believe I will go to London."

VI

MADELEINE, dusting powder from her face with a hare's foot and seemingly absorbed in this delicate operation, had nevertheless a clear view of her daughter's expression in the mirror. She disliked the droop of the pretty mouth which had held a sweet curve in childhood. It would trouble her when Eugenie returned to that godforsaken place in Lancashire. Very likely it would spoil her enjoyment of a ball or a play.

"You should get your portrait painted while you are in London. There is an excellent man, a Mr. Stillington. He is no Lely, but I have seen his work, and it is better than average."

"My portrait?" Eugenie looked up in bewilderment. "But what should I do with a likeness? Athel would not wish for it."

"Of course he would! He has simply never thought of it. Besides, I would like to have your likeness and Mr. Stillington might easily make a copy. . . . I imagine he will be glad of the work."

"*Chère Maman*, confess! This is another of your protégés!"

Madeleine shrugged. "One must amuse one's self with something."

"And you think this will divert us both?"

"He is a very handsome young man."

"I do not find myself beguiled by handsome young men."

Madeleine turned herself around on her dressing-table stool and considered her daughter with an anxious frown.

"I do hope you are lying, *petite*. When one grows bored with everything, one becomes so very plain."

Eugenie laughed at that.

"But really, I assure you that it is essential for a woman to entertain herself or at least to allow herself to be entertained."

"With trivialities . . . like the vanities of handsome men?"

"Why not, if that is all that life affords us? I have told you before, one must take what one can."

"And giving? Is there no room for giving in your philosophy, *Maman*?" Eugenie asked teasingly.

"Giving is uncomfortable. That, too, renders one plain. It puts lines about the corners of the mouth."

"You are incorrigible!"

"I have adjusted myself very well to the life I live. Pray you do the same." Madeleine turned back to her mirror and placed a patch by her mouth with a steady hand and a nicely judged artistry. "How are the children?"

"They grow more like their father every day."

"That at least must please him."

"And how is *my* father? I have not had a letter from him in a long time."

"He is not in good health." Her mother hesitated above her rouge pots. "Ah, the palest pink tonight, I confess I am not in best looks and the red will be too

103

strong. . . . Your father does not have a care for himself,"
she continued. "He drinks too deep and eats too hearty. I
offered to go up to Blowick and stay the whole summer,
but he misliked the idea. . . . What can one do?"

"Has he consulted a physician?"

"No, he has not. But *I* have consulted *mine*. He says that
your father's symptoms would seem to indicate some
choleric condition of the stomach lining. Perhaps an
abscess. He advises the waters at Scarborough, but of
course, Carle will have none of them. I even went to the
trouble of having some bottled and sent to him. He said
he had never tasted anything so vile in his life and that he
would not even pour it in his cattle trough!"

"So like him," Eugenie said. "Perhaps I had better go
to Blowick."

"I wouldn't dissuade you for the world. But if you go, it
will be for your own satisfaction, not for his. You might
take Thurstan, and that would bring him some pleasure.
I have learned by long and bitter experience that a
woman's company only plagues him."

Eugenie stayed with her mother in London for nearly
eight weeks. She had her portrait painted by the good-
looking Mr. Stillington. "In a revel gown . . . with a mask
in your hand," her mother had suggested. And it was
done and everyone pleased with the effect. "Mysterious,
inviting," the artist complimented himself. "It must be
one of my best portraits." "Captivating," Madeleine said.
"People for centuries to come will be tormented to know
what you were thinking about at the time."

Eugenie looked at herself framed in gilt and wondered
over the woman everyone else appeared to recognize
and she did not. Long eyes rather than the round shape
that beauty decreed and a quizzical curl at the corners of
the mouth. In one hand she held a black velvet mask
upon a stick. The other clasped a fold or two of the satin
domino that trailed beside her on the floor.

Auguste de Mulignac came to view the portrait. He

looked from the subject to its image and raised carefully painted eyebrows.

"*Dieu sait comme,* Madeleine, for once your painter has earned his fee. Here he shows a woman ever so slightly *ennuyante* from the dance . . . or from life. It is all one. A small masterpiece." And then: "Why do you not come with me to France, *ma belle* Eugenie? We will divert you there."

"I am going to Blowick," Eugenie said.

Blowick was not a good thought. Her mother had lent Ferne to her and an experienced majordomo took much of the fatigue out of a journey. Nevertheless, Northumberland was a long way, and the carrier, with a quantity of the luggage, had not kept pace with them. Then there was advice of a load of purchases gone to York, instead of to Lancaster. It was all most troublesome.

"Well," Hannah said. "You would come!" And went to see her parents.

"Eugenie!" The thick, dark scowl Eugenie remembered so well from childhood. "Have you brought any of your boys?"

"No, I came direct from London. But I will send Thurstan to you this autumn if you would like to see him."

"Never mind." Lord Carle shook his head, his disappointment plain.

"Mother tells me you have not been in the best of health."

They sat, each at the farthest extremity of an oak table thirty feet long, and took their supper.

"Not at all! Your mother is mistaken. I am very well." He raised his voice to make himself heard, and the echoes rang back from the vaulted roof of the hall.

Great dogs prowled around the back of the carved and smoke-blackened oak chair in which he sat, and he threw them bones and kicked out at them when they fought and generally behaved as if he were alone.

There were sixteen dishes offered, and he sampled

most of them, constantly signaling a footman forward to refill his cup.

"Perhaps you would like me to play for you," Eugenie said after supper.

"Why, that is a thought! I do not have much music here. We'll go into the gallery and you shall give me the old north-country ballads . . . not court music, mind. I have no ear for that kind of thing . . . but 'A-weavin' of the ribbons' or a 'Tommy at Ashdale Fair,' I shall like that. Sing 'em loud, m'dear. Let 'em rip through these rafters, as they did in m'father's time, and I'll give you such a bass as you've never heard!"

It *was* a good bass, too. Awesome, Eugenie thought, how he could still summon strength for the things he enjoyed, but in between times she could sense the aching weariness about him. He had always lived vigorously, and he would rather wear himself out quickly than let sickness or age waste him away in its own time.

"Daughter, I shall not ride my boundaries much longer." He silenced her protests with an impatient hand. "They will bury me this Christmas, or the next, what matter which one, and then Blowick will be yours. Now mark what I say. I leave this place to you because it is your right to have it, but I do not want you to keep it—"

"Not keep it? I had thought you would want Blowick to stay in the family at all costs."

"I would have it stay in *my* family, to be sure. I would not have it become a mere appendage to the Athelson property."

Eugenie frowned. She understood what her father was thinking. If Athel should ever have the means of getting his hands on Blowick, he would bleed the estate to improve Clere Athel.

"Thurstan and Dickon will get no land from their father."

"They will get money from you when they are grown and may buy land. I'll not secure Blowick to a child. And you needn't think you could hold it in good order from the distance of Lancashire, for you couldn't. It's three times the size of Clere Athel, and it needs a master, not an absent mistress or a minority."

Eugenie tested her own feelings briefly, then bowed her assent. "Naturally I shall do as you wish."

"You accuse me of a maudlin sentiment, perhaps?" He looked at her suspiciously. "Let me tell you I have nothing in mind but the practicalities of managing a large and scattered property. It is true I have had some affection for this place. I would not wish it sold piecemeal or fallen into disrepair." He reflected on the admission and did not care for it. "There is no weakness in that," he continued sternly. "I have taken my profit from these people. Men are bred hard on the borderland, and I have ridden 'em hard. Rent on quarter days and the edge of my tongue for the man who could not pay it."

Eugenie smiled in her rare way. A glowing smile illuminated her still face and startled him. "Yes, Father," she said. "I know what you are trying to say. I understand. Trust me."

"A woman—" He shook his head, leaving the sentence unfinished.

Soon he would go "over the hill." He had declined to entertain the county that summer. He had disparaged the company of his wife. He looked at his daughter. "A man thinks he lives a long time, but in reality it is a moment."

The glow faded out of Eugenie's smile, and her eyes hardened. Her father was a fine man. She admired him. But she had disappointed him the day she was born. Now they faced each other, perhaps for the last time. She wanted to embrace him, not formally—they would do that for the benefit of the watching servants, when he saw her into her coach—but wildly, clinging, like a small child. Had she ever done that? She doubted it. He wanted a son, and when he looked at her, he felt cheated.

107

Yet he was sorry that it should be so, and therefore, he groped for something kindly and approving to say to her at this parting.

"I am glad you called Thurstan after my father. The boy has a look of him . . . handsome lad. . . . You might give him my seal ring when he comes of age. I should like him to have it."

"I shall wear your seal ring so long as I live." Eugenie's chin came up sharply, and her voice was firm. "Thurstan can have it after *my* death."

Lord Carle was vaguely surprised by her decisiveness, but its cause did not touch him. "I daresay you are right," he said with indifference. "Aye, that would be fitting."

Eugenie was silent on the journey back to Clere Athel, so silent that she did not even bestir herself to complain of the jolts and starts, the dust or the indifferent inns, which were to be had along the route back to Lancashire.

"You are thinking of your father." Hannah took a liberty and anticipated forgiveness. "You mustn't brood, lady. He has had his life and a good one by all accounts."

"A good life." Eugenie repeated the words as though they sounded strange to her. "I wonder—what is a good life?"

Hannah looked at her doubtfully, trying to assess her mood. "That's the sort of question you might argue a whole evening with Master Giles. Me, I'm just a simple countrywoman. I'd say a good life was plenty of everything—kindling for a fire, food in the larder, a stone house to keep out wind and weather."

Eugenie smiled faintly. "Then you and I—we both have a good life."

"That we do. Everyday things are worth being thankful for and when I go home to Blowick, I'm mindful of it. A lady of your station in life can't be expected to see these things, but a cotter's family in Blowick are lucky to raise two children out of six."

"Are you saying that my father has not been a good landlord? You must be run mad, woman!"

108

"He's as reasonable a master as he knows how to be." Hannah answered hesitantly. "His tenant farmers live well as any in England. But it's the laborers. They grind them terribly hard in a lean year, and their homes are just hovels of wattle and thatch with a bare earth floor."

"Tenants are responsible for the cottages on their property. My father cannot be expected to see after the repairs to every shepherd's hut on the estate."

"I know that, lady, and you may be sure I told my family roundly what I thought of them."

"I am glad you do not reserve every piece of your mind for me alone. It seems fair that their should be an even distribution." Eugenie spoke dryly enough. Nevertheless, she was too appreciative of Hannah's many excellent qualities not to attend to her. "And what did they have to say? I imagine your father would have liked to box your ears."

"He would. Only he daresn't for the sake of the position I hold with you." Hannah chuckled. "He was fair mad, though."

"The tenant farmers in Clere Athel," Eugenie resumed, curiously, "they keep their laborers better housed?"

"Indeed, yes. There are stone floors and windows that open in the cottages. Mistress Warrener told me that the master visits every dwelling yearly. He makes the rounds just before Lady Day to see how roofs have weathered the winter and gives orders for repairs. If the cotters are on tenants' land, he adds the expenses to the rent due at the witan in the following November."

"Ah, yes, to be sure. The witan." Eugenie thought for a moment. This institution, as old as the subdued land itself, had been handed down the generations. Held each November, when stocks were garnered and root crops gathered, it straddled the centuries—a cross between manorial court and a local parliament. It was a time for paying dues, for voicing grievances and getting justice, for assigning new tenancies, for generally transacting the business of the land. The witenagemot. Men put everything forward to that event. They dated documents by it: "an agreement for Roger Bigod to wed Tabitha Toller when she comes of likely age . . . dated eight weeks after the witenagemot, in the year one thousand, five hundred and fifty-four" . . . "an appointment of the blacksmith's first son, Ned Pointner, to the working of the acres known betimes as The Drove and granting him and his heirs this property in perpetuity, in exception of any default . . . dated the witenagemot of 1721 . . ." and so on. She had read through some of the old records in the library.

There was nothing comparable to the witan in Blowick, and it might be that this annual confrontation served to goad the conscience of a community toward its humbler members. Her father loved Blowick and prided himself on knowing all his people by name. But in recent years and in failing health, familiarity had perhaps blinded him to the needs of some of them.

"You do well to tell me these things against the time when I inherit Blowick. I will see what may be done." She paused. "One should remember, however that there are lean years when crops fail. A generous landlord supports tenants through them, and any benevolence beyond that needs a deep pocket; otherwise, it is soon called mismanagement, and ultimately there is a harsher word—ruin. . . . The Clere Athel accounts have often shown a deficit. What balances the books now is nothing other than my bride price."

There was a tartness about the last words, and the two women were equally aware of it.

"Forgive me," Hannah said suddenly. "I spoke my mind too freely."

"Not at all. Your honesty is useful to me."

They returned home to a grudging welcome.

"Well," Athel said. "You came in your own good time.

110

We have trouble here, lady, and your son is locked in his room."

"Which son? Do you mean Athel?"

"Of course." Her husband spoke as though there was no other. "He tells me I am 'in error,' I stripped the hide off him two days since and I shall do the same two days *hence*, unless he changes his mind and makes a proper apology."

Walter Corby was at the root of the disturbance, it seemed. "All I did was tell him to conduct household prayers one morning," Athel explained irritably, "and the next thing I knew the servants was in an uproar and now there's young Athel vowing he will not go to the Mablethorpes' harvest supper because they are of the old faith."

Giles found the situation amusing. "I warned Athel." He shook his head at her. "I offered to wager him ten guineas that Humphrey had placed Corby here deliberately. But he wouldn't listen."

Eugenie was bewildered. "Whatever can you mean?"

"It turns out," Giles explained kindly, "that Corby is that breed of Protestant who must be forever protestin'."

"But the Mablethorpes—" Eugenie began.

"Are our oldest friends and our best neighbors," Athel roared. "Their harvest celebration is next Saturday night. You are back just in time, and if you do not bring your son to his senses, by God I will disown him!"

"Giles!" she appealed, when Athel had left the room.

"No use talkin' to me. I didn't engage Corby."

"He seemed such an upright young man."

"You didn't engage him either. It is Athel's problem. Humphrey never made any secret of his political ambitions, and we worry him, here in Catholic Lancashire."

"But the Athelsons have not been Catholic since the reign of Queen Elizabeth. He must know there is no rebellion here."

"Oh, to be sure, he knows we wouldn't involve our-

111

selves directly. But as long as there's a Stuart claimant to the throne, folk like the Mablethorpes will hope, and Humphrey would rather we had nothing to do with them. I doubt if Corby intentionally set Athel up against his father. He is not such a fool. But he might try to steer him to a strong Protestant line."

"Well, Athel has only to send him away. It is for him to hire or dismiss a tutor as he pleases."

Giles looked thoughtful. "It ain't as simple as that. Athel don't want us tainted Jacobite."

"What did Corby say to the household that upset them?"

"Told them that erroneous practices were creeping into their worship and that they must be rooted out. Got very excited on the subject of their loyalty to the Crown—downright abusive to Heskettson when he spoke up a protest."

"And Wortham?" Eugenie considered the vicar of their parish, querulous, old and slightly deaf. He was hardly an answer to an ardent young man with a mission.

"No one's tried to explain the situation to Wortham. Have to shout from here to Beacon Cross, and then he'd only get half the story. Besides, as I pointed out to Athel, Corby's a good tutor. Far better tame him than turn him off. Might even make a good successor to Wortham in this living." He spread his hands. "He is a man of great ability."

It was true that Corby had appeared to form a good relationship with her sons. Eugenie approved his manner from the start. He was firm, but not harsh, and he now appeared to want no other diversion than their constant companionship and the opportunity to develop their minds. It would be hard to find another tutor of similar academic caliber.

"Has Athel spoken to Corby?"

"No. The storm only blew up the day before yesterday. All Corby knows is that he is one pupil short. I was to tell him the boy had been disobedient and was locked in his room for punishment."

"Well, this is a pretty kettle of porridge to come home to! I had better go and see what Athel has to say for himself."

"Heskettson has the key to the door. No one else has been near him . . . and don't let him cajole you too easily. The boy was both defiant and impertinent. I was there, and I may tell you my brother hung onto his patience far longer than I should have done."

Now he was twelve years old, Athel had a large room to himself, next door to his father's bedchamber. Thurstan and Dickon shared a room in the new wing, close to her own apartment, and since it was past seven o'clock, they would be in bed.

There was a light showing under the door of the nursery, which had lately become the schoolroom. Very likely Walter Corby was preparing lessons for next day. She passed by softly, not wanting to confront him at this stage.

Athel was sitting on his bed with his knees drawn up under his chin. She noticed that they were very dirty knees. It would not have occurred to Heskettson to see that he took a bath. A blotched, tear-ravaged face glowered at her over the knees and then hid itself, more for the shame of apparent weakness, she guessed, than any other reason.

A feeling of tenderness overtook her and something else, more painful. Memory stirred. A huddled child alone in the limbo of parental disapproval. Then, remembering his manners, Athel stood up. Even in the indignity of his underbreeches, he was no nursling, and she would do no good by treating him as one.

"My dear boy, I'm afraid you have made your father very angry. Bring forward a chair for me, and we will sit and talk about it."

Athel did as he was told, but his eyebrows drew down

113

in a sulky, slanted union, and she knew that look from his earliest childhood. He had never been an easy boy to govern, quiet, serious-minded, lacking in humor, she sometimes thought regretfully. When his determination was fixed, it was hard to find an argument which would persuade him. Until now he had always obeyed his father because he cared passionately about his inheritance. Perhaps too passionately, for a boy of his years. Was it, after all, not so much Corby's influence which now made him rebel, but simply that in sounding some note of threat to Clere Athel, the tutor had inadvertently struck a reverberating response?

"You do not wish to visit the Mablethorpes?"

"We should have no truckle with the minions of Rome. We are not Jacobites here."

"No, we are not," Eugenie determined not to lose her temper at the tone of this response. "But I hope we are folk who can base judgments of our fellow men on our own good sense, rather than on cant and prejudice." She hesitated. "Where did you get these notions?"

"Master Corby gave me a pamphlet to read. My uncle Humphrey contributed to it."

"What did it say?"

"It was about peace. It said the country could not flourish when there were wars over succession. And it said King George was the right man to govern England and those who wanted a Stuart were traitors."

"And you think that because the Mablethorpes are Catholic, they are plotting rebellion? Well, really, Athel, I would have thought you had more sense! It isn't as if they were a family with any influential connections. They live a quiet life on the land, as we do. If they have clung to an old faith, they have suffered for it time and again. The Athelsons were Catholic once, remember."

He glared at her. "A long time ago."

Eugenie shrugged. "Some people find it easier to adapt to changing times than others."

"But Master Corby says—"

"Master Corby is an excellent teacher, but he is young. Discuss mathematics and grammar and geography with him. Take your moral precepts from him, for I am sure that they are excellent. But when it comes to theology, philosophy and history, have the greatest care. A young man takes what he wants from these subjects and is not always wise."

Athel stared at her. "I like Master Corby."

"So do I."

The boy was silent, and she let him think over what she had said.

"Will *you* go to the Mablethorpes, Mother?"

"Certainly. So will Master Corby." It was an idea that had just occurred to her. If this tutor was the right man for his post and she wanted to keep him, then he must be educated, too. He had never met the Mablethorpes. They were warm, hospitable people and could work their own charm if he was introduced into their midst. She affected a yawn. "You had best not accompany us, however. Your feelings might get the better of you and embarrass us. I will make your apologies and say you have the fever."

Eugenie rose and shook out the folds of her gown. "I must go and change and you had better get ready for bed. I will ask Heskettson to send up some water. You might oblige me infinitely by washing. . . . A *boy* of your age"—she stressed the word slightly, "really should not have dirty knees."

Athel stood up and opened the door for her. "Shall I get supper?"

Food, it seemed, would in no wise compromise his principles.

For a moment she cupped his chin in her hand, and he did not jerk his head away as he would ordinarily have done.

"Will you make a fair apology to your father tomorrow morning?"

There was the frown again. "I think he is mistaken to

115

keep good friends with the Mablethorpes." At least this answer was more pliable.

Eugenie nodded. "If he ever asks for your opinion, you may give it. In the meantime, I think you would be wise simply to ask his pardon."

At supper Eugenie was as conciliatory to her husband as she could possibly be. Giles' knowing smile did not deter her, and she drew Athel to her bed that night with every skill she could command. Once they were behind the curtains, she argued his son's youth, and Master Corby's virtues, and her own plan.

The Mablethorpes, she pointed out, had no less than five pretty daughters, and a young man such as Corby would be susceptible. In the midst of charming and innocent company he might learn to moderate his opinions.

"It will do him the world of good to find himself enjoying the atmosphere of a solid Roman Catholic household. Moreover, their old priest has wit and learning enough to give him a good debate if he wants one."

"But what if he refuses to go? Then we shall have him ranged alongside Athel, and devil-a-fool I shall look."

"He will not refuse to squire me, I think, and I will arrange it so that I must leave earlier in the day than you and Giles. I could say I have promised to help Mistress Mablethorpe with her preparations and that I must leave at first light. I will say I have a fear of that highwayman—what is his name? Beacon Brentneath."

"What of Athel?"

"He shall not go. Believe me, that will seem a punishment rather than a triumph when we return with glowing tales of the festivities."

Her husband gave up whatever other enterprise he had in mind and twitched back the hanging, the better to consider her by the bedside candle.

"You have this well worked out, madam, but I think it will not do. Can I countenance a man who will stir up my own son to defy me?"

"I am sure there was no deliberate intent to do anything of the kind," Eugenie said quickly. She explained about the pamphlet. "Athel put his own construction on what he read and applied it to the Mablethorpes. It may be that you . . . we . . . underestimate the depth of feeling he has about Clere Athel. In his imagination he sees us called traitor and the land taken from us."

The flickering light made it difficult to read his face, but when he spoke again Athel's tone was more relaxed.

"It is possible, you are right. I had certainly thought Corby a fool to go against *me*. . . . Why, I might give him the living when the boys are schooled. Wortham cannot go on forever."

"Precisely. And when we send Thurstan and Dickon to Eton, Corby might go with them. He knows their lodgings will be of the best. . . . Perhaps later a tour of Europe. . . ."

"Well"—Athel was still reluctant to be cajoled, unwilling to admit that any scheme a woman devised could bring a happy solution to the disturbance which had only this morning ruined his breakfast—"I daresay he is as good a tutor as we should find anywhere, and since young Athel will have no other formal education. . . . But the boy made me very angry. The way he spoke back at me! You wouldn't have liked to have heard it."

"I should not," Eugenie said firmly. "It would have distressed me beyond measure."

"I didn't beat him as hard as I might have done."

"You were forebearing, sir."

Athel blew out the candle, and they were in darkness. "Truth to tell, I was moved by his courage. But he can be bullheaded, and I won't have it!"

"I know he is grieved for what he has done. He will apologize tomorrow."

"See that he does."

She most certainly would.

The plan had worked well, and the surface of life at Clere Athel was smooth again as the duck pond on its common land. Master Corby was no longer invited to take the household prayers, and on the rare occasion when Athel was absent, Giles directed their devotions in as cursory a fashion as anyone could wish. There was one mildly diverting sequel to the party at the Mablethorpes. Master Corby fell so much enamored of their youngest daughter, Eveline, that he was found to have carved her name on the writing table in his bedchamber. Eugenie told the maid, who reported the matter, to rub in some wax and stain over the scratches.

VII

A scatter of shingle can set a landslide in motion, and sometimes a slight incident, not of any importance in itself, starts a series of happenings so that in conclusion it is possible to look back and say it all began on that day: Athel had bought a pair of boots at a fair. They were fine boots, made of the softest leather. Normally they would not have been sold. The Italian who fashioned them extra large had no customer in mind. They were a sample, and to show his skill, he fringed the tops and added swinging leather tassels.

They were not such boots as the master of Clere Athel would normally wear. But having tried them and found them a perfect fit, he would have them.

Giles teased him for a dandy, and Eugenie permitted herself a smile.

"Said he never thought to meet a man with such a big

foot and such a length of leg." Athel cast a triumphant look at his wife. "Marvelously comfortable." There was just a trace of defiance.

"And very pretty, too," Giles said. "Perhaps he will make me *one*."

The tassels swung when Athel walked and it happened that on a certain day, Eugenie's lapdog—the same that Jennie had given her, though now grey in the muzzle and somewhat blind in one eye—should take exception to the adornment and, leaping from the cushion at her mistress' feet suddenly, for no accountable reason, fastened her teeth upon one of them.

Startled, Athel kicked out his foot to shake her off, and she lost her grip and flew through the air, breaking her neck against a stone pillar.

"Oh!" Eugenie was across the hall in an instant and on her knees. "Poor little creature." She turned reproachful eyes on her husband. "She was only playing."

"Damme," said Athel, "is she dead?"

Giles limped over to inspect the inert bundle of fur. "Quite dead," he said coldly.

"God, Eugenie, I am *deuced* sorry! I didn't know what she was about."

"Well, she was hardly going to do you any serious injury," Giles said. The tears in Eugenie's eyes exasperated him. "She was very old, anyway," he added severely.

Eugenie nodded. "Yes." It was an effort to speak. "Of course. A quick end. Merciful."

Some weeks later Giles was in a fuss about the arrival of the carrier from Upstrand. When it came, it brought the servant of a Westmorland family, the Dracotts. Giles had been at school with Jarvis Dracott and knew that his family long cultivated a breed of wolfhounds from Ireland. The servant was accompanied by a five-month-old dog, called Fionn.

"There you are," Giles introduced his gift to Eugenie with a complacent smile. "Athel will think twice before he kicks that!"

It was the biggest dog Eugenie had ever seen, nearly three feet at the shoulder.

"Not fully grown yet, of course," Giles said.

"Of course," Eugenie agreed faintly. "What will I do with him?"

"Be a companion and guard for you. Let him go wherever you go. Run beside the carriage when you go to Lancaster."

"Surely that would be too far even for this dog."

"Well, then, when he's tired, let him ride. No highwayman going to take your purse, or your pearl choker, with Fionn up beside you." Giles stroked the rough coat admiringly and felt the broad chest. "Powerful, ain't you, though?"

The dog lifted its great head and looked at him adoringly.

"I believe he takes to you more than me." It had occurred to Eugenie that Giles was rather partial to the company of dogs and that he never had one because he did not hunt. "Why don't *you* keep him?"

But he wouldn't have that. "Bought him for you." He frowned. "Gone to the trouble of writing for him. Fionn!" He pointed at Eugenie. "Guard this woman. Guard her well. Don't let her out of your sight."

The dog rose and stood looking from one to the other of them and then strolled over and settled down beside Eugenie's chair.

Giles was delighted. "There you are, you see! Understood what I was saying. Now go out into the hall for a minute and then come back again."

Eugenie complied with a tolerant smile. Somewhat to her surprise the dog rose and followed her. She went back into the library. Fionn was at her heels and looking up into her face when she turned around, clearly wondering where the rather purposeless exercise would lead.

"Fionn," she said. And the dog wagged its tail and moved closer to her, holding up its head. Without bending down, her hand could rest on it. "Where should he sleep? Mignon used to lie on a silk cushion at the foot of my bed, but this creature is more in want of stabling."

"Let him throw himself down outside your door. If you lay a rug there, he'll take to it."

"He really is a splendid animal."

"Thought you'd like him. Give you an interest now the boys are away at school."

Thurstan had gone to Oxford that year. Dickon was still at Eton with Master Corby minding his wild ways for him.

Dickon. Eugenie's face would soften every time she thought of him. Such a loving, impetuous boy. Always at cross swords with authority and running back home to her whenever he thought he would. Thurstan was steadier, studying law as his Uncle Giles had done. Young Athel had left her long ago, in the spirit, and already, at eighteen, he was betrothed to Kitty Hatton.

Eugenie met the girl and liked her, but thought small chance of happiness for any bride when her suitor studied the dower agreement closely for two nights and then asked his father's advice about her portion in the family silver.

"Well, she's a fine, strong girl. I wouldn't quibble." Even his father had been less parsimonious about the details. So the betrothal contract was signed.

"Such a pretty child." Eugenie tried to implant the enthusiasm her son seemed to lack. "I shall enjoy having her for a daughter-in-law. Shall I ask her to stay? Her aunt might be chaperone."

"Better wait," her son advised, "until the contract is finished." He was in no hurry. Very likely his father had been the same, and yet her own betrothal months had seemed long and she drifting through them, dreaming of life in a countryside where it was always summer. The contrast with reality was poignant.

The Hattons were a wealthy Cheshire family, but they had three boys and three girls to provide for. Kitty would come with a substantial, not a great, portion. Yet it was a good match on both sides, the interests being long-term from the reversion of Hatton property, and Eugenie settling an annual income on the bride, which her mother and father found more than reassuring.

"They'd have laid more on the line if you could have given the boy even a fifth share of Blowick lands," Athel said. "The rents need only have been small, but the acreage would have looked good."

It was an irritation to him that she, or rather her trustees, had sold Blowick. Seven years since her father died, and Athel still resented the terms of the will. He felt he had been cheated.

It was a clever will, indicating Lord Carle's wish that Blowick be sold intact and the capital reinvested as part of the trust fund from which his daughter drew her income. Carle House in London had gone to Madeleine. Only the Leicestershire property could be realized, and Athel got nine thousand pounds from that.

There had come about such a fortunate circumstance with regard to Blowick that Eugenie wondered whether perhaps her father had paved the way for it. Writing to her Uncle William in Barbados, she learned by the quickest possible return post that his elder son must settle in England and was in search of an estate. The climate, it seemed, did not suit his health.

Eugenie dictated the answer to her man of business. "Tell him Blowick is for sale at the price he can afford." Cousin Robert would succeed to the title after *his* father. One day there would again be a Lord Carle at Blowick.

These were her letter-writing years. Sometimes Eugenie filled a whole day driving her tiring pen across the sheets of fine, hand-cut paper, or in dictating pages for clerks to copy. "Money," as her father had often told her, "does not manage itself." He was certainly right. Business letters were a prodigious effort. Twice a week she wrote to Thurstan and Dickon, and once a month to Jennie. The livelier correspondence was with her mother, who continued to enjoy life as she had always done and now spent the larger part of the year in lodgings at the French court.

Eugenie had taken to riding more frequently. It was not an exercise she particularly enjoyed—the weather in Lancashire was frequently bluster and showers—but she did it as a duty to her health.

Sometimes she would see things about the estate. "The river piece needs draining," she told Athel.

"What do *you* know about it!"

"Fionn was up to his hocks and could scarcely struggle through the Warreners' west meadow."

"You shouldn't have been riding there. That's best grazing land."

"It's boggy and trampled by the cattle, and it will go to waste if you don't watch it."

Little Rip had changed its course over the years. It was putting out an elbow and nudging the good meadowland.

"I can't afford ditches across that section, and anyway the men can't spare the time to dig them."

"I'll buy the labor."

"Very well then." Athel shrugged. "If you've a fancy to do that, I'll speak to Warrener."

"They tell me Cotter Thorpe's boy is promising on the fiddle. I heard him playing for the little lasses to dance yesterday noon, and 'twas a pretty sound."

"There's a boy in every village promisin' on the fiddle," Athel said flatly.

"Let us at least hear this one up at the house, and if he has talent, we might set him to study."

"I suppose you must needs do something with your money. But I'd rather you didn't fill folks' heads with nonsense."

He sounded irritable. In fact, he did not dislike her indulging the village in this haphazard manner. "Well, well, you've a care for them. Another woman would spend more on fripperies for herself. I daresay you are less extravagant than most people would be on your inheritance."

Athel had a hunting dog, a great gray bitch, all muscle and bone. She would work the whole day for him without rest or water and manifested both the qualities of a retriever and a gazehound. He would have liked a litter from her, but none of the males could get within reach when she was in season. As soon as they tried to get to grips, she would sink her teeth into the nose or shoulder of the dog bold enough to be concerned.

"A natural virgin," Giles said. "A true Diana of the chase. She'll not let you slow her down with mating."

That was how matters stood when Fionn came, and apparently the bitch, Corinna, had only been waiting for a worthy sire. Seeing Fionn, she was provocative, even playful, leaning down on her elbows, waving her rump in the air. Very shortly, as might have been anticipated, she was in whelp.

Athel was amused. "Well, I'll say this for Fionn—he wasn't behind the door when the good Lord gave courage. Giles, can you imagine what the crossbreed of Fionn and my Corinna will be?"

Giles shook his head. "Best not feed the pups red meat, or they'll have us all by the throat."

It was January when Corinna was due to have her litter, the weather bitterly cold, promising snow every day with lowering, yellowish skies. She had tried to make a bed in the stable, it seemed, and in doing so ferreted out a good deal of straw in a corner that one of the lads had just tidied.

He booted her, none too roughly for knowledge of her temper and the place she held in the master's affections, but it was enough to make her take off into the darkness of late afternoon. And she was gone, and the snow began to fall.

"Where's Corinna?" Suddenly after supper Athel had a fancy to look for the bitch. "She must be near her time.

I've a mind to tell one of the lads to stay up with her. Fionn's pups will be large and she may need help."

"She'll have found a warm place in someone's byre, Master," Heskettson said. "I'll send a man down to the cattle shelter on the home farm and another to Warrener's place. They are nearest and most likely."

But they could not find her.

"She's a dog of the woods. Near wild, I sometimes think." Athel was staring out into the darkness. "She'll have gone where she hunts." He was restless, and it occurred to Eugenie that he had never shown such anxiety for any of their children. "The snow's not stopping. There's a real blizzard out there."

"Well, as you say," Giles pointed out, "she's near wild. She'll find a place in a hollow tree."

"The whelps will perish in this cold."

At eleven o'clock Athel said he was going out to look for the bitch.

They protested that it was an impossible night and did what they could to dissuade him. In the end Heskettson roused up four of the house servants, and the men set out through the driving snow and the drifts, floundering their way across the home park, by the flicker of lanterns.

Three hours passed before the search party returned. When they stumbled into the porch, they were exhausted, their frozen lips unable at first to frame words. Athel was not with them. He had sent them separate ways with instructions to meet again on the old stone bridge over Little Rip. They last saw him taking the track along the bottom of the home farm.

"Keeping to the leeside of the big thorn hedge he were, and the ground looked to be none so bad." Tobias Thatcher spoke for the rest. "When he didn't come to t'bridge, we reckoned as how he'd called in on Haldane."

"We'll know that soon enough," Giles interrupted. "I sent Shaw to fetch Haldane an hour since."

Almost while he was speaking there was the scrape of boots and men's voices at the door.

"Haldane! Is the master not with you?"

"No. I've not seen him this night. Looks bad. Does anyone know which way he was heading."

"Aye, he said he'd make for the woods."

Haldane shook his head. "Well I've brought five o' the lads from t'farm, and the snow does seem to be slackenin' off a bit now. But there'll be no tracks. . . . Happen he found some shelter if he reached the woods."

"Take Fionn with you. He might be able to find the bitch. Take some of the other dogs. Try anything!" Giles said.

Conscious as he always was of his own helplessness in times of crisis, Giles drove on relays of men to search throughout the remainder of the night, drove them ruthlessly.

"What, nothing yet! Then you must go out again! Take a mug of hot ale and be on your way."

And no one answered him back, as all had a right to do, that the limit of his own endurance was reached or that his clothes were frozen stiff on him from falling into drifts.

Eugenie, sitting with her hands clasped and numb, in the hall, thought it a great wonder. Such hard, rough folk as these Lancashire farmers were—did they never give in?

The dawn came up quite suddenly, the sky was clear, and there was a brilliant beauty in the morning when they found Athel. He was just alive, lying between the broad limb and the trunk of a fallen tree. He had found the bitch, and man and animal huddled together to survive the storm. The pups, born into a frozen world, had died.

They carried Athel home on a rough lattice of yew branches, the bitch still beside him for warmth under the blankets. Two days in a straw-filled box by the kitchen stove, pampered with hot milk laced with brandy, and Corinna would regain her strength. But upstairs in the great dark oak bed Athel was dying.

126

"A powerful man, a powerful frame!" The physician shut up his case of potions and powders with a snap. "Only a most remarkable constitution could have fought so hard . . . but. . . ." He spread his hands. "The breathing is very labored. Another twelve hours, perhaps. Not more."

"Can nothing be done?"

"If it could, madam, I should stay and do it." He answered tetchily because he was tired. The roads between Upstrand and Clere Athel were still axle-deep in snow, and he had made three visits in the last two days to try to save Athel Athelson. "There's a gathering of fluid in the lungs. I have tried what physic I can to expel it, without avail."

Eugenie accepted the rebuke. "Be good enough to see my brother-in-law before you leave, and tell him what you have told me. He is in the library."

She returned with slow steps to the room where Athel lay. The air was pungent with some special salts, which the physician recommended be sprinkled on the fire to aid breathing. Not an unpleasant odor. Distinctive. It would be a part of the memory of this scene forever. She approached the bed cautiously. Athel was not sleeping. His eyes moved restlessly about the room, but the agonized twisting of his body under the covers had ceased, rather as though he were now aware that the fight was over and he might just as well conserve what little strength he had left.

Eugenie stood beside him for a moment before he was aware of her presence. A powerful man, as the physician had said—a powerful man with the vigor ebbing out of him so fast that it was like blood from an unstaunchable wound. She listened to the short gasping breaths with infinite pity. And something else. A sense almost of bewilderment. Her union with this man, which had existed for twenty years, was about to end. She had borne him three children and spent the larger part of a lifetime studying his moods and attending to his pleasures. His habits, his attitudes, his speech, every gesture, they were all familiar to her. It was rather as though she had devoted herself to learning a difficult language only to be told that the use for it was now extinct.

Athel turned his head slightly on the pillows and saw her.

"Eugenie . . . I am a-dying."

The calm simplicity of the statement and the dignity of its utterance brought tears to her eyes.

"No cause to grieve . . . must go sometime . . . got three sons. . . ."

Four sons, Eugenie thought. Four sons. The woman he had loved best was also the mother of a son. The boy was grown to manhood now, and they called him Poor Ned. They'd have called him Daft Ned if he'd been any other man's son but Athel's.

Would Athel ask for Sally Bowden? He must surely want to see her before he died. He had visited her not five days since and spent the night with her. Earnestly desiring to bring him every comfort that she could, Eugenie gathered her courage together. It was not an easy matter to speak of, but she was remembering that in all the years of her marriage Athel never allowed Sally to come to the house. He had been very proper in that respect, even when she herself was away in London or Northumberland.

"I have been thinking," she began quietly. "It might be there are people you would wish to see. . . . Would you wish me to send for Sal Bowden?"

Athel's eyes fastened upon her, and his face grew flushed. With heaven alone knew what effort he levered himself up against the head screen of the bed.

"What the devil are you saying, woman!" he demanded, and there was such rage in him as she had never provoked in the whole of their married life. "What the devil should a man want with his mistress when he is dying? When he is in health and vigor, then fetch him a doxy by all means!" He saw the shock in her face and relished it, even while he panted with the exertion of his anger. "I have a few hours left to me, madam. I would see my heir, my brother and then the priest, in that order. If there is still time, you may return to me and take your leave."

There was no more to be said. She curtsied and left him.

Young Athel was in his father's room for an hour or more. That gave Giles plenty of time to recover from the struggle up the stairs with two footmen to help him. He, too, was with Athel for a long while. The Reverend Mr. Wortham entered next and sketched the beginnings of a prayer for the sick before he discovered his mistake and amended it to one for the dead.

The only leave-taking for Eugenie was to close her husband's eyes.

At twenty years of age Athel was in possession of his property and the date set for his marriage to Kitty Hatton. He would go to Cheshire for the wedding, and his Uncle Humphrey and Thurstan would go with him. As a widow observing the formal mourning period of a year and a day, Eugenie decided not to accompany them.

It was when she stood in the drive to wave off a son and knew that she would welcome home another woman's husband that the full significance of her own changed position came to her. With the carriage lost to view under the broad spreading trees, she turned to look at the house. She had never liked it. It was cold and uncomfortable. Her own apartments, the wing she had added, were pleasing to her. But she shivered just to think of the dining hall—and how the chimney smoked in there, to say nothing of the one in the hall!

These would be Kitty's problems very soon. It was she who must learn to chase after the pantry maids to see they kept out summer vermin; she who must scold the cook when large joints went to waste or, worse still, unaccountably disappeared; she who must check that linen was properly mended, and properly washed, and properly stored, and properly aired. Mrs. Murchitt had retired several months ago. She was in her sixties and not in good health, and since then Eugenie had contrived, with Hannah's help, thinking it best that the bride-to-be made her own appointment for such an important post as housekeeper.

I am free now, Eugenie thought. *I don't have to stay here. I could go anywhere, live in a house of my own choosing where everything was arranged just as I wished it to be.*

"I have been considering," she confided to Giles later that evening, "where I might live now that Athel is bringing a new mistress to this house."

"What are you talking about? Where else should you live but here? And as for Kitty Hatton . . . well, the servants won't accept a chit of a girl for mistress in your lifetime."

"Precisely!" She was quick to seize upon a point he did not intend making. "All the more reason why it is desirable for me to live elsewhere. Athel's wife must learn to be mistress of his home, and she will do it the quicker for not having a mother-in-law peering over her shoulder."

"But she's so young. She'll never manage without your help."

"I was only a few months older, and I managed well enough."

"Ah, things were different then."

"Yes, indeed they were." Eugenie's eyes transfixed him across the supper table. "In the years after your mother's death the entire household appeared to have gone to pieces. There were no accounts kept for food, fire or candles. You had let the servants grow slack. The rooms were dirty, and most of them were damp, and when you wanted something, instead of ringing, you bellowed for it."

Giles scowled but then grinned reluctantly. "Aye, we did live rough in those days. I had forgot. . . . Well, you have spoiled us, d'you see? We are grown very nice in our ways and cannot do without you."

"And there's no use to try and charm me"—she pointed an accusing dessert spoon at him—"for I have made up my mind to build myself a house. I leave this one well ordered and the servants well trained. Kitty is a sensible girl. She has but to engage a good housekeeper. You will never notice I have gone."

Giles pushed his savory away untouched. He was not smiling.

"Athel won't like it."

"Probably not. He never likes me spending *my money*. He thinks it is his already." Did she sound hard? she wondered. Yes, she must allow that she did. *They have made me hard*, she thought.

Giles was watching her warily, perhaps assessing the strength of her determination, looking for a weakness through which she could be persuaded to change her mind. He would take Athel's part. That much was apparent from his reception of the idea. But whether because he disapproved of the expense or because he placed any value on her company, who could say? Better not to know the answer.

She kept her eyes carefully averted and gave the conversation a fresh direction.

The time until Athel's return with Kitty passed quickly enough. Eugenie was full of plans, her dream of a house with not too many rooms, but every one of them light and in a good proportion. A house that would need only a modest complement of servants to maintain it and would give her peace and leisure to study.

She wrote to her mother about the scheme, and Madeleine replied that there was no need for her to go to the trouble of building a home when she might have the use of Carle House for the rest of her life. "No woman can be entirely dull in London, and while I choose to live in France, because it is my soul's home, the place of my birth, yet I think *you* might do very well there. . . . At the moment it is let but on a short lease and I can easily repossess it for you within the year. . . ."

Carle House. Her mother used it now only in September and October. It suited her to renew English acquaintances, and she claimed that these months of the year offered a more benign climate and a livelier social diversion than any other.

But Carle House was too big and formal for the life Eugenie had in mind. Moreover, twenty years of married life in the country had caused her to lose touch with the acquaintance of her youth.

"A widow," her mother wrote, "is rather like the leftovers of a meal. She can fill her life with new interests and thus, as it were, serve herself *rechauffée* to the world, or else she may languish on a side table—*peu ragoûtante*. Of course, you may marry again. For my own part, I was never inclined to do so, considering your father more than sufficient experience for one lifetime."

Eugenie smiled over the letter. It was so typical of her mother. At least she seemed to enjoy herself at Versailles, lodging with a widowed sister, full of their doings and the gossip of Louis XV's court, playing piquet and comete and usually winning more than she lost.

Blowick. Eugenie considered Blowick at some length, still retaining a great affection for it. Her Cousin Robert would readily lease her a parcel of land. After all, he owed it to her. Not merely in money, that was nothing, or at least—she was consciously self-mocking—it was nothing to *her*. But had she not found him a wife? The Wade girl from Thirlwall Manor . . . an amiable wife, who brought him a good and old connection in the neighborhood.

Blowick. Windswept, barren, handsome Blowick. Its farms and lands spread below its own commanding site were left to be taken by any enemy—but the castle? Never.

She remembered, then, the day when she had handed

it over to her cousin. She traveled up over those dreadful roads, which never seemed to be improved by any covenant of landowners along the way, and arrived at the castle in an ill temper and worse health. With Hannah's help she had stirred up the servants to make some sort of welcome for their new master.

"You'm mistress here." The old steward was querulous. He would have to go, but she hoped that Robert would allow him to go in his own good time.

"My cousin will be your new master. One day he will be Lord Carle, as my father was. He comes from Barbados, where it is always warm. Light fires . . . light fires in every room. Air the beds. We do not know how many family and household may accompany him. We must make him feel comfortable even in this chilly spring!"

"Doan't seem fair!" The old man was stubborn. "When you played here as a child, we always thought the place were your'n."

Eugenie overcame her impatience. "It was mine," she explained, "but I have sold it to my cousin, who can live here and take care of you all, as I could never do."

The steward looked at her as if she had struck him and Eugenie turned away, clapping her hands for the maids. "Those hangings are full of dust. Take them down and give them a good shaking. See that they are rehung within the hour."

She would have liked, above everything, to be mistress of Blowick, yet it seemed useless to try to explain.

Her Cousin Robert arrived three days later. By then she had made the best of a reception for him. But by no range of fancy had she conceived of him arriving with only one body servant and a disproportionate *six* carrier loads of luggage.

The servant was a full-blooded black. No one about Blowick had ever seen such a representative of the human race in their lives. He was immensely tall and built like an oak tree, and the magnificent livery with which he was equipped set him off so spectacularly that the footmen fell back when he jumped out of the coach to lower the steps for his master.

Eugenie, warned of their coming, was waiting at the doorway of the castle to receive them. It was not an auspicious arrival. Her Cousin Robert was a slightly built young man and his tanned face, with large dark eyes, gave him an altogether exotic appearance, which she was aware would not endear him to his prospective tenants. She could almost hear the servants stiffening in disapproval along their lines ranged respectfully in the great hall behind her. Moreover, he was swathed from head to foot in a blanket against the cold and then with a valorous disregard for appearance had topped the lot off with a knitted shawl about the head. It was necessary to adjust her expression before she gave him her hand in greeting.

But "unbandaged" in the hall, he proved to be a wiry, vigorous young man, striding up and down, examining everything with the greatest interest, quick in his observations and with a ready, short infectious laugh. Wherever he walked, Lumson, his slave, prowled behind him.

Robert introduced them.

"Lumson?" Eugenie queried the name.

"Son of Lum."

"Oh, yes. Naturally."

"Give him your hand."

Eugenie was faintly surprised. One did not normally give any servant one's hand.

She was even more astonished when instead of kissing it or bowing over it, as she had anticipated, the man commenced to sniff at it, the back and the palm and the wrist. She restrained the impulse to give him a box on the ears.

"What the devil is he at?" She turned appealingly to her cousin.

"Smell good." Lumson announced with satisfaction. "Smell like something growing. Body and thought in head all good."

"I am so glad," Eugenie said faintly.

Robert found her discomfort vastly amusing.

"Lumson is a remarkable fellow. I value his advice beyond that of anyone. He has memorized all that I could teach him, and yet he has never disowned those primitive, natural instincts which can sometimes keep a man alive in a hostile environment."

"This environment is friendly."

"Is it? I hope so. But I have to feel my way. Lumson understands this."

Eugenie said, "I shall be gone in a week's time. Earlier if you wish. I only came here to help you settle in."

"Of course. Do not think me ungrateful. I make a poor appearance of—what do you say in England?—a squire. But I shall learn."

Careful to suppress any appearance of doubt, Eugenie volunteered that the rooms he would be likely to occupy had been carefully aired. Nor was she ashamed when she personally led him to the master bedchamber, for her mother had refurbished the tapestries and hangings to her own choice, not so very long ago. The colors were rich and somber, such as a man might find to his liking, the fittings of silver, bright in the firelight from a handsome porphyry hearth.

Her cousin was not disappointed. He turned to her with his sudden smile, a young man's generous enthusiasm.

"But this is magnificent—like the castle of one's imagination." He took her hand with the same un-English gesture he had shown on arrival. "My dear Cousin Eugenie, I was not mistaken to come here!"

"I hope not. This is the home of the Carles."

Robert crossed to the deep casement, set cornerwise at one end of the irregular-shaped room and stood looking down on a broad spread of the land. It was late, and the light was going. Eugenie watched him, trying to gauge his judgment of what he saw. It was of the utmost importance that he could feel some sympathy immediately. Later he might grow to love it as her father had done. A strange, elusive relationship . . . this of a man or a woman for his or her native land. Sometimes so deep buried that one supposed it to be imprinted on the soul. But Cousin Robert had been born and reared in a far-off country where blossoms half a foot across grew like weeds and where the heat induced languor. Could he, and would he, change? He looked for a long time down the valley. The wind had shifted and was bending such weather-bitten trees as existed with a new malice.

"Does anything grow here?" he asked in wonder.

"Sheep."

Eugenie had intended to stay only a few days to establish her cousin, but the weeks slid into months before she left him. She must see him settled as an unquestioned master of Blowick, and as he said, there was much he had to learn. Moreover, the tenants were become accustomed to the castle without a lord. The land steward's visits had been less frequent. Dues were paid indifferently, and the cottages and dry-stone walling showed a neglect which made her sorry the first time she rode out with Robert.

Perhaps he expected no better, for he did not complain, but she felt it her duty to point out to him everything that needed attention.

"It was not like this in my father's time. It takes only a year's weathering up here and much tidy work undone." She hesitated. "Also my father was not in good health for several years."

"I understand. You must not apologize."

"I was not doing so," she answered sharply. "I was questioning whether you think you have the strength to keep an estate of this size and in this rough country." She looked briefly at the shawl he still wore about his shoulders, although the worsted traveling cloak should surely give protection enough to a strong-blooded man.

He laughed quietly. "Little cousin, you look fragile, but I understand that you are a true woman of the north . . . a very princess of the snows! Do you never feel the chill of the wind on your back?"

"No, Cousin. Only in my spirits." It was said lightly enough, in one of those quick changes of mood she could sometimes have—from irritation to teasing. But she could recognize the truth of it in her own heart as they turned their horses for home.

Returned to the castle, she made an excuse to leave her cousin and called at once for her father's steward. She waited for him in the library, where there was a good fire. The hall was too vast to warm with any one blaze even in summer.

"Master Bolton has arrived, my lady. Will you receive him here?"

"No," she told the butler. "He may wait in the hall."

That would be well. Let him cool his heels ... and more than his heels!

Bolton needed a reprimand. She must give it for Robert's sake. She waited deliberately and after exactly fifteen minutes went out into the hall.

"My lady. You wished to see me?"

"I did indeed." If the hall was cold, her voice was colder. "Is this how you keep house for my father, now that he is dead? I have ridden around Blowick this day and never scorned a place so much."

"My lady." The man bowed awkwardly. Hastily summoned, he had appeared in string-tied gaiters with every appearance of his own smallholding still clinging to him.

Eugenie looked him over from head to foot. "I see you have been busy about *some* land. Was it by any chance *ours*?"

"My lady," the man said again, "your father, Lord Carle, is dead."

"So he is. But I imagine that you have continued to draw your stipend? Yes? Just as I thought. Are you earning it, do you think? You may like to know that I did not show my cousin the outlying farms. Those close to home were wanting enough in good governance." He stared at her, and she outstared him. A slight woman in a black velvet riding habit, she was as much unlike the late

137

Lord Carle as any man in his wits could imagine. Yet Bolton had the uncomfortable feeling that his office and his small piece of land had never been in so much danger.

"We have been waiting for Master Robert to arrive," he said lamely.

"Waiting to perform those duties for which I have paid you in the meantime?"

"It has not been a good year at the markets. . . ."

"It has been a very good year at the markets. I ascertained that before I came. It was my duty to see after the castle and I trusted the land to you."

"Now we have a master here, things will be different," Bolton assured her earnestly.

"A new master. Will he find it easy?"

"Well . . . that is to say . . . a strange master. One we ain't accustomed to. . . . That manservant of his doan't help."

"It is no concern of yours *who* waits on my cousin."

Bolton conceded this with a slight bow but then straightened suddenly as though he had made up his mind to something and it must be said.

"My lady, you may not take to our folks' point of view but"—he shook his head—"but for a man to come wrapped in a shawl like an old biddy and with a fancy Negro slave. . . .

She had intended to scold Bolton, but instead, he must be answered and Eugenie knew that whatever she said would be repeated.

She considered briefly and then waved a dismissive hand. "We are simple folk in these parts, but not so slow-witted that we cannot appreciate the change from a hot climate to our own north country. As for the servant, he is no boy tricked out for the amusement of a lady of fashion, as one sees in London. I daresay he can use his fists. Or"—an inspiration came to her—"his muscles!" Bolton reacted visibly. "Yes. What about the tug-o'-war with Netherlode? This man would surely be an asset to our side."

So simple and yet so successful. The argument should having occurred to her before. Bolton was the leader of the tug-o'-war side, and this annual struggle between the men of Blowick and the men of Netherlode was an event which aroused more feeling in the countryside than it rightly deserved. Blowick had lost these many years.

And thus it was that Lumson, proving his strength on a rope against the weight of a birch-whipped ox won more respect for his master than could have been bought with round pounds. He was enrolled at once to the Blowick team and, being witnessed to have downed a yard of ale after his exertions, without drawing a breath, made a man in the eyes of every Blowick farm laborer.

Eugenie decided that what Robert needed next was a wife.

"You must seem to have settled here. These people want a long future, as they have a long past. It is just the same on my husband's property," she told him.

"The English," pronounced Robert in his slightly accented speech, "have no spirit for adventure. Everything must be going on and on. . . ." But he laughed, and she understood that he did not dislike the traditions he mocked.

"You must give a ball. I will make out the list of guests, and I will take care to include those families in the neighborhood with eligible daughters."

"And if I do not care for any of them?"

"Then you will be a very difficult man to please," she answered crisply.

There must be all the families included who had always expected her father's hospitality. She would offend no one. The list was carefully made. But there was an added diversion in matchmaking, and so Eugenie found herself, with Hannah's help, sorting through such accounts as they could glean, of the beauties of the county.

"Dark," said Hannah. "Coming from Barbados. Raised there, he is bound to favor a dark girl."

"Fair," said Eugenie. "Something quite different from what he has had."

In the end he chose a nut-brown girl. Rosamund Wade.

The castle was a fine setting for a ball. Something of a task for the guests to reach, but plenty of good stabling for the coach horses at the end of the journey and accommodation for all, even with their servants. Stone-walled rooms opened up and, provided with good fires, not too chill in the spring turning to summer. Massive tapestried beds pulled over and inside out. A shower of moths, and even a bat or two in the turret ends, but these were chased out with a broom.

Down in the hall, tables were laden with the game, which tenants had been bringing in for weeks. Huge haunches of venison were the central dishes. But crown roast lamb and wild duck, and patties of hare, and stuffed carp were also displayed. There were twelve puddings. Eugenie worried over whether that would be sufficient. In London her mother never offered less than fifteen. But they liked the berry pies in Northumberland. Maybe the lack of variety would pass notice.

It was perfectly clear to her that just so soon as she had introduced her cousin to the eldest unattached Wade girl she made a marriage. Nothing of the shawl-clad figure who had first appeared among them. Robert was the gallant that night.

Rosamund Wade wore satin of a brilliant buttercup yellow. "I could never wear that shade," Eugenie said, and Hannah readily agreed with her. "She must have some white flowers for her hair . . . and my pear-shaped pearl around her neck. See to it."

Eugenie watched the girls complete their dress and go down. And then when she had led Rosamund to Robert, there was the satisfaction of knowing she had chosen the winner. Her cousin's eyes, and the girl's demeanor while they danced. Quite delightful to see an attraction bloom

140

between two young people. She spent the latter part of the night talking to the Wade parents. By dawn the marriage was as good as arranged.

"You are pleased with the Wade girl?" Eugenie signaled with a feeble hand that the curtains should be taken back from the deep-set casements. Their guests were asleep, and it was first light.

"Yes. She is very pretty."

"She brings you little money. But she's a healthy girl. The whole family is prolific."

"Thank you, Cousin. Shall I be happy with her, do you think?"

Eugenie said, "I don't see why not." She hesitated, then added: "One must not hope too much of marriage. Lawyers marry you. Not angels. This child, Rosamund, will do very well."

But no. She would not go to Blowick. She had become an "outlander" there, just as she had been to her husband's people when she came as a bride to his country. Perhaps the ultimate irony lay in this. She had never felt at home in Clere Athel, and yet after so many years she was more at home in Clere Athel than anywhere else.

With the whole world to choose from, she would bargain with her son for a couple of acres of the home park. She would build a dower house.

It was a chilly autumn evening, and a large fire, burning with a bluish edge to its flame, reflected in the polished, paneled walls of the library and picked out the gilt lettering on the spines of the books. Giles was reading, and Eugenie worked a tapestry with little industry, while she thought of the next day when Athel was expected home with his new wife.

"I do hope," she said suddenly, "that Athel and Kitty will be happy. . . . I wish . . . I only wish he were a little more in love with her." She sighed. "He doesn't seem to me to show any signs of being in love."

141

Giles looked up sharply. "I should hope not. Tiresome thing, love. Takes a man's mind off a game of cards." He disappeared behind his book again.

Eugenie laughed. "You don't mean that!"

"Don't I?" He seemed to be waiting for an answer, but she let it pass.

VIII

AFTER the diversions of a visit to Versailles, the road to Dijon was not the most interesting route to be taking. Eugenie's eyes followed the contours of the landscape, but her thoughts were hundreds of miles away.

Strange. She had wanted so much to escape from Lancashire, and now, well sped on her journey, she could think only of Clere Athel and the house, nearing completion close inside the gates of the park. It would be a good house, a home. A simple, yet pleasing design. Three stories, but not more than four rooms on each level and all of them large. The windows of the principal apartments came to within twelve inches of the floor, and the long salon would open onto a terrace leading down to an enclosed garden at the rear.

"Let it be a house for a woman such as I am," she told the architect, "a house for a woman alone. I want many aspects, with light to read wherever I sit. I want a well-turned staircase, with the steps shallow for the years that lie ahead of me. I want a large salon and a small dining room, for I shall entertain very seldom. Let there be an

142

ample bedchamber with the best view that is to be had of the trees in the park, and see that the kitchens are comfortable and convenient for the servants. Set them immediately beyond the dining room in a single story, so that there is no annoyance from the smell of cooking rising to any place but the heavens."

Most of the notions for the house came out of her own head, but Master Cloud added one or two touches of his own. The library, which would also serve as a morning room, was hexagonal. That was a charming idea. No doubt about it, he drew well. The sketches for the plastering were conceived with an airy delicacy, and he avoided those busy flourishes which she so disliked at Carle House. She told him he might have his way with the marble for the stairs and the hall, provided the colors were muted and the design such as might rest the eye. "For the rest of the decoration, little gilt and much paneling will be the thing."

Athel resented the project of a dower house, of course. He did not want to lease her the modest plot of land and she had to be artful in argument. She smiled to herself now, thinking of it. But she was bound to win in the end. She would leave him a valuable addition to his property. If he did not allow her to build in Clere Athel, she threatened, she would go to France and according to French law, Louis XV might then claim her personal possessions—her jewels and her silver—when she died. Athel, grown first red and then white, said she might have the land.

The consent was ungracious, and he could not forbear to add the condition that she should kneel to him at the next witan and make the old gesture of fealty for tenure. Giles conveyed the message, and she laughed outright.

"What? Kneel to my own son? Him I gave birth and shall leave possessed of better fortune nor any Athelson ever had?"

"You must do it for his dignity's sake," Giles said. "It is the tradition." He was unwontedly stern with her.

"We shall see. We will wait until the house is completed and I take possession of it."

First, she resolved to make a visit to Italy to collect works of art with which to adorn her new property. On the way she would see her mother at Versailles, and then she would pay a call on her old friend, the Chevalier de Mulignac, now retired to his estates just beyond Dijon. Her plans for the journey were carefully made.

She ordered a traveling coach. "It looks like a jewel box on wheels!" Giles disparaged the quilted interior.

"Do you begrudge me my comfort?"

"I wonder you don't order a gilded barge to cross to France."

"I may do that. I am a very rich woman, you know."

"We all know."

If Giles and Athel had fought her over the dower house, that was nothing to their endeavors to stop her from going to Italy. Athel even summoned Thurstan and Dickon—the one from the inns of court, and the other from schooling. She saw a letter Athel wrote to Thurstan. He left it on his desk, half-completed, and she read it accidentally but without shame: "Mother is impossible. She intends to build a house of her own in our grounds and talks of a protracted visit to Italy to buy furnishings. I have tried to dissuade her without success and can only wish that you will return home and add your voice to mine. The expense will clearly be considerable and one must feel alarm at the danger of such an expedition for a woman of her age with only servants to guard her. . . .'"

Eugenie smiled again. The expense. Of course, that *would* be uppermost in Athel's mind. As for her well-being, surely Dickon was the only one to care. "Let me come with you, Mother. School is nothing to me. I am no scholar. Thurstan says there are wolves in the Alpine passes. Let me come."

"My dearest child, you are overly concerned. Wolves will come nowhere near us. The journey has been made

144

by hundreds of travelers. Besides," she added, "nothing *ever* happens to me. I am one of those dull people who may wander as they please without drama. If a wolf sees me, either I shall seem too thin, else he will not be hungry. Continue your lessons at Eton. You can be perfectly sure I shall return."

"Is this wise?" Thurstan asked. Thurstan was always restrained both in inquiry and judgment. "Athel would much prefer that you did not go."

"Yes, Athel has put his opinions at my service many times these past months. And for my part I have tried to overlook the impertinence of some of them, remembering that while he is now head of the family, he is also very young."

She saw that Thurstan was taken aback by her tone and instantly regretted the sharpness of it, so that she added more gently: "I have always had a fancy to see my mother's country, you know, and the art of Italy is worth a pilgrimage."

Thurstan frowned, thoughtfully. "I suppose I might leave my studies and escort you myself."

"No, no . . . it has always been my idea that you should make the tour with Dickon, when he is old enough. *Then* you will have the benefit of Master Corby's company. You will find that much more to your taste."

She would prefer to have no one's whims to consult except her own. And it was no part of this modest adventure she had planned with such pleasure, to find herself in the charge of her nineteen-year-old son, who would clearly protect her from any interesting experience the journey might afford.

All had gone well so far. She made the crossing from Dover to Calais in a little more than three hours and was met by one of the stewards from her mother's household. The man, Pierre Barac, smoothed her way through the customhouse, without the officers seeking to open even one of her jewel cases. She was quickly persuaded of his value to her party. In addition to Barac, she had the company of Hannah, and Tom, her coachman, with Ezra, the groom, on the box beside him. The baggage coach, following behind, was driven by a young lad, green out of the stables at Clere Athel. But there was a footman, who could use a brace of pistols. Well pleased with her arrangements, she traveled directly to Versailles.

Madeleine was with her sister, the Marquise de Fontenand, who, by virtue of her late husband's former post at court, had a suite of apartments in the palace.

"You are more than welcome, child," her mother told her. "My sister has a reputation for piety and a talent for performing card tricks. This has been quite sufficient to secure her the favor of the queen. We move in the very first circles of respectability. . . . You will overlook that they are also the dullest!"

The queen, Eugenie was shortly bound to agree with her mother, had very limited interests. A healthy woman, who got healthy children, she held her place in her husband's affections. She was even handsome, in a dignified, matronly way. But attractive or entertaining, she most certainly was not.

"Louis is a family man," her mother observed shrewdly. "He would like to love the queen, but as it is, he merely respects her. Such a dreary thing for a man —respect without enchantment!"

Madeleine would have prefered to mix with the livelier company at court. The king had recently taken a mistress, Madame de Mailly. The parties in her rooms sent music along the corridors and woke sleeping equerries, where they sat in the gilded chairs to await dispatch on some improbable errand for the pleasure of the company.

"They say Louis is developing a fancy for his mistress' sister, Madame de Vintimille," Madeleine told her. "A mistake. That one will cause trouble."

Eugenie was intrigued by the undercurrents of the French court. The unchallengeable etiquette bewildered

146

and amused her. Ladies of the court could not move without employing a certain gliding step, which made them look as if they had wheels, rather than feet, beneath their spreading skirts. And there was a fashionable laugh—not a natural sound, but a short exclamation, with which they must register delight.

"I am clumsy," she told her mother. "I have a countrywomen's clumsiness. I cannot play these games."

"You could learn." Her mother sounded almost wistful.

"No," Eugenie said. "After all these years people must take me as I am."

"Sometimes I am bored with the queen." Madeleine pouted. "Maria Leszczýnska has a Polish fancy for obscure saints. It is nothing to me if she keeps the king from her bed on saints' days . . . but if she will use the same dates merely to keep us from supper and cards. . . ."

"Why do you stay here?" Eugenie asked.

Her mother smiled wryly. "I am amused for *nearly* half the time. Somewhat less in London."

But the life seemed very restricted to Eugenie. She found herself longing to throw open the windows of their elegant painted rooms or to run on the carefully tended lawns she saw beyond them. Quite uncharacteristic inclinations, and she wondered at herself.

"The firstborn of the queen's twin daughters has the fever," the courtiers said. "*Quel dommage!* She might die." But there must be no betrayal of anxiety or grief. . . . That would be unseemly. . . . Madame Première was better. . . . "*Plus heureuse*." . . . A turn of the head sideways and a mere elevation of the corners of the mouth. . . . Very proper. . . . Very mannerly. Emotion must be subdued. One must never show *maladresse*.

"I shall set out tomorrow for Dijon." Eugenie was unable to raise any of that elegant doubt, that *longueur*, about her plans which would have made them more acceptable to her mother.

Madeleine suppressed a yawn. "Well, if you are determined to go, it is of no purpose to argue. The queen seems to favor you, and there is an invitation to supper this evening. I'm sure I do not know why you will not settle here . . . two rich *English* widows . . . we have a certain *train de maison*, which is noticed. . . . Will you see De Mulignac?"

"Yes, I have written to him that I shall visit for a day or so."

"He is an old man. Tell him I will come in the summer."

"It is May now. Do you mean within the next two months?"

Madeleine yawned again. "Perhaps."

And so there was the road to Dijon. Not a fine road for its prospects or the inns along the way, but a reasonable traveling road. Eugenie sent her courier ahead and had the best rooms reserved

The Chevalier de Mulignac did not rise before noon, and then he put on only his small clothes and a silk robe. He was quite bald, not by shaving but by nature. He wore a small round cap with a tassel. At nine o'clock in the evening he had his valet dress him with infinite care in a full-skirted coat and satin breeches. A curled and scented wig was tied with a ribbon to match his vest. Diamond-buckled shoes were chosen and, lastly, a small dress sword. He made this toilette even when he was alone. In Eugenie's honor he added diamond studs and a fob which represented a fortune to most men.

To De Mulignac, nearing the close of his life and conscious of it, the gesture was a small compliment he paid to his guest. Nothing more. Even the trouble to direct his valet to ask his steward for the key of the box where he kept his most valuable jewels seemed more than it was worth. But for Eugenie? Yes, he would do it. He had always been fond of Eugenie. He loved her mother. He had loved her mother for many years.

148

"Eugenie, you have grown into a most beautiful woman." This said across the supper table.

"Monsieur, le Chevalier, you are kind. My son is married now. No doubt I shall soon be a grandmother."

De Mulignac considered her critically.

"You have that quality of porcelain fired with skill —delicate and yet with considerable ability to last. I admire that."

Eugenie laughed. "And I deplore it! Who would wish to outlive their time? Perhaps as a widow I have already outlived myself."

"Were you happy in your marriage? . . . No, no—I rephrase the question—were you contented?"

They had finished supper. Eugenie left the table and walked across the room to examine a miniature which hung on the wall above a buhl table.

"You are not interested in that trifle," the chevalier said. "Why do you not answer me? You forget I have known you from your nursery days . . . won't you honor a bored old man despite the impertinence of his questions?"

"It is not . . . it has never been possible for me to confide in anyone."

"This is to be understood—of the past. Even as a childless bachelor I saw that you were too often alone. But you may talk to me and be assured of my discretion. I am nearly eighty, and there is no better place to bury a confidence than in a grave."

Eugenie returned to sit opposite him across the vast hearth with its deeply carved armorial device. The chevalier always liked well-heated rooms, and even on this summer evening in France there was a small companionable glow.

"You are grown very gloomy. You will live to be a hundred!"

"Do you really believe so? More cognac will reassure me." De Mulignac reached for the tapestry bell rope

149

beside him and, when the footman appeared, ordered the same. Also the table removed and a number of the scented candles snuffed. The service was instant and expert, and then they were alone again.

"You were about to tell me more of your life in Clere Athel."

Eugenie laughed. "I was about to do nothing of the kind."

De Mulignac's eyes narrowed, and he said, "One may assume that there have been painful disappointments."

His persistence was too compelling.

"Some. I would not say that every day in my life had been a festival day, but then neither was it always a rainy Thursday afternoon!" She smiled faintly. "I had great pleasure from my children when they were small and still in my care."

"And now? Surely they are grown into fine young men. At least your mother wrote to me that it was so."

Eugenie hesitated before answering. "Thurstan and Dickon do very well." That was an understatement, of course. Thurstan shared her own love of books and study, a young man with quiet eyes and a neatly ironic sense of humor. Odd how she could view him with a detached appreciation as well as deep affection. Dickon was different. He had been, and always would be, whatever the injustice of it, the one who turned her heart whenever she looked at him. Parents were supposed to love all their children equally, but that was an ideal. The truth was that children began in only a very few years to show their potential in both character and inclination, and everyone was unique. Maternal *interest* would surely persist forever. But the deeper maternal *instinct* might fade along with the dependence of infancy.

"And your eldest son, Athel?"

De Mulignac slipped his question into her thoughts.

This time she was quick and firm. "Athel has never been like my own. He has shades of his father, but he

150

lacks that generosity of spirit which allows forgiveness of other failings or neglects." Confidences once begun grew easier. "I had always a great respect for his father. . . . Perhaps they took Athel away from me too young. They showed him his property, and by the time he was eight years old it seemed to me that there was more of avarice in his attitude to it and less of that responsibility toward the people who live off it than I would have wished to see." She stopped abruptly. "Now you have urged me, I am saying too much. I am becoming tedious company."

"Not at all. You are fascinating. It is impossible to be bored by human nature." De Mulignac tapped his snuff-box thoughtfully. "This boy knows, of course, that he will inherit great wealth from you?"

"Oh, yes. I daresay he knows to within pence what I am worth."

"You sound bitter, *ma chère*."

"Those I would have loved have too often weighed my fortune when they looked at me." For a moment her eyes were bleak. Then she smiled. "*Alors!* It is only what is to be anticipated. Now I go to look for adventure in Italy while I still have health and strength. I shall live out my days quietly in the dower house which I am building at Clere Athel."

"You might meet with *un galant* and lose your heart. You might marry again."

"No, I shall not do that." She stared into the heart of the fire for a moment and then, conscious of her complexion as Madeleine had always taught her to be, unfurled a delicately gilded fan to fend off the heat.

De Mulignac saw her away the next noon with reluctance, raising a hand to her in farewell from the cypress-lined drive of his chateau. It would be remarkable if he saw her again. "My mother says that she will visit you very soon," she told him on parting. "I am waiting for her," he answered. "Some women keep a man waiting all their lives!"

She traveled to Turin without incident, and then to Milan, where she had a desire to visit the Borromean Library. There was another English family lodging at the same address.

"Did you come by chair over the mountains?" Mistress Morrison was prepared to believe anything.

"No," Eugenie said, "although I understand it is a reasonable means for bolder travelers."

"And you are quite alone except for servants? My dear, you must continue your journey with our party. If you are on my conscience, I cannot sleep in my bed!"

"I set out for Venice tomorrow . . . but you are very kind."

Mistress Morrison's eyes narrowed. "I think you will find yourself remarkably uncomfortable without an escort. We are ourselves bound for Venice, and I am told that the entrée is not to be had so easily. My husband might be of service to you. Why do you not wait a day or two?"

"Well, you see, I am very impatient," Eugenie replied. "Moreover, I have lodgings reserved on the Grand Canal, and there is a carnival."

She detached herself with determination from the Morrisons.

In Venice there was a certain freedom. One might go anywhere in a mask. The lodgings were good—better than she had expected—and the English consul was helpful.

She dined with the Spanish ambassador and went to the comedies and the opera whenever she felt inclined.

During her days she purchased gouaches, viewed and made a successful bid for a large oil painting of the waterfalls at Terni, failed to buy a Vernet, but acquired a Titarella of no distinction. Her decision to visit the galleries of Florence was largely induced by the arrival of the tiresome Morrisons a few days later, in company with a pair of insufferable *petits maitres* making the tour. The manners and excesses of these young men, fresh escaped

152

from country estates in Dorset and let loose without control in a city like Venice, reflected little credit on other English visitors. Mistress Morrison might pretend to find their pranks amusing, but Eugenie thought them embarrassing and boorish and said so.

It also became apparent that far from being well furnished with introductions, as she had claimed, Mistress Morrison was looking to Eugenie to connect her with embassy staff and thence with the nobility. She might have done this in respect of the family, but Eugenie had no intention of inflicting their raw, young acquaintances on people who had shown her hospitality.

A somewhat hasty withdrawal to Florence recommended itself.

Having no lodgings bespoke, she was grateful to accept Lord Keyne's offer of a villa which he had taken for the summer. Lord Keyne was forced to return to England on urgent family business, and meeting him briefly at an inn along the road, she confided her difficulties over a shared supper in the only public room available. He at once wrote a letter to his steward and urged her to make full use of his house and his staff. Moreover, he refused to discuss any question of rent, saying only that he was happy to have been of service.

"By-the-by"—he turned back, before their coaches set off in opposite directions, next morning—"there is only a courtyard to my property, but you have the use of gardens belonging to the Vardi villa, next door. It is in the lease. There's a splendid avenue, and you can drive there comfortably on a hot day."

Eugenie was so delighted with Florence that it was several days before she recalled this piece of advice. She exhausted herself in the meantime with sightseeing. She gazed at the Uffizi Palace, the Brunelleschi dome on the cathedral and Giotto's marble tower, crossed and recrossed the Arno River on a tour of the city's medieval churches and made a thorough examination of the Roman baths and the amphitheater.

It was now high summer. The sun stood in splendor from early morning, and even the shadows were stifling. The Vardi gardens suddenly looked wonderfully inviting from her windows. There were arbors of cypress, and the long avenue led to a square filled with fountains and cascades.

Lord Keyne had left behind a light carriage, which was just the thing for a drive in such surroundings, and she at once ordered it.

"Come, Hannah, we will take our embroidery and find some ideal, little spot where we can spend the afternoon quietly and rest our feet."

"Shall I bring a footstool then, as well as cushions?"

"Certainly not!" Eugenie said tartly. "I said 'rest our feet'—not cosset them. We are not old women yet."

"We aren't fledglings, neither." Hannah sighed. "However, leave be. I'm only thankful you'll let us take our ease for once. It seemed to me one of us must surely run a fever from exhaustion if we carried on any longer at that pace."

"What an impertinent wench you are." Eugenie laughed. "And where's the gratitude you owe me for showing you one of the most beautiful cities in Europe, this magnificent art and architecture? Don't you feel your whole spirit being uplifted?"

"No," Hannah answered stolidly. "I only know that I reek of incense."

They found a miniature grove of chestnuts and cypress, where a delicate column of water rose and fell in a stone basin. There was a copper ball dancing on the spray, with something inside it that kept up a pretty sound. Eugenie had never seen such a thing before and at once settled herself down beside it with her needlework, having instructed the carriage to wait for them in the shade of the avenue.

They had been working pleasantly for about an hour when Eugenie saw two women approaching across the lawn. Even while she watched, the slighter figure stag-

154

gered and appeared to swoon. Her companion clearly had difficulty in supporting her, and Eugenie, exclaiming to Hannah, hurried to help.

"Let me take the girl."

"My daughter!" The older woman gasped. "She has not been in good health. We took a walk for the air, and I have sent our carriage away until five o'clock."

"Bring her to this seat. Hannah—wring out my handkerchief in the fountain, and we will apply it to the nape of her neck."

The child was perhaps sixteen. Eugenie thought how fragile the bowed shoulders looked. After a few minutes of their anxious attentions they were successful, and the girl stirred in her mother's arms, attempting to sit up by herself.

"Gently, *mia figlia*."

"But I feel better now."

They were speaking in Italian. Eugenie turned and translated for Hannah. "The girl says she feels recovered. Will you call the carriage? Tell the driver *'Presto, presto.'* "

"The *donna inglesa* is very kind." The girl's mother hesitated, looking doubtfully at her daughter's shadowed face, "I am reluctant to trouble you, but. . . ."

"There is no trouble in such a small service. Please do not even speak of it. Only give me the direction of your villa and we will take you there at once."

"The villa Franciosa then, if you please. We are staying there with my sister."

On the short journey Eugenie had the opportunity to consider the woman—handsome in the tradition of her country. Rather more ample than English fashion would allow to be beautiful, but having expressive eyes and mouth and an abundance of silky-black hair, dressed without powder, under a black lace veil. Her face was puckered with motherly concern, and she fluttered small, plump hands about the pale girl, who leaned back wearily.

155

"I should introduce myself, I think." Eugenie deprecated the formality with a gesture. "I am Eugenie Athelson. I have the use of Lord Keyne's villa for a short time, while I visit Florence."

"*Piacere di conoscerla.* I am Seraphina di Palacco. This is my youngest daughter, Lucia. Do you make a long stay in Florence?"

"I do not know. I am recently widowed, and my time is my own. Perhaps I may stay here another month."

The Contessa di Palacco bent her head sideways, implying that widowhood was a state demanding tender sympathy. "You have children, donna?"

"Three sons."

"Ah! You are blessed. I have six daughters."

"I would have liked a daughter." Eugenie's voice was deliberately cool. "I had a girl, but she died at birth."

Seraphina's eyes widened with womanly understanding. "You must visit us. Here is the Franciosa Villa. But you must come and see us."

"Perhaps I might call tomorrow to see that the child is better." Did she sound too eager? Eugenie leaned back in an attitude of careful boredom. "My driver will carry the child inside."

The villa was a handsome affair of peach-colored stone. Footmen appeared down its wide steps as soon as the carriage stopped. Eugenie watched them help the plump figure of the contessa inside, with her daughter borne tenderly as though she were a sacrament.

"*She* won't make old bones," Hannah said flatly.

And for once Eugenie answered in a short, snappish way and said, "What do you know about it? A girl is often delicate at that age and comes on very strong in womanhood."

The next day she restrained herself from calling to see how Lucia did. But on the second afternoon she ordered the carriage to drive to the Franciosa villa and had the groom announce her.

156

Seraphina herself came out, quick and eager with her gratitude, begging Eugenie to step down.

"My husband is home. He is in Lucia's room now, and the physician is with him. Please to come in. It was our intention to wait on you and give you thanks."

She showed Eugenie into a long drawing room where a servant was already folding back the slatted shutters.

"You will take a glass of wine or some cordial. I will go and tell my husband you are here. He had left us for a few days to see after our estates near Siena. He returned late last night."

"I am afraid I make my call at an inconvenient time."

"Not at all. Not at all. I only beg you to wait one moment. He will be delighted to meet you and have an opportunity of adding his thanks to mine. . . . Our Lucia is such a precious child to us . . . always so delicate . . . nearly lost to us so many times. . . . You understand."

"Perfectly."

"Then you will excuse me."

"Of course."

There was a book open on a bronze lectern by the windows. Eugenie crossed the room to examine it, in the idleness of waiting.

A single paragraph illuminated upon the page. Martial, from the *Epigrammata*. As usual, Eugenie reflected wryly, she was outclassed. Latin. If Giles had been there, he could have read it with ease and made an elegant translation. In the first line the design intruded to such an extent that the letters must be illegible unless one was familiar with the passage. The rest read: "*Sera nimis vita est crastina: vive hodie.*"

"Life . . . will be. . . ." She labored over the words, unconsciously speaking them aloud.

"The life of tomorrow is too late; live today!"

Eugenie looked up from the page. A man had come silently into the room and now stood looking at her, leaning easily on the back of a chair. There was a lithe grace in his attitude, and his face had the proportions of fine sculpture.

"You are Donna Eugenie Athelson and I am Matteo di Palacco . . . most particularly at your service." He straightened, bowed very slightly and moved across the room and for some reason, when she held out her hand, it trembled.

IX

"THE PALACCOS' manservant is below again." Hannah gave a disapproving twitch to Eugenie's bedcurtains and handed her first a cup of hot chocolate and then a note upon a silver dish. "Will there be a reply?"

Eugenie yawned and opened her arms luxuriously to another day. "I will tell you when I have read the note. Why do you sound such a bear this morning?"

"Seems to me we shall be here forever if these folks keep suggesting some new pleasuring. All these parties, and tripping about palaces, and the like. When shall we go home to Lancashire, that's what I want to know?"

"When I'm ready." Eugenie reached out and tweaked the thick cream paper off the dish. She read the direction. "It is from Matteo di Palacco, not his wife." She was faintly surprised.

"I see that. Most improper if you ask me."

"I don't." She was reading. "Lucia is much better, and

they have decided to take her back to Siena. . . . They urge us to go with them."

Hannah scowled. "And I suppose you are of a mind to accept."

"Yes, I think so. Why not? There is the Donatello bronze of John the Baptist to see in the cathedral and—"

"Do not tell me the rest. I would rather not know."

Eugenie laughed. "Poor Hannah! You really *do* want to go home, don't you? Well, I promise you that when we to go home, don't you? Well, I promise you that when we have been to Siena, I will make arrangements for shipping the pictures home, and then we will be on our way."

The Palacco estates included some of the richest acres in Tuscany. The white stone villa, set on a hill above the umber plain, seemed to have an unattainable quality as one approached it. Like a citadel, Eugenie thought, and promptly fell in love with it.

"We live very simply here," Seraphina said complacently, waving a plump hand at the peasants who knelt at the roadside as the coach horses struggled on the winding climb to the villa. "One may do so when one lives remote."

Matteo di Palacco had reservations. "I only hope you will be comfortable. It may be that we cannot offer what the Donna Eugenie has been accustomed to think of as necessities to living."

Eugenie smiled about her. "If you had seen Clere Athel, you would have no doubts. We are very primitive in the north of England."

The Palacco villa was more a miniature castle than a house. Its fortifications were still kept in reasonable repair. Older parts were carved out of the rocky hill on which it stood, and the main hall, where most of the household took meals, was a round tower with walls of seemingly impregnable thickness.

And yet there was nothing grim or sinister about the dim, cool interiors. The atmosphere was happy, Eugenie

159

felt. Secure as a family home should be. There was the echo of girlish laughter and Seraphina's own warm contralto voice along the corridors. Rich tapestries glowed upon the walls, and portraits peopled the rooms even when they were unoccupied.

Seraphina had an affectionate nature and overwhelmed Eugenie with kindness, giving every appearance of pleasure in additional female company. Of her daughters, three had married within the past two years and another had "answered the call of Holy Church." That was Constantia. Seraphina was both proud and afraid of this daughter. She sighed whenever she mentioned her, because although Constantia would surely one day be an abbess of her order, she was lost to man and marriage and motherhood—all the blessings her mother could comprehend.

Two daughters remained at home. There was Lucia, who had been such a delicate child and so heart-rending to rear that both parents had come to look upon every birthday she celebrated as a triumph, and Teresa, a plain, shortsighted girl who disliked the company of any man save her father and had begged him therefore not to find her a suitor.

"*Aiyee-a,*" said Seraphina, "she will be a spinster that one for sure." And then, because she was on good terms with human nature; "Well, well! Every family has need of a *zia.*"

There was already one grandchild—a boy, praise be!—and a great many of Seraphina's prayers were going into the making of another, due within the month. It was all very gratifying. Nevertheless, she missed the daughters who had left her.

She was curious about Eugenie's sons and wondered how she could bear to be parted from them.

"You will want letters! My husband has made arrangements for your letters to be redirected from Florence. Oh, how very happy you will be when news comes."

"Yes, there may be some letters by now." Eugenie was

160

mildly amused, thinking that the contents would disappoint Seraphina and perfectly sure that she would be expected to impart them. Dickon might write that he had overspent his allowance or complain that Master Corby kept him on too tight a rein. Thurstan would send her an impeccable page of family news, and Athel would grumble about the additional expenditure which she had lately authorized.

As it happened, worse befell. For the post, fetched at no small trouble by the priest, Father Jessolino himself, consisted of a single letter and that one of the strange communications she sometimes received from Giles. Father Jessolino brought the letter to Eugenie as she sat sewing on the terrace.

Seraphina clapped her hands with gratification. "It will be from your eldest son, I make no doubt. He, it will be, who has written for his brothers. Ah, the love and the tenderness. . . . The letter to travel so far. . . . You must long to read it at once!" She eyed Eugenie with bright anticipation.

Eugenie's heart sank. Impossible to lay the letter aside without hurting Seraphina's feelings—Father Jessolino's, too, since he had settled himself down comfortably with them and wore the same expression of interest. And yet how could she possibly read aloud any letter from Giles to people who did not know him? How explain the subtle, and often not so subtle, gibes that made their appearance in practically every passage? There would be asides in Greek and Latin, which he wrote deliberately, knowing she could not translate them, and he would say a great deal around some subject, in a witty, clever way, and then leave undisclosed precisely what his reader most desired—the outcome of the matter, a reassurance, even a judgment—so that in the end he had raised only a series of anxieties, or at best a ravenous curiosity.

She did not want to read the letter, not even for herself, let alone a simple, kindly woman like Seraphina and a good-hearted priest, who had gone off his route on a private pilgrimage to perform a service, which he thought would please her.

"The letter is not from my son." She hesitated. "I see by the direction that it is from my brother-in-law." She turned the packet over in her hands uncertainly.

"The brother of your lamented husband?" Seraphina sounded surprised. But if she had been cheated of her first hope, she would make the best of it. "The *uncle* of your sons. It is clear that he writes to you of the wonders of their achievements."

Eugenie surrendered. "If you will excuse me, then, I will see what he says."

"Do, do, daughter!" Father Jessolino urged. And added, transparently: "Letters from England are rare here . . . quite an event, in fact. It will make me happy to know that your mind is set at peace about your loved ones."

She broke the seal with reluctance. The original cipher had already been cut, since no letter crossing so many frontiers could hope to travel unexamined. A wonder that it had not been detained on suspicion of code, she thought bitterly, her eyes racing down the close-written pages.

It was quite as bad as she feared. She could picture Giles, writing in his study when the rest of the household was asleep. As usual he gave the impression of having more to tell than he told: "I will not trouble you with that since you are so far away and can do nothing." . . . Athel's wife was with child, but looking very frail. Heavy rain had beaten down crops. The dower house was completed, but Athel declined to put in any staff to mind it. "It has a very damp feel," Giles wrote gleefully. "I wonder if the soil drainage is good at that end of the park."

Eugenie did what she could. She gave her audience the news about the grandchild that was to be.

"We will light a candle for her this evening." Seraphina nodded.

162

"The house I have built for myself is finished," Eugenie said. It was a fortunate item to have selected. She had not talked about the dower house before, and Seraphina was both amazed and intrigued.

"You mean you will not live with your son and daughter-in-law in the so big palace?"

By the time that Eugenie had finished explaining the difference between Clere Athel and the palazzo of Seraphina's imagination, to say nothing of attempting to justify her own desire for an independent establishment, it was time to dress for supper.

"What does he say of your sons?"

"They are in good health. Study has kept Dickon and Thurstan from writing, and Athel has been very much occupied with the estate," Eugenie lied firmly.

There was, of course, no mention of her sons. It was as if they did not exist. Seraphina accepted these excuses and folded her needlework with a sigh.

"One's children grow up. That is in the nature of things." She considered Eugenie thoughtfully for a moment. "How wise you are to be the first to leave."

During the first two weeks of her visit to the Palacco villa Eugenie had seen very little of her host.

"Matteo, *Matt-e-o . . . per favore. . . .*" Seraphina's voice was operatic in appeal. Her husband answered her soothingly, but he would still go out from early morning until dusk. They were building a new tower on the village church. Eugenie watching from the terrace, could see the dust rising like puffs of sulfurous smoke where they worked the yellow stone in the valley below.

Matteo di Palacco was supervising the work. It was one of his chief joys to build things. He had designed the tower, making careful calculations of the weight the walls must bear, buttressing it in against the main structure with bold, spreading pinions of his native rock.

"But, Matteo," Seraphina wailed, "there is no need for you to exhaust yourself day after day among your own workmen. Are you not *padrone* here? Father Jessolino tells me you stripped off your shirt and labored until you were so caked with sweat and dust that he could not tell you from your masons."

"Surely the worthy father did not condemn me for that?" Matteo's mouth curved ironically.

"Why, no . . . he said it was to the greater glory of God. . . ." Seraphina sounded doubtful.

"So it is, then."

"But think of your position, your *dignity*."

"A man's dignity is not impaired by wholesome labor," was the mild answer.

"Your own father would never have done such a thing."

"That is perfectly true. My honored father never turned his hand to anything but a game of cards."

Still, Seraphina would not let the subject rest.

Finally she wore through her husband's patience until he said sharply, "Oh, do be quiet, Seraphina. Can you not see that you are embarrassing Donna Eugenie by prolonging this conversation?"

His wife had lapsed then into an aggrieved silence and after a few moments excused herself to Eugenie with elaborate courtesy and left them.

They were in the salon, a long, low-ceilinged room with many casement windows looking across the plain. Eugenie continued to work a tapestry, enjoying the glorious quality of the late-evening light. After a while she became conscious that Matteo di Palacco was watching her and looked at him directly to invite conversation if he wished it. There was a brooding weariness about his expression which surprised her.

"A woman can fill her life with her children," he said suddenly. "She should understand that a man must have occupation also. Seraphina does not seem to see this. She thinks I can spend every hour of my life either eating or sleeping. . . ." If this called for an answer, Eugenie could not find one. He walked over to one of the windows and stared morosely down at the tiered gardens falling away below the terrace. "I made these gardens, you know."

"They are very pleasant. The whole scheme is excellent. Did you employ anyone with experience of landscaping?"

"No. It was my own design. I gave each of my gardeners a simple sketch to work by. Every man had his allotted task. We labored side by side with the digging and the planting. The statues I bought in Florence." He spoke rapidly and in a low voice, more as though to remind himself how it had been than to inform her. Obviously it was an achievement which had given him great pleasure.

"And now the church tower."

He nodded and then, without turning his head, added: "You must understand how I feel. My wife told me about the house you built. I believe we are *simpatico*—you and I."

Eugenie selected a hank of azure blue and drew three strands from it with infinite care. "I do not build to occupy myself. My house is to live in, sir, not to pass my time." She looked at him over her needle and then threaded the strands. Their eyes met and held while she knotted the silk.

"Would you like to come and see my tower?" He sounded almost wistful.

"Very much. I have it in my mind to rebuild the church at Clere Athel when I go home. Perhaps you can give me an idea for the plans."

He drew forward a chair and sat down close to her, resting his small, broad hands on his knees. Capable hands, Eugenie thought, strong, and of a fine, even color. They were hands that were made to create.

"Tell me about your house. . . . No—better still draw it!"

"I cannot draw. I have no skill at all with the charcoal."

"Mark out the number of rooms in squares, their approximate shape. And on this sheet the elevation."

"I cannot—"

"Yes, you can!"

Eugenie put aside the tapestry. No one could withstand such enthusiasm. With Matteo's charcoal and the pad of paper he gave her she attempted to evoke the dower house. It was a poor attempt, but he seemed satisfied.

"There are broad spreading trees about it? One must have trees to soften these classic lines."

"Yes, there are trees and the park—over six acres, before one reaches the old manor house."

"That is well. You want a circular carriage sweep in front of the house"—he was sketching busily—"and here, at the center, a piece of statuary—something distinctive. Something evocative of you!"

Eugenie laughed. "I don't think—"

"That you will find such a piece? Leave it to me! Something aloof, graceful. I know the very man for the commission. Ricorro. You will sit for sketches. It will be the only inspiration he requires."

"You flatter me. I am an old woman and not such a one as will make a model for any figure."

"Don't say that. You are beautiful."

Eugenie looked away before the intense expression in his eyes. *Mother of heaven,* she thought, *have I played the coquette? All unwittingly have I invited this and spoiled my stay with an amiable acquaintance?*

"I have shocked you?"

"No, indeed. You are very kind."

"I am not kind. I speak of what I see."

"Then perhaps you are not seeing too clearly. It is the light . . . the rose of evening is kind."

"I am not looking only at your face. I see the tilt of your head. The lift of your eyebrows. The fragile wrists. . . ."

"Sir! I beg you! For pity's sake, say no more. These are not proper sentiments between us, and I mustn't hear you." Eugenie gathered up her work in haste, dropping skeins from her workbasket, and then a packet of needles, suddenly clumsy as she never was since a girl.

166

Matteo bent to pick up her workpieces, and she stood, frozen while he placed them in her hands and folded her fingers over them with his own. "We have not spoken before," he said. "But our eyes exchanged understanding—did they not?"

"It may be that I have not understood you," Eugenie protested faintly.

"Oh, yes, you have." Matteo, still detaining her, gazed intently into her eyes. "You understood me perfectly, Donna Eugenie."

Then he released her, and Eugenie sped from the room, the assurance of her maturity deserting her. The bed she slept in was cool and wide that night. Her own skin silkier to her own touch and her hair longer by a yard when she brushed it. Would any man ever have found her desirable without her fortune? Common sense told her it was possible. *But I wanted Athel and I thought that he wanted me.* She had never looked farther than Athel. That was a poor answer now that Athel was dead. *He never loved me.* The truth of that startled her up out of a nest of ruched silk and lace. *I am nearly forty years old, and I never was loved.* Oh, why did she turn so feverishly in the dark? Italy. *I am far from home. I must not be ill in Italy.* Why not? What difference did it make?

In the morning it was apparent that she was very sick indeed.

There was some fever in Tuscany that season. A dry, hard, racking fever that caused the victims to shiver and burn in a debilitating cycle for several days. Eugenie succumbed to the infection. She lay ill for five or six days, and then: "She needs fresh air, the wind off the sea to recover her." Matteo nodded to his wife. "There is no doubt that a visit to Elba would be beneficial."

Seraphina agreed.

"My husband has a villa on the isle of Elba. It is nothing elaborate, you understand. A small house above Porto Azzurro. We have taken Lucia there on several occasions, and the air has always revived her. If the accom-

167

modation was larger, we might come with you but in the circumstances perhaps. . . ." Seraphina frowned uncertainly. "Of course it might be possible to rent another house on the island. . . ."

"Indeed, no! You must not think of putting yourself to such trouble. I am perfectly sure you had no intention to remove to Elba until I fell ill. However"—Eugenie chose her words carefully, not wishing to offend Seraphina or belittle her solicitious care—"I believe I should feel better for a sea breeze, and I should very much like to see the island of Elba. Your husband tells me that it is extremely beautiful and also that fine stone is quarried and carved there."

"Say no more! If you like the idea, everything shall be arranged." Seraphina was delighted to please her. "My husband will hire a boat for you and you may go from Piombino to Portoferraio in a few hours. I will send a servant at once to give warning to the housekeeper. The necessary preparations can be made in two or three days."

Eugenie was still weak from the fever. When she set her feet on the floor for the first time, the contact was unreliable and she swayed weakly.

"There, now," Hannah said indignantly, "a fine case you are in to be jaunting off to some wild, raggedy island."

But Eugenie's fever had frightened her, and the heat in Tuscany was intense. Perhaps a sight of the sea would do them both good. Hannah performed her part readily enough in the preparations for the journey.

Eugenie would leave the coaches and the horses, but her servants would go with her—all except the young lad from the Clere Athel stables, who would stay behind to groom. He was learning a pertinent phrase or two in Italian and had a laughing, black-haired peasant farmer's daughter tucked in the crook of his arm most times that you looked for him.

168

"I think you will find plenty to interest you on Elba," Matteo said when he saw Eugenie onto the boat. "I am always happy there. When the church tower is nearly completed, I will come to escort you home."

"Home," Eugenie had repeated the word. "Yes, I must soon go home to Clere Athel."

"You will not think of going while the winter lasts. When I said home, I meant that you should return here. No one goes back to England in the winter."

The island of Elba, it seemed to Eugenie, was scented through to its core with thyme and rosemary. When she stood on the balcony of the Palaccos' small house and drew in a breath of herbs and salt and evergreen trees and the scent of the wild flowers that grew down its rugged slopes to the edge of the sea, she knew that she would never forget it.

There are some places in life's experience which transfix themselves in recollection. Ever after a single note out of the whole chord carries one back. So it was for her. Let the cook use rosemary with a side of lamb on the spit. Let the breath of some English garden flower carry only a tone of bougainvillea or a hint of the laurel, and Eugenie would close her eyes and know again the warm happiness she felt on Elba.

The house, as Seraphina had said, was not designed for formal living, and Eugenie, eating prodigiously and sleeping well at nights with her window open to the sound of the sea, filled out the hollows under her cheekbones, left her hair unpowdered and went about in comfortable *déshabille* and a wide straw hat.

There was no stabling at the villa, but Matteo di Palacco had arranged the hire of a carriage for Eugenie and after the first week she made good use of it to explore the island.

"I believe I will begin a journal," she told Hannah. But she did not keep it. It was not in her nature to set her

169

most intimate reflections and moods down on paper, and the first few entries were turned instead into a long letter to Giles.

"Elba is not large," she wrote. "One may drive across it in a few hours or (if one has a mind to have one's internal organs jolted up and rearranged) around it in a single day. . . . I have the introduction to a number of dignitaries here, and they are extreme helpful and courteous in their manner, giving me plentiful advice of what to see and where to take my drives. You would be impressed by the immense fortifications, which Cosimo de' Medici built above the bay at Portoferraio. Forte Falconi stands on a rock well over two hundred and fifty feet in height, and the Forte Stella is near as high. No doubt but the Medici knew how to hold their acquisitions. I must see if I can find you a book about this remarkable, self-nominated Grand Duke of Tuscany. I am sure that he would interest you, and I have, in the meantime, made a sketch of the Cellini bust of him at Forte Stella. It depicts a mighty implaccable face. . . ." Eugenie paused. Would Giles recognize the amateurish likeness in the face she had drawn? The truth was that Cosimo had something of disapproval in his expression when he looked at her, and it put her strongly in mind of Athel. Perhaps it would be better to strike out the reference to the drawing. Giles was so quick. She stared across the small lawn splashed red with oleanders. But why should Giles not see what she had seen? Where was the harm?

"Yesterday we went to Porto Azzurro to see the men who had been tunny fishing haul in their catch. We were advised not to watch too close since it is a bloody, sickening slaughter. The tunny are vast—the size of well-grown children—and so trusting and simpleminded that they are no match for the web of nets spread to trap them on their habitual course. I must confess to being on the side of the tunny when I saw how easy they were to take. But Hannah tells me this is wrongheaded and that I should think of the needs of the fisherfolk and their families!"

170

She hesitated again, drawing the quill through her hands. There was room for one last paragraph. Should she tell him of the journey she had made to the sanctuary of the Madonna del Monte? No, better not, for any account must take in the remarkable climb on hands and knees to reach it, and Giles was always resentful of pursuits which his disability made impossible. Instead, she sent affectionate thoughts to her sons and daughter-in-law, her duty to Giles and the assurance of her concern in the harvest to all the people of Clere Athel.

Three weeks later Matteo came.

"The church tower?"

"It is finished. I told Seraphina that I felt we were inhospitable to leave you so long alone here. For propriety's sake I will lodge with the Delspozzo family, but at least I may escort you while you see what our island has to offer."

"You do me too much kindness."

"No matter. I had some work I wanted to put in hand on a new road to reach our villa."

"Building again!" She smiled at him, gently teasing.

"Yes, building again." His response to the smile was quick and warm; then he frowned. "It will be a good road. I shall have it rise on a better line than the present track. It will be easier if we need to use a litter for Lucia when we next bring her."

"Is Lucia unwell again?" Engenie asked quickly.

"No. But neither is she any better. I would have brought her with me only sometimes there are storms in July and heaviness oppresses her."

In the next few days Eugenie found herself engaged in a whirlwind tour of the island. Matteo would not let her be lazy. "We *must* go to Poggio! The natural springs weep down the hillside to the sea." . . . Or again, "What? You mean you have not walked through the chestnut forests of Monte Capanne? We will take our luncheon there. . . ."

They stood on the rocks at Cavo. "Sometimes pirates come," Matteo said. "Will you be afraid?"

"No pirate would ever carry *me* off." Eugenie laughed. "I would be tough meat. Tough old English meat. Poor fare for a Mediterranean robber. Besides, I would barter with my jewel case."

"You deceive yourself. The pirates would take you and the jewels. The rogues in these parts are connoisseurs."

"Thank you." Eugenie dropped him a mocking curtsy. "But I am not decieved. At least I am not self-deceived, which is better."

"You must," Matteo said, suddenly intent, "have been very little loved."

She turned away. "When do we go to see the mines at Rio Marina?"

"Tomorrow, if you like."

When Eugenie saw the quality of the stone that was worked, she could almost forgive the clefts and the untidy outcrops of the quarries.

"The Romans came for iron ore, and the Greeks. And the Etruscans. All down the ages Elba has been ravaged for her mineral wealth. . . . Here"—Matteo held out a piece of rock to her, a curious vibrant metallic green—"take a little plunder. You might buy a piece of onyx marble and have it worked in Florence. You will be filled with wonder when it is polished."

"How will I convey such heavy stone home?"

"Leave the arrangements to me."

Eugenie looked at the heaps of colored rock and ore, dazzling in the sun. "Buy for me, then, I leave it to you. Choose the workmen yourself and commission only the best."

"You will have a fancy for small, pretty things too," Matteo said. "There is good garnet, beryl and tourmaline. I will take you to visit one of the most skilled men in the fashioning of these semiprecious stones. He knows the legends of them and their magic properties. I promise you some fine tales."

Eugenie regarded him with a sudden gravity. "Yes, I have need of a little magic."

He was staring back at her. The myriad particles of shimmering splendor heaped behind her on the hills about the mine were an effective foil to her pale skin and hair. "Eugenie," he said with a sudden intensity, "Donna Eugenie."

It seemed she was looking at him more closely than ever before, observing as though for the first time his perfect features and the expressive eyes under strongly marked brows. He was of a slight, almost insignificant build after the Athelson men. What was it about him that made him memorable, poignant . . . every adjective that must put a woman in mind of him?

Eugenie walked over to a wooden prop, which stood at the entrance of one of the quarry corridors, and leaned against it for an instant. *I am a fool*, she told herself. *In the rather dim mirror of my southwest facing room the light is kind. But I am old.* She clung to the prop. *My life is more than half over. So is his. What purpose is there in our meeting now?*

The pause gave her strength and restored her complacency.

"Come. We have kept Hannah waiting a long time in the carriage." She indicated the road above with a tilt of her head and began to walk in that direction, lifting her lilac silk skirts from the dust.

"Eugenie! Stop! Don't run away!"

"We shall dine by the light of many candles tonight." She added with deliberation, "*Many* candles. Do not be fooled, dear friend. See me as I am."

But after that they had a tendency to walk hand in hand. A ridiculous inclination to look a long time and smile at nothing.

"Eugenie." He would keep saying her name. "Eugenie!"

There was no other word between them that the servants might not have heard.

Why am I always happy with him? Eugenie wondered over his ability to make her laugh at trivial things. *Why is there excitement when he is near and boredom when he is not present?*

173

And why, when she closed her eyes to sleep, could she see the curve of his lips and the soft line of his graying black hair where it gathered about the temples? Such soft, vulnerable places, with the pulse beneath the skin. It was a form of enchantment. Something to run from and deny.

And then finally, in the soft, shaded looking glass, that was overkind, in the fifth week of her stay in Elba, Eugenie admitted she was in love.

X

NOW Eugenie's feet touched the ground lightly when she went to meet Matteo on the terrace. Hannah remarked on her gaiety. Everything amused her. It was as though the veil of boredom she had been wearing for most of her life were suddenly snatched away and she were young and eager in the heart as a girl. But it could not last.

There is Seraphina, she told herself. *Matteo is not free, and I am several times a fool.*

Nevertheless, she would have these days. They attended parties given by local residents. The vines were harvested, and there was dancing. Long hours of talk and Matteo was always entertaining. Perhaps not so sharply witty as Giles, but with a gentle humor, which suited her mood. She laughed softly in the warm, caressing night when they stood above Porto Azzurro, with the soft gleam of lamps in the harbor below, reflected in the midnight sea.

"Eugenie, don't go back to England. From what you have told me there is no life for you there that you cannot abandon."

"And if I stayed here, what should I be to you?"

That was a hard, an impossible question to answer, and Matteo was silent. She could be his mistress. . . . *But I am too old to be any man's courtesan.* Her sensitivity rebelled against the idea.

At a loss for words he had simply enfolded her in his arms, and she knew for the first time in her life the sweetness of welcoming the experience of love for its own sake, not seeking to take anything, as in youth.

"Stay on any terms you like—only stay!"

"You know I cannot."

"I swear there would be no other woman except you."

"There is Seraphina," Eugenie voiced her thoughts. "I like Seraphina. Could I live on some estate close by and have you visit me, and meet her from time and time, and smile and lie? And you . . . would you like to confess to Father Jessolino that I am your *amante*?"

His lips and his caresses pleaded with her.

"I was married to Seraphina when I was very young. She is a good woman, mother to my children. But a man has his dreams, and I believe that all my life I have been dreaming of such a woman as you. Do we not have the right—"

"No." Better to resist now than to be swept away on this tide of tender yearning. She tried to keep her voice reasoning, unemotional. "We should regret it, you know, and in a little while there would be reproaches between us."

"How can you think of that? . . . Perhaps it is true when they say the English are cold."

She understood that she had hurt him, and his almost boyish protests made her twice as vulnerable.

175

"Please . . . let us have this little while. It is not easy for me to deny you anything but—oh, Matteo, I have such a need of one love in my life that is not shadowed by defeat." She was thinking of Athel. *Not lost*, she thought wryly, *but simply never won*.

"You know, I believe I have never learned the craft of love."

Matteo released her, scowling. The assumed lightness of her tone affronted him. "The *craft* of love? I do not understand what you mean. Is love a craft?"

"I think it must be. There are some lines by Chaucer: 'The life so short, the craft so long to learn.' Yes, I think he is right. One should start to learn very young." She smiled at him faintly. "I have left it too late, and I should make an indifferent lover now."

But an odd thing was happening. The moonlight, the lanterns on the terrace were beginning to blur and dissolve behind Matteo's head while she looked at him. Suddenly, without even the rising of a sob to warn her, uncontrollable tears gathered and overflowed.

"Ah, you are crying! The wonder of it!" She could not see him clearly, but she could hear the gladness and triumph in his voice. "One moment you stand there with the face of a statue and then behold the miracle—the statue weeps!" He snatched hold of both her hands, denying her the right to conceal her tears from him. "No. Let me look at you. I love you, I want you, Eugenie. You try to deny me, but you cannot hide these tears from me. They are mine."

"Please let me go." She turned her head away. "The servants will see us."

"Then we will go where they cannot see." Matteo scooped her up in his arms and carried her down into the smothering fragrance of the garden. There, in just a little while, her tears ceased.

It was nearly one o'clock in the morning when Eugenie went up to her room and Hannah was waiting, wide-awake and disapproving.

"Have you been in the gardens with Palacco until this hour? I was about to send a man out with a light to search for you."

"You would have done nothing of the kind. You would not have been so indiscreet." Eugenie yawned. "But I am tired now. You may brush out my hair."

"Looks as if it has been brushed out already," Hannah snorted.

Eugenie's eyes met hers with a look of lazy amusement in the mirror. "What a good thing you have been with me so many years, Hannah; otherwise I might be forced to dismiss you." Hannah snorted again. "I am very much afraid you are a Puritan at heart."

"I know what's right," Hannah said stoutly. "And better still, I know what's wise."

"But you should not presume to know what is wise for someone else. I have earned a little summer madness."

"It'll get out of hand," Hannah warned.

"Well, when it does, I am sure you will be the first to tell me."

Eugenie felt strangely confident. The truth was that there was just so much of her engaged with Matteo and no more. Not all. She had made her protests. There had been the struggle with her own reason and her inclinations. a short tempest of tears. Now she was in control again.

When I am a very old woman I shall look back and say I was enchanted at the time, she told herself. *Everyone should be enchanted just once in her life.*

Matteo had to go back and visit his family.

"At the same time I will take the stone and commission the piece I have in mind to make a portrait of you. You shall have it in the front of the villa I will buy for you."

Eugenie knew that ultimately it must be shipped to England, but she did not say so. *It will stand in front of the dower house—another memory for my old age*, she thought.

"Seraphina must be wondering what you are doing to stay so long here on Elba with me."

"No. The work on the road goes forward. She will accept that I am supervising that. She is very happy, left to her own domestic concerns."

Eugenie wondered at him. Were all men so dismissive of their wives when their own desires were in question? Had Athel said the same thing of *her* when he spoke to Sally Bowden?

But she waved Matteo off from the quayside with reluctance. When he returned, she must tell him of her decision to return to England. The time to reawaken from the dream was very close at hand.

While Matteo was away, she resolved to visit the old man they called Madrileno, the storyteller. Madrileno was the guardian of legends concerning the magic properties of semiprecious stones and rocks, but more than that he was a fine worker of pretty statuettes and trinkets.

She had seen some of his carving up at the villa. It was delicate and unusual and would make pretty gifts to take home to her family.

Giacomo Madrileno was a small, shriveled man. There were such scars of existence down his cheeks that one could no longer trace expression. He sat on a flat rock outside the front door of his house—nothing more than a rough shelter built against the face of the quarry—and worked cameos and small boxes, which were bought by a dealer from Florence and sold for four times what they earned the old craftsman.

Such merchandise as he had was arranged on a length of tattered black velvet. He had been warned of Eugenie's coming and did his best to please her.

"Exquisite." She handled the pieces with reverence. He told her that malachite bestowed the power to read the thoughts of others; that if one drank from a cup set with amethyst, one could never become intoxicated; that beryl had the strongest magic to grant a wish.

She chose a selection of the gifts she thought might charm or amuse her sons and her daughter-in-law.

"And what is this little box?"

The trifle she had picked up was onyx, the lid a smooth oval of brown, merging to black at its heart. Irregular milky stripes at the edge of the stone had been echoed in the shape of the gold rim, and the whole dainty creation stood on four thin, bowed legs of solid gold.

"Onyx," Giacomo said firmly, "has the strongest power of all. There is a story told of this very island which concerns the onyx."

"I should like to hear it." Eugenie smiled up at him warmly. "I think this is a charming toy, and I will buy it, if I may."

"To give?" Giacomo considered her, with his head on one side. "If so, you must be careful where you give it. . . . I will tell you the story and then you shall decide. . . . There is a legend goes back many centuries in these islands, off the shore of Tuscany. Once they were governed by a witch, who bought her immortality a year at a time for every sailor she drowned. She would climb on the rocks and sing a strange song, born of the wail of the wind, and sailors would hear it and row in close and be dashed to pieces. It happened, one day, that she had taken a rich prize, a royal galley with a prince aboard. She slew the sailors, but on some whim rescued the handsome boy, who was their lord, and caused him to be her slave.

"Tales spread of the witch song. The sailors were growing more cautious and stopping up their ears when they neared these parts. So she happened on the idea that she might force the young prince to stand upon a high ledge of rock, wave the shirt off his back and look like any innocent sailor marooned. Then the ship would try to rescue him, and she would whip up a terrible storm by her magic and bring the sailors to their death as she had done before.

"Now the prince, whose name was Talvo, worked for her for some years. He loathed his task, but he was under her spell and could do nothing but obey. Sometimes the witch left the island, flying on the tail of the sirocco to

179

make mischief elsewhere, and then he would study in her books of magic law . . . Thus it was that he learned the power of a gift of onyx." Giacomo paused, nodding toward the sea and then glancing at the little box and looking out to sea again. He seemed to have forgotten Eugenie.

She prompted him gently. "And what was the power?"

"I am just going to tell you that, am I not?" Giacomo said, irritated by the interruption. "The unique power of onyx—if it is openly given and freely accepted—is that it can break an enchantment. Talvo looked along the shore and in the rockfalls, and eventually he found what he was searching for. The problem was how to get the witch to take it from him. She must surely know the lore that was in her own books.

"It happened that soon afterward the witch sighted a quinquereme going by, with many oarsmen, and ordered Talvo to perform his part. But Talvo pretended that he had twisted his ankle, and the witch, beside herself with rage to lose a rich prize, climbed onto a rocky ledge at Capo Cavo and began in desperation to sing her magic song.

"Now witches, as you probably know, weigh next to nothing at all. It is one of the ways by which you may discover them, if you are sharp. Set one in the balance, and it is the surest test than can be devised. The wind caught the cloak of this evil woman, and she was in danger of being blown off the rock, so she called out to Talvo to hand her up some stones from the beach that she might put them in her pockets to hold herself down. 'Will this stone do?' he asked, holding up the piece of onyx. 'Yes, yes! Any stone. Only make haste and give it to me!' "

Giacomo sighed with satisfaction. "He gave her the onyx, and instantly the spell was broken. Talvo, standing below, seized the witch by the ankles and dashed her down the cliff. Her body blew like fine paper on the wind, into the sea, and a great wave curled over her. A

180

witch," Giacomo added by way of explanation, "is best destroyed by drowning. Burning will do, but it does not always kill the strong flame of her spirit."

Eugenie heard the end of the tale in silence, and then she laughed softly. "And so good triumphed over evil."

"Of course. Isn't that your experience of life?"

"Only sometimes in fact, *nonno*. Always in fable."

"Do you still have a use for the onyx?"

"Maybe," she said. "For the time being I will take these other pretty things and leave the little box."

Matteo returned eagerly, as a lover should, and brought her letters. There was one from Dickon, sweet Dickon, whom she loved above all but must discourage from being too close to her because his inheritance would be small. A thousand pounds a year. It couldn't be more. He might make a modest gentlemen farmer, or he might marry a rich wife. Now, as usual, he had overspent his allowance. Dear God! And it was generous enough. Better than Thurstan had when he was at school. There was also a letter from Giles.

"You write of Elba in a thoroughly tedious fashion," he said. "A verbose traveler needs a better eye and better prose. . . . No, I am not interested in the Medici. Their violence and their cruelty throw up the stomach, and they had an unlikable tendency to incest." She almost set the letter aside. But there was a postcript. "You have been too long absent—*Nil mihi rescribas, tu tamen ipse veni!*"

Since she could not translate this, she showed it to Matteo.

"Who is this who writes?"

"It is my brother-in-law."

"He quotes Ovid." Matteo looked at her searchingly. "It means something like 'Write nothing back to me, but come yourself.' "

Eugenie considered the words and experienced a strange sensation like a tightening about the heart. She

181

looked at the letter again. The writing of the postcript was different from the rest of Giles' careful, scholarly lines. The half-formed characters dashed across the foot of the page.

"You are very close to him—this brother-in-law? He writes to you often."

"Giles is"—for some reason she was reluctant to talk about him to Matteo—"in delicate health. I daresay he is lonely. I play chess with him sometimes to amuse him."

"And he entreats you to return."

"Entreats" was a strong word. Was it the right one? Were the sharp-toned letters Giles' way of reproaching her, and did he send this final plea in Latin because he could not bring himself to say what he wanted to say in English.

"You won't go." Matteo sounded decisive. "There is no reason why you should consider yourself obliged to do so."

Eugenie looked at him unhappily. "My dear, I haven't known how to tell you this, but indeed I must go back to England. . . . No, wait. Please listen and don't be angry. It isn't just this letter. I must go home to Clere Athel because that is where I belong. I have always known this, and so have you."

"But I love you! And you—you are not a woman for a casual affair of the heart. Do you think I took you lightly?"

"No." The quiet answer infuriated him.

"Well, perhaps you were amusing yourself with me. The English milady on the grand tour, sampling all that Italy has to offer and taking back a few trophies, including my heart!"

The extravagance of his language served only to strengthen her resolve. She found his attempts to wound her easy to forgive, but at the same time she was thinking, *We two could never belong together. For a little while it has seemed as though we did, but it was only an illusion.* His anger was a gesture. When it had subsided, Matteo would rec-

182

ognize the same truth. She allowed him to go on a while longer and then interrupted.

"Dearest Matteo, you don't believe a word of what you are saying, and neither do I."

All my life, she was thinking, *I shall remember this man's face. On a summer's night I shall remember his soft voice and his gentle hands. On this beautiful island I was wanted, just once, for the woman I am, and not as a property.*

Matteo accepted her decision at last. The few remaining days they spent together were not stormy.

"You are a grandfather," Eugenie reminded him. "I am almost a grandmother. We cannot play out a high tragedy at parting. Not at our age."

She asked him to buy her a keepsake. It was their last day on Elba. On the next they would return to the mainland, and she would stay with Seraphina, before setting out for Leghorn and the experience of a sea voyage home.

"While you were away, I visited Giacomo Madrileno. There was a little box of onyx. I wish you would buy it for me. Don't stop to hear the tale he tells, or you will never return in time for supper. But let it suffice when I say it should make our parting easier." A little self-mockery helped, and she wanted a remembrance.

"Mysterious! Of course I shall ask him the meaning of his onyx. I have never heard of it."

Later he brought her the box. "You were right. I have need of these magic properties."

"So have I."

They smiled, looking into each other's eyes.

"Such a wondrous thing that we should meet," she said.

There had been a great deal to do before she sailed. Matteo saw her safely aboard the ship on which he had arranged passage. There was the worry of seeing that her valuable cargo was safely packed and securely lashed down.

"The statue cannot be completed on time. I will dispatch it to you within a month or so. I have threatened the captain on the soul of his mother that he sees you safely arrived."

"I don't know how I should have contrived without you." She looked around her cabin. The dressing room, where Hannah would sleep, led out of it. "The accommodation is far better than I hoped for."

"I have told the officers that you are a principessa. They will do their best to serve you."

There was little left to say.

"It will be October by the time you get back to England."

"Yes," Eugenie said. "A wistful month in my climate. A good month for regret." She tried not to look at him. "I am glad you can use the horses. I should have been worried about them below decks."

"Your traveling carriage is well braced. There are bales of calico to cushion it, if it rolls."

They offered each other the conventional exchanges, preliminary to a journey, a parting.

"Give my best duties to Seraphina. She has been so kind. Tell her I will write when my grandchild is born."

"That will please her."

The captain presented himself with a flourish, seeking to impress everyone favorably and insisted on escorting Matteo ashore, as a matter of courtesy. Eugenie extended her hand, and Matteo bowed over it, very correct, very formal.

There was a driving rain coming in off the sea, so he would not let her go up on deck to see him leave the ship. The idyll was over.

Eugenie's decision to return to England, once made, had been speedily carried through. The journey, whether overland or by sea, was best undertaken before autumn closed in, and she was pleased that she had found the courage to round off her travels with a sea voyage. She wondered whether the letters she had sent to

184

announce her return would fail to reach Clere Athel before she did. They had been dispatched through the messenger service of a Sienese banker, but delays were always possible.

She would stay at Carle House for a few days while she arranged customs clearance. It would be no easy matter to find carriers for the furniture and pictures she had bought. Would three wagons suffice? Better leave several family servants to escort them over the rough roads to Lancashire. One-half of her thoughts were already sped ahead of her; the other half looked back over the ship's wake to Italy and Matteo.

There was a timelessness, despite the ship's bells, an enforced idleness about life for a passenger at sea. She had needed this uneventful period of transition. The weather was calm—remarkably so, the captain said. It seemed fitting. *I am gliding on into the quiet waters of my life, and there is just a trace of disturbance, a slight froth of agitation left behind.*

XI

EUGENIE had not expected that there would be much of a stir over her homecoming, and she was both surprised and touched to find a sizable crowd gathered at the gates of the park to raise a cheer for her as she came by.

"Tell Matthew to stop the horses and let the steps down."

"You'll surely not get out." Hannah was astonished. "It's bitter cold and raining, too."

"Well, if folk have waited to see me in such weather, the least I can do is give them a greeting."

The people of Clere Athel made no great show of their feelings upon any occasion, but there was a surge of enthusiasm when they saw what Matthew was about. One of the tenant farmers stepped forward and made a gallant bow and handed her out of the coach. There was an audible sigh of satisfaction at the way that was done.

But once she stood among them they were tongue-tied. To smooth over the small awkwardness of the silence, she held out her hand to Mistress Warrener, who was to the fore of the crowd.

"I am happy to see you, madam, I hope your family is in good health?"

"Aye, thank you, my lady. And may I say we're reet glad to give you welcome? Back safe and sound from foreign parts, that's a mercy that is!"

This speech had put quite a different heart into her neighbors. What Mistress Warrener could do they could equal. They pressed forward, each one with a few words of greeting and fine, strong, workaday hands, calloused and etched by the earth, or washday raw, and children's, sticky with the juice of apples given to keep them quiet. Eugenie took every one that was offered, thanked them, and smiled, and asked after the root crops and the fruiting.

Back in the coach Hannah said, "Well, bless me! I never knew you do a thing like that before. Why, you're soaked to the skin standing in that drizzle and your dress all muddied."

"It was an impulse." Eugenie shrugged. "They seemed pleased that I got out. I thought they were quite pleased to see me, didn't you?" She sounded as though she thought that remarkable.

"Of course they were," Hannah snapped. "Folks round here take a pride in you, I've always told you so.

186

Like to see you wrapped up in your sables, traveling in a fine coach. They feel"—she searched for words to explain—"well, you might say they feel they own you."

Athel and Kitty were waiting in the porch to greet her. "So, Mother, here you are. You look to be in good health. Tom Jarrod ran up from the gatehouse. He said you got out of the coach to speak to our people. That was well thought of." He kissed her lightly on the brow. "Good of them to turn out for you. Weren't asked, you know. Did it of their own accord."

"I'm glad," Eugenie said. She turned to her daughter-in-law. "Kitty, my dear, how you glow! It becomes you to be *enceinte*."

There was the bustle of arrival, Heskettson taking her wet furs and clucking disapproval over them. The servants, lined up with a strict regard for hierarchical tradition, waiting to pay their respects.

"But where is your Uncle Giles?" she asked Athel at last. "Is he ill?"

"Oh, no, not in the least. You know what he's like. He's been stumping around in the deuce of a mood all morning. Then he goes and shuts himself in his study and says you're to go to him there. I can't understand him. Should have thought he'd be glad to welcome you back."

Kitty said quietly, "He has missed you dreadfully."

Athel looked doubtful. "He never said anything to me about it."

Eugenie found Giles sitting in near darkness in his study. There was a single candle on the table beside him and the fire was low.

"So you've condescended to come home at last, have you?"

His tone was disagreeable.

"Why are you sulking in the dark?" she challenged in return. "Do you want me to think you have been neglected while I was away?"

She lit the large candelabra on the desk and put split logs and kindling on the fire.

"Leave that! One of the servants can do it."

"Why didn't you ring for them, then? It's cheerless in here when you let the fire die."

"You weren't asked to come in here."

"Yes, I was. Athel said you wanted to see me."

"I can't think why!"

"Well, perhaps if I just sit quietly here for a while, you will remember," Eugenie said kindly.

He directed an almost malign concentration on her face.

"Why did you bother to come back? Nothing you like about Clere Athel, as you have often remarked."

"I have never said that. Not even," she added sweetly, "when I have thought it."

She must acknowledge to herself that she had actually missed crossing swords with Giles. There could be no sensible explanation, yet his verbal attacks stimulated her to a keener feminine response than the flattery of other men could ever achieve.

Kitty's son was born on November the 15. Two weeks before, Eugenie had completed her removal into the dower house and left the silk-hung bedroom, in which she had borne her own children, to her daughter-in-law.

"Oh, Madame. . . . Mother—it is a beautiful room!"

"It is close to the nursery. And your maid and the wet nurse may reasonably share the dressing room. Plenty of space for two pallets."

"But Athel will not allow me to stay here after the child is born." Kitty bit her lip, regretfully. "I asked him once if we should ever use this as our bedchamber, and he said he couldn't abide a boudoir and that he preferred his father's room."

Eugenie laughed. "So like him. But I don't mean to interfere, my dear. Such matters will be for you to resolve between yourselves."

She touched her daughter-in-law's hair, fleetingly, smoothing back a strand of it which had escaped the curl tongs. She liked Kitty. The girl had a quiet, modest manner, but she was far from spiritless. "You will persuade him to whatever you want when you have a son."

The dower house was taking shape. The furniture and the china and ormulu pieces were in place. The curtains hung, the tapestries stretched, the carpets trodden. There remained the garden to be civilized.

No shortage of labor for the digging over and the autumn planting of shrubs. Half of Clere Athel, it seemed, would be glad of extra coin in the pocket, and the Lady Eugenie paid handsomely.

She had appointed Ralph Jarrod, from the gatehouse, to be her head gardener. Athel did not mislike the idea. He would still have Ralph's services to mind the entrance to his park, and that for nothing.

Mounds of earth were moved and raised beds swept along grass-set walks. Trees were planted, and a fountain of pink marble, bought in Florence, was set up, tested and failed to work.

"Happen we'll get it right in t'spring," Ralph said. Eugenie showed him the fountain bell and explained the principle of it. Ralph sucked his teeth, dug the toe of his boot into the soft earth and said he didn't know about *that*. Foreign things might not be expected to work in England.

"I don't see why not . . . if you have the skill to work the fountain. Perhaps Noah Tyte from the smithy could help."

"Noah Tyte? I'll not have that know-it-all sticking his oar in here," Ralph said indignantly. "Yon's my garden and what works in it will work on account o' me. Or not at all!"

You could not push a north-countryman. Eugenie had learned that long ago at Blowick. She merely gave Ralph a level look and said that she trusted him to know what he was about.

The gray dog, Fionn, followed her out onto the newly built terrace and stood leaning against her knee. Fionn was said never to have left Giles' side while she was away in Italy. But now that she had returned, he took up his quarters in the dower house with her, just as though his duties were apparent to him.

"You'll not let that beast wander the garden? He'll step on the young plants," Ralph warned.

"He will keep to the walks." Eugenie stroked one of the dog's ears, idly. "He is extremely well conducted in his habits."

"Well, it don't seem right to have a brute like that in a dainty house like this."

"Oh, come now, Ralph! I must have some company."

"Here comes more company, if you've a mind for it!"

Like everyone else in Clere Athel, Ralph was wary of Giles and his moods. Yet as brother of the late master he carried an authority among them which they would never have disowned.

"Looking over your property?"

"Yes. I think it will do very well when the garden is set out."

"What are these plants couched into the wall here? Nothing will take in such an unpromising place."

"That plant can survive anywhere." Eugenie smiled. "I brought it from Tuscany. They call it *speranza*—hope. It is a pretty white flower, growing virtually wild and never giving up."

The look of interest faded from his face, and Giles said flatly, "Then it is just as I have always suspected. Hope is no better than a weed and should be rooted out."

"I've just set it in," Ralph said indignantly. "I aren't going to take it out!"

"No, of course not," Eugenie reassured him. "Master Giles does not mean that you should."

"Sounds as though he do." Ralph continued to eye Giles with suspicion. "What I always say is a man canna tak' orders from two different bodies," and he went off grumbling about his work.

"Come into the salon and see if you approve my ar-

190

rangement of the furniture. There are one or two pieces of interest, and I think the pictures look well." Giles followed her back into the house.

She moved a deep-padded seat closer to the fire for him. "See! I have thought of you. This shall be your own particular place whenever you come to share my fireside. Over here there is a new chess set. I bought it in Venice. The carving is exceptional, I think."

Eugenie watched Giles covertly, seeing that one of his moods threatened and trying to divert him. So often he would invoke depression with just such a trifling remark as he had made about the rock plants. Now he relaxed in the smallest degree.

"Can I offer you a glass of madeira?"

"Brandy."

"But you hardly ever drink brandy."

"I hardly ever permit myself to be humped across the park in a sedan to see a wayward woman who hasn't the grace to come to me!"

"Oh, dear. Didn't Harry and Tom carry you comfortably? Never mind. They will soon learn the knack of it."

The sedan chair had been Eugenie's idea—her present to Giles on return from her travels.

"No one in Clere Athel goes about in a chair."

"But you will want to visit me often and you can't have a pony put in the shafts *every* time you come down the drive. Besides, I have no stables here. Where would the beast stand when you sup with me?"

"Who said I was going to have supper with you?"

Eugenie merely smiled. "A chair is the answer. You must get used to it."

Giles considered her for a moment, and then his eyes narrowed, pleasureably. "Well, I have a message for you—an idea you must also get used to. . . . Athel will have his fealty oath from you at the witan in two days' time."

"Hah! So he will not relent over this stupid matter?"

"No. He is firm."

Eugenie's thoughts ran quickly. Two days. She had been optimistic to hope that Athel, knowing her feelings on the subject, would let well alone. "I'll be damned if I'll kneel to my own son," she said.

Giles continued to watch her with a slight, triumphant smile. "There'll be bad blood between you if you don't. You know what a stickler the boy is for tradition. He won't have it flouted. And he'll have Thurstan to back him up, remember."

Thurstan! Of course! He was now a qualified man of law, and she had recently appointed him to represent her in matters of legal business. Thurstan was due to arrive the next day. Time enough to brief him.

But she merely said, "I shall have to think on what Athel has said."

When her second son arrived at Clere Athel the next evening, it was his natural duty to wait upon his mother. He had been looking forward to the occasion with a reasonable degree of confidence. Since taking over her interests, he had worked diligently to show that her patronage was not misplaced and there were already a number of items for approval. The interview did not go as he had expected, however.

"Yes, yes, Thurstan. . . . I am sure that is very well done." She dismissed the documents he would have set before her. "You are a good, conscientious boy, and I am sure that anything you recommend will be for the best. But I want to speak to you of some urgent business *here*. It will be necessary for you to represent me tomorrow at the witan."

"At the witan?" Thurstan's mouth dropped open in astonishment. "You mean—represent you legally?"

"Certainly. I understand that it is permitted for anyone who has business at the witan to be represented."

"Why, yes. But whatever can you want me to do?"

She told him, and when she had finished, telling him, he was both less confident and less happy than he had been on his arrival in Clere Athel.

"Folks will say they never saw the like of it!" In his confusion he dropped the slightly pompous language, reminiscent of his Uncle Humphrey and took on homelier, Lancashire words.

"Nevertheless," his mother said relentlessly, "this is the way it must be done. Indeed this is the only way I will do it."

Servants listen beyond brocade screens and paneled kitchen doors. They listen behind stone pillars and the other side of yew hedges on the lawn. The whole of Clere Athel knew that Eugenie would be called upon to take her oath for her land at the witan.

Just the fact of her attendance there had given the meeting an added excitement. Women did not customarily attend the witan, save in the rare instances of a widow woman holding a farm tenancy until sons came of age. The last time Eugenie had graced such an occasion with her presence had been when Athel was sixteen and took his place beside his father for the first time. There hadn't been a new tenancy granted in a long while, and the ceremony was a small spectacle, which broke the monotony of routine . . . rent fixing, boundary marking, small disputes and the like.

They said, "This'd be summat to see." The Lady Eugenie would be dressed "reet grand," and even the possibility that she might wear the coronet of her father's earldom was not derided.

The witan was held in the old hall at the back of the house. Once, back in the eleventh century, it had been the sole accommodation of the lord of the manor and his family. They and those close about them slept, lived and ate in it. The gallery rooms had sometime been pulled out. The hall was left—a great beamed cavern of a place—and the later manor house built on the front of it,

193

so that a short passage and great double doors made it part of the whole building.

But though joined, it stood apart. The atmosphere was heavy. The first time Eugenie entered she felt it full of ghosts. Sullen Saxon eyes under ox-stubborn brows. She had felt them directed at her from every corner.

It was full of wood beetle, of course. "They'll eat the hall away one day, and it will fall down around your ears," she had said to her husband.

He laughed. "Not in my time—nor in yours." She could still recall the way he threw back his fine head on the strong shaft of his neck and looked up at the huge beams of the roof as though he worshiped them. "This is the very heart of Clere Athel," he said simply. "The old place won't rot until the heart stops."

Tenants filled the benches long before the appointed hour of the witan on the day that Eugenie was due to give her pledge. Everyone wanted the best seats at the front, with an uninterrupted view of the high chair where Athel would sit with the long table before him and the great scrolls of the manor laws set out upon it. Giles, the elder of the family, would sit at his right hand. Young Thurstan would be at his left. If Humphrey or Dickon chanced to be visiting, which they were not, they would have sat below in that order.

Haldane and his eldest son, who was his clerk and would succeed him, sat at a smaller table to one side, with the rent book before them. And the priest, lending a becoming touch of godliness without interference, sat just above the benches and just behind the rent table—a nice judgment of his influence on the proceedings.

When everyone was assembled, Athel called the meeting to order with three thuds of his fist upon the table. The tenants gave him their fullest attention. Customary business was dealt with. Grievances laid, rents paid, decisions made.

Athel's fist pounded the table again. "Is there any other matter before us?"

194

As if he didn't know full well the colorful treat they had still to enjoy!

The double doors were opened at the end of the hall. The candlelight from the tall sconces, which stood the height of man in wrought iron, flickered in a sharp draft. Eugenie walked in, her soft slippers making no sound, down the aisle to the high table.

She had dressed no more carefully for this occasion than she did for any evening, but her dress of pale-blue velvet with silver lace and a matching cloak, trimmed with the ermine that was her right, did not disappoint them. Moreover, she was heavy with diamonds.

The villagers gasped at the spectacle of so much wealth.

Very slowly she advanced toward the high chair.

Haldane said stiffly, "The Lady Eugenie, widow of Athel Athelson, has something to say here," and overcome by the effort of this announcement collapsed rather abruptly into his chair.

Eugenie made a deep curtsy to her son.

"Thurstan Athelson, who is my legal representative, will speak for me." It was pronounced in a clear, firm voice.

Thurstan got to his feet. Somewhat husky—"Yes ... er ... well, the Lady Eugenie, who is our mother, has some thoughts upon this occasion which she wishes me to make known to you. . . . She wishes me to say that she both admires and upholds the custom of the fealty oath. She says . . . in her own words . . . that it is a good thing, and that it binds men together in an endeavor of the land which is not to be despised. . . ." Thurstan hesitated, glancing nervously at his elder brother. The set of Athel's mouth and the lowering brows were uncomfortably reminiscent of his father. "The Lady Eugenie"—Thurstan's eyes were now redirected, uneasily toward the slight, glittering figure of his mother —"adds that she appreciates the gesture of her son, Athel, in allowing her the use of some acres of his parkland for the building of a dower house. But she asks me to say that her gratitude may already be measured by the value of the property she has set upon them and will leave behind her."

A flicker of annoyance on Athel's face showed Eugenie that the point had been taken and resented.

Thurstan, his harassment plain for everyone to see, continued with the most difficult part of his statement: "Our mother, whom I have the honor to represent here today, has considered what is expected of her on this occasion. She tells me that she cannot think it seemly for our father's widow to be kneeling to a child of her own body." There was an audible gasp around the hall, the collective amazement of Clere Athel at such a flouting of custom. "However, she considers that tradition may be satisfactorily upheld if she gives the fealty oath to our Uncle Giles!"

Men turned and looked at their neighbors, astonished at this suggestion. Master Giles—well! But he was the senior member of the family, her husband's brother. There was no precedent for such a thing. But then there was no precedent for a widow of the Lady Eugenie's status in such a fix. They asked themselves how they would like to kneel to their own offspring and found the idea little to their liking.

"Aye, aye. . . ." The murmur was faint, respectful to Athel. Nevertheless, the general feeling in the stuffy air of the hall assented.

Athel fought with himself. He was not subtle, and he was still very young, and the fight was visible. Eugenie's eyes met his, calmly waiting for his decision. Thurstan twisted his notes in his hands.

The silence grew intense. "Very well, then." Athel snapped out the words. He had lost face. The only dignity left to him was in consent. "Uncle Giles?"

The focus of concentration changed in an instant, and they saw Giles staring at Eugenie with such intensity that

for a moment they shrank back, afraid rather than glee-
ful at the scene they were witnessing.

"Come here," Giles said coldly.

Eugenie walked unhurriedly to the very edge of the
high table.

"Kneel!"

Even then the Lady Eugenie looked around with inquiry for a stool, and there was the younger Haldane son,
quick to produce one and place it for her. She smiled her
thanks and knelt gracefully, in a sweep of rustling silk
underskirts and a hush of velvet.

Giles leaned across the table, placing his hands, palm
upward, with the little fingers touching, a cup to receive
hers.

Eugenie put her own hands, joined as though for
prayer, within the compass of them.

"What do you say?" Giles asked sternly.

"I owe fealty to the lord of this manor and, with the
land granted unto me, I accept also the duty to honor
him, serve him in peace or war, and to render to him
those dues he shall demand, in season and out of season,
in times of hardship or in plenty."

"So shall we, in return, give you claim."

The ceremony was over. A short ceremony with a long
history.

Eugenie turned and left the hall. She went in search of
Kitty and stayed to drink a dish of tea with her in the
salon.

"I am afraid I have made Athel angry tonight. I hope
he does not use his irritation on you."

She had the chair fetched. Athel stayed behind in the
old hall with Haldane. He was looking over the accounts,
he said, and sent his excuses. A mark of his displeasure
with her, of course, but she was untroubled by it.

Giles was waiting by the front door.

Eugenie hesitated when she saw him.

"I give you good-night, Giles. The men have brought

197

my chair." She would have gone past him without more words, only he detained her, leaning against the door, barring her path.

"Why?" he asked simply. "Why me?"

There was something in his eyes, softened—a plea, even.

"Did you not always know," she answered slowly, "that if you held out your hand to me, I should put mine in it, willingly?"

She slipped past him, and as she was stepping into the chair, she could hear him following her, his crutch a staccato crunch on the gravel.

"You annoyed Athel. That was foolish. A high price to pay for your dignity!" His voice bit harshly through the darkness.

She smiled to herself unseen, considering what answer would annoy him most. "I can afford my dignity.... I can afford almost anything which money, and the power of money, can buy."

Eugenie's life settled down to a pattern. In the new year she found her household established very much to her liking. Hannah acted as housekeeper and filled this new role along with her duties as personal maid. The cook, Mistress Hindley, endeavored to please and was honest with the joints. The girls kept themselves clean.

"I shall require of my maids, who are waiting about my person and my rooms, that they bath at least twice a week and change their linen, their dresses and their caps at least as frequently. Or more often if they have a need," Eugenie wrote in her elaborate script. To guide Hannah, she had made a housekeeping book. There were instructions in it, her favorite recipes. Household accounts were kept at the back. "Cook may have the leavings of joints and game after Tuesdays. . . . All linen should be embroidered as to its purpose, with symbols and the year of purchase, which will help greatly in the sorting. . . . The sun comes into the salon at noon. If the room is not in use, curtains should be drawn to keep it out, or it will spoil the carpets and the pictures. . . . The girandoles, which are hung with pendant jewels, shall not be dusted save by the Lady Eugenie herself. A housemaid will attend her on Mondays, Wednesdays and Fridays when she performs this duty at half past eleven o'clock. Likewise the harpsichord. Tea leaves should be used to clean the carpet in the morning room. The sun comes in here very early and the blinds should always be let down for the sake of the bookbindings. . . . The carvings on mahogany pieces should be kept free from dust by use of a painters' brush. . . ."

It was April—heavy, slanting showers, darkening the earth and breaking it up between the newly set ornamental trees and the slender cuttings of shrubs. Eugenie looked out the windows at her garden and thought it would be a pretty place, a sheltered, colorful, scented place to sit.

"We must raise the walls another six feet," she told Ralph Jarrod. "We must trap in the sun of every summer."

"What do you mean 'raise the walls'? You canna do that just by saying 'Have it done!' There'd be masons and mason's rubble. New plantin' trampled 'neath their boots, the ground hard and miserly, long after."

"Come, Jarrod. One cannot make a garden and get it right the first time. We must adapt ourselves to modifications. . . . Better you should trouble yourself now with the bricklayers than later when shrubs are well established. You might put in nectarines with more shelter," she added, placating him.

"Nectarines is a load of trouble," Ralph said sulkily. "You nurse 'em and cosset 'em, and nowt comes to table."

Eugenie considered him. "What about the fountain bell?"

It was always the ace in her pocket.

Still, Jarrod could not get the fountain bell to work. It maddened him, and although he would not have admitted it for the world, he loved the idea of it, like a child with a toy.

"You really must get Noah Tyte to try his luck. I believe I will speak to him after church this Sunday."

"Doan do no such thing!" Jarrod's indignation gave him the courage to be thoroughly disrespectful. "I'll have yon working yet. And as for t'wall—you can leave that to me."

She left it to him, and it was done.

In May the statue arrived. It came by special carrier and drew a deal of attention, riding through Clere Athel, shrouded in canvas and enclosed within a wooden cage. A letter from Matteo had been delivered a week earlier, and Giles brought it to the dower house.

"Someone gone to a length of trouble. . . . Who writes you from Tuscany?"

"Matteo di Palacco. He commissioned a piece of sculpture for me. It should be here any day now."

When Giles saw the piece, he was a long time circling it, and considering, and saying "Humph!" rather often, in a tone which gave nothing away.

"Do you like it?"

They viewed the work together. There was no doubt—could be no doubt in anyone who knew her —that the subject had a look of Eugenie. She was depicted as a mermaid, sitting with her tail curled about a rock. Her hair was unbound, and her face wore a strange expression, mystical and taunting.

"It's a good piece of sculpture, I think," Eugenie said carefully.

"Who's the artist?" Giles demanded.

"He's little known. They call him Ricotto, the Profeta."

"And this man, Palacco, he had the work executed for you?"

"Yes."

"You have talked a good deal about Palacco."

Eugenie did not answer him. She turned and walked back into the dower house, and Giles followed her.

200

"You will keep this statue where you have put it now, in the center of your carriage sweep?"

"I think it goes well there. Yes, I believe that I shall have it mounted as a centerpiece to the drive."

Eugenie went into the salon, allowing Giles to keep pace with her. He swung himself into his usual chair and set his crutches to one side with a deliberate thump.

"Bring me that little box you have upon the table." He indicated the object with a peremptory gesture.

"This box?" She hesitated. "Why should that suddenly be of interest to you? There is nothing in it, you know."

"Bring it to me." Giles turned the trinket over in his hands. "Hannah said it was a keepsake from this fellow Palacco."

"So it was."

"I see nothing on it—no inscription. What was Palacco to you?"

Eugenie resented his manner. She did not like the directness of the question, but answered steadily: "He was my very good friend. He showed me every kindness and civility." She turned away, dismissing the subject.

"I am sure he did!" The sneer was unmistakable. "It seems plain to me, madam, that you have given him such favors as would be like to make any man *kind*."

The accuracy of the hit astonished her. She had betrayed nothing and it could only be intuition, that discomforting, uncanny intuition, so formidable in a man of Giles' temperament.

She wondered how to answer him, caution at war with outraged pride. Pride won.

"It is of no consequence to me what you suspect," she said coldly. "You are not—I think—the keeper of my morals. I might take twenty lovers for my pleasure without its being the leastwise your concern."

"*Not my concern?*" Giles' fury gave him an unaccustomed strength to raise himself from the chair in one abrupt movement. He stood, swaying slightly, groping for his crutches, and nonetheless awesome in this situa-

201

tion. "Not my concern when my brother's widow, a woman of *your* age and living under my protection, plays the wanton." His voice thundered in her ears, and she longed to shut out the words.

"A woman of *your* age"—that was harsh, unnecessary. No! He should not compel her to feel guilty or foolish or spoil the little happiness she had known with Matteo.

"It was not wantoness," she cried out wildly. "It was love!"

Giles' breathing rasped in the ensuing silence; two patches of color flamed above the tightening muscles of his jaw. "Do you admit then that this man was your lover . . . that he seduced you?" He asked at last.

"It was the moonlight . . . the gardens were very beautiful." Despite her determination, Eugenie's words faltered. She was already regretting the admission, but it could not be recalled.

Giles had recovered his control. He leaned on the back of the chair, staring at her, and then he laughed in a short, unpleasant way.

"A love scene enacted in a moonlit garden must have all the impact of the totally predictable. Why didn't you stay with him? Did you tire of him, or he of you?"

She shook her head wearily. "Neither. The time to end a liaison is before it spoils. . . . Giles, what is the point of this? I left Matteo and came back here because this is my home. There was no harm done and I was always discreet."

"But not chaste."

"Chastity is sometimes in the mind."

"Are you trying to claim that when you lay on your back with your knees in the air, your heart was pure?"

"I did not feel ashamed." She met his eyes steadily.

He straightened up and swung his crutches into position. "I shall not stay for supper this evening."

"No. I think it would be better if you went back to the house. Don't come to see me again until you feel you can forget what has been said between us today." She did not

202

pull the bellrope but saw him to the door herself. "Try not to reproach me. I never reproached your brother, you know." Eugenie's anger had left her, and now she spoke in a flat, calm way which made him look searchingly at her. "And perhaps when you come to think this over, you can make allowances for my conduct. I never had the opportunity before to give my love where it was really wanted."

"Are you sure of that?"

XII

HARVESTTIME brought Dickon home from school with Master Corby. Eugenie had looked forward to the return of this favorite child for weeks but characteristically chose to conceal the fact, and it was Hannah who was continually at the window on the day of his expected arrival, clucking with impatience and exasperation.

At last the coach turned into the park and stopped outside the dower house. The door was flung open, and a tall young man jumped down without waiting for the steps.

"Why, bless my soul! Whoever can this be? It's not...*it can't* be Master Dickon!"

Eugenie joined Hannah at the window, and for a moment she, too, stared in wonder. She had sent away a boy with a tasseled cap and a long buttoned coat. Now he was a man, with lace at his throat and wrists and a traveling cloak slung negligently about his broad shoulders.

"How he has grown!" Hannah exclaimed.

"Aye—grown in conceit of himself, I make no doubt." But Eugenie's eyes were tender. The stamp of his boots was already in the hall, and his impatient voice was seeking her out.

"So, my son," she said when she had embraced him, "I see that your last year at school has wrought some change in you."

"Yes. I look well, do I not?" Dickon fingered deep cuffs with satisfaction and spread out the skirts of his coat—for all the world, Eugenie thought, like a young cockerel pleased with his tail feathers. "You see that I haven't wasted the extra allowance you sent me."

"No," Eugenie answered solemnly. "It is evident that my money has gone to a most worthy cause. I am the benefactress of an excellent tailor."

"There you are, Corby." Dickon glanced over his shoulder at the tutor waiting discreetly behind him. "It is just as I told you. Mother don't mind a bit that I tipped the gig on a few clothes."

"Tipped the gig?" Eugenie inquired faintly. "You mean you spent the whole of the last draft I sent you on your wardrobe?"

"Well"—the boy was momentarily abashed, but then—"boots is deuced expensive, you know, and my feet are forever growing."

"I regret to tell you that he has been exceedingly extravagant," Master Corby intervened. "Dickon knows my opinion of such vanities, but he has chosen to defy my disapproval."

Eugenie gave the tutor her hand in greeting. "Never mind. I am sure you did your best to restrain him. We will forgive a little excess this once. His judgment may not be admirable, but his taste certainly is."

Master Corby must be the only man on earth who could bow without bending, she concluded. What a humorless fellow he was. There was no flicker of response in his face. No doubt he had been a sober and conscientious tutor, and he would certainly look after Dickon if, as she hoped, the boy elected to complete his education by visiting Europe. But he would hardly make an amiable traveling companion.

"Now you must go and pay your respects to your brother." Her eyes lingered over Dickon. What a beautiful young man he had become. People said Athel was the image of his father, but this youngest son was his father with a warmer heart and a gentler nature rounding out every feature.

"Oh, I doubt Athel will be looking for me," was the cheerful response. "He'll want me to be on my way now I'm done with schooling."

"My dear! That is not a proper remark. Your brother has the greatest care for you."

"In a pig's ear, he has!" Dickon laughed, and Eugenie thought how sad. Three brothers. They should have been close. Born of the same stock and they had been reared in more or less the same way. Yet the land was all for Athel. And Athel would hold every acre of it. He would even begrudge the modest provision she might make from her income for Dickon and for Thurstan. Nor could she entirely blame him, for his motives were not entirely self-interested. He had inherited from his father at least *some* of that sense of responsibility to his inheritance that must be forever guarding an almost abstract notion. Property. Land. Something a man could hold for a brief tenure of a generation. Something he worked on and then must leave behind—a gigantic canvas that was never completed.

"I shall join you for supper up at the house. Tomorrow noon you may visit me again and tell me what you plan to do next."

She gave him her hand to kiss before he left. Dear Dickon. The one with the loving arms and the moist, eager lips. Very soon she must part from him again.

Nevertheless, his plans, when she heard them, came as a shock to her.

"Mother, I don't want to waste my time on a trek about France and Italy. I want to go to Barbados."

"Barbados?" He might just as well have said he was bound for the moon. "Whatever possesses you to think of such a thing? You know nothing of life out there, and I am told the voyage is fearful."

"My Cousin Robert told me about it when I was last up at Blowick. It sounds a fine place for a man to make a fortune, and I may stay with my cousins there until I am settled."

"You will not make a fortune out of nothing."

"Ah, but you will give me a stake, won't you, Mother? Then one day I shall come back to you with my hands full of opals and diamonds. I shall pour them into your lap in a shining cascade until your eyes are dazzled."

She tried to talk him out of the notion, but in the end she wrote to her Cousin Edward, who was Robert's elder brother, and to her man of business and arranged the passage.

Dickon was just a boy. A very young boy. He would be gone to a treacherous, fever-ridden climate, and she might never see him again.

"Write to me as often as you can find the time, I shall be anxious, you know."

It was spring when he set out on his journey. He would take ship from Liverpool. "A seven-night and you'll be under sail. I shall lie in my bed and listen to the wind. For God's let me know you are arrived safe. Send me word by the returning ship."

"Don't come out in the drive to see me off," Dickon said. "I would remember you standing in that doorway in your gold dress with the sunlight behind you."

It was too much for her to bear, and as usual she took refuge in some slight, meaningless remark. "Oh, yes indeed. . . . Remember me with the light behind me. Every woman past forty would have it so!"

Thurstan was betrothed in the summer of the follow-ing year, 1743.

"A good match, I think." Athel rubbed his hands with satisfaction. "A cousin by marriage of the Countess of Pomfret and with a comfortable settlement. Thurstan may consider himself fortunate."

Giles nodded.

"Is she pretty?" Eugenie viewed the wine backed by the candlelight.

"I'll wager Thurstan thinks she is. She's got property in Berkshire and more to come in Surrey when her mother dies."

"Then their happiness is assured." Eugenie lifted her glass briefly. "To you—Kitty Hatton." She drained it, set it down and left the table.

"Now, what the devil made my mother go off like that?" Athel asked. But Kitty had followed her mother-in-law out of the room.

The question remained for his uncle.

"Well," Giles said, "women have their moods. Some-times they have their reasons."

The old vicar of Clere Athel died in his ninety-third year. Wortham, who had baptized and married and buried two generations of practically every family on the estate, finally succumbed to the erosion of time and followed souls he had had in keeping.

Athel appointed Corby in his place as had been prom-ised and expected.

"God help us!" said Eugenie, after four successive Sundays of two-hour sermons.

"*He* may not . . . but you could." Giles had a sudden inspiration. "Why don't you give Corby something to keep him busy? Why don't you build a new church? . . . Could give him a house to match, alongside it. Capital idea!"

"A church. That would cost a great deal of money."

"Well, you've got a great deal of money."

"I hadn't considered investing it in the afterlife," Eugenie said tartly.

But that was not true. She *had* thought of rebuilding the church. She had told Matteo of her plans and he liked them. What was it he said: "We make such little tracks in a lifetime. We should build and plant . . . plant and build. How else can we leave behind the message we learned?"

She had built her house, and she had set a garden. Now she would create a church. It should be of modest proportions. Sandstone—that was the material. Morning and evening sun enriched it. The bell tower might be Italianate, the windows like jewels. She would work tapestries for the family pew with her own hands.

She wrote, summoning an architect, the next day.

"But we've got a church," Athel said. "Perfectly good church. Norman. Nothing much wrong with it."

"Nothing much right with it, either," Eugenie pointed out. "It's exceedingly cramped and deuced uncomfortable."

"Moreover, it is in the process of falling down." Giles was prepared for once to ally himself with the project he had instigated.

Athel scowled. It was clear that he was upset by the thought of the cost. "Couldn't you simply repair the existing building?"

"I could," Eugenie agreed. "But I'm not going to. That would not interest me."

"You'll not touch the family vault—that was only just put up and a fine fat sum paid for it, too!"

"It was built in sixteen hundred and four, and since it is considerably more substantial and attractive than the church, I would not dream of disturbing it. Indeed I shall myself be a tenant one day. Pray you, have a care I am not in a draft."

"Well, sir?" Athel glanced across the fireplace at Master Corby. "What do you have to say about my mother's notion?"

Athel had ever a reverence for his old tutor and since

his return tended to consult him on matters far less his province than the one under discussion.

"Ah, yes . . . certainly. That is to say, a new church —one would be grateful. . . . Always provided that there is no undue decoration. . . . Man worshiping in a plain, honest fashion. . . . No painting on the walls, mind you . . ."

Giles leaned across toward Eugenie. "Master Corby likes the gesture, but he will have you restrain yourself in the execution of it." He smiled at her wickedly.

"We will keep it as simple as a barn," she said. "Likewise the residence I shall provide for Master Corby!"

Auguste de Mulignac died, and Eugenie felt sorry that her sea voyage home had made it impossible to pay him a second visit.

"Ma chère fille," Madeleine wrote, "we are the poorer of a very good friend. . . ." In fact they were the richer from a banking point of view. The bulk of his fortune, his chateaux and land, went to a nephew. But he had made personal bequests to Madeleine and Eugenie of some twenty thousand pounds. "You need not feel obliged to accept this inheritance," her mother continued, "but it is my sincere hope that you will do so for the sake of the affection Auguste always had for you since you were a child. I know that your father misliked the relationship. However, in the security of our naturally advancing years, I feel able to tell you that there was nothing improper in it. I believe you and I were the nearest experience to a family relationship that Auguste ever knew. . . ."

The money would do very well for Dickon. A discreet word to her banking house and Athel need never know about it.

Money, money, money. Sometimes she stared into her mirror and tried to imagine what life would have been like if she had been shorn of her property and her wealth.

209

I could never have been a Sally Bowden! she thought, and laughed. For one thing she did not have the physical attributes of a Sally Bowden. She lifted a fragile hand, heavy with jewels, and attempted to smudge out the lines that wrote her age beneath her eyes.

"Why do you powder your hair all the time?" Giles demanded. "Never used to. I remember when you first came to Clere Athel . . . deuced pretty hair, I used to think. Color of the wheat in Godwin's Field."

"You've answered your own question." Eugenie toyed with the long ringlet that lay over one bare shoulder. "Powder conceals the passing of the years. Coloring fades in a woman. Now you do not know whether my hair is gold or gray."

"I know it is still gold. It will always be gold," he answered her almost fiercely.

"There is another reason why I have fallen into the habit of always being *en poudre.*"

Giles lifted an inquiring eyebrow.

"Yes. When I was on my travels and stopping over-night in so many wayside inns, it kept away the lice! My mother gave me some recipe she had from a skilled chemist. I promise you it was most effective."

They shared their laughter.

There were many such evenings, with Giles sitting across the hearth from her. And his wit would spice a good wine.

Other times she had to fight his moods.

There was news from the outside world. Walpole had resigned but, before he left office, gave Humphrey a knighthood.

Giles was disparaging of the honor. Nevertheless, Eugenie realized, he was jealous of it.

"So Jennie will be 'milady' now."

"Yes, she will."

"You, as an earl's daughter, won't make anything of it."

210

"Why not? I am sure Humphrey has worked hard for it."

"*Sir* Humphrey and Lady Jennie, indeed!"

"I thought we were playing chess."

"Go along then. I have you in check."

Eugenie extricated herself. "You have not. And if you don't pay more attention, I shall win."

Giles glared at the board for several minutes and then his face cleared. " 'Full craftier to play she was,/Than Athalus, that made the game.' "

"Chaucer," Eugenie said. "And check to you."

"Damme! Well, I don't mind sacrificing a *knight*."

Eugenie regarded him levelly. "You cannot get Humphrey out of your thoughts tonight, can you? . . . If you were as limbless as a blasted tree, you would still be worth ten of him. And yet you persist in resenting him."

"Ain't it natural?"

"Perhaps. But it isn't worthy of you." She sighed. "Poor Humphrey—I find him almost pathetic with his ridiculous pomposity and his larded body laced into a corset. Oh, come on, Giles. See the ridiculous side of your own behavior, for I vow I will play no more of this game."

His mouth twisted in a rueful smile. "You will call for my chair and send me home in disgrace, I suppose? You are always doing that!"

"Only when you are intolerable company."

Giles scowled. "I imagine an embittered cripple is seldom an amiable companion. Not like your Italian friend, what's-his-name."

Eugenie looked beyond him toward the silhouetted trees in the darkening garden. "No. You are not in the least like Matteo. . . . Now it is your move."

She could understand how he was feeling, but she had a duty to prevent him from making a fool of himself. Humphrey was clearly in favor with the family at the present time. It was he who introduced Thurstan to his future bride and an excellent match for a second son

211

with no prospects save the ten thousand pounds which she was able to promise from her personal income.

"A man with poor relations is a poor man," Humphrey had written to her in his dull way. "It has therefore been my most energetic endeavor to see my nephews well provided. You have established Dickon in an adventurous undertaking. I pray he will prosper. I think I may congratulate myself on having secured such a wife for Thurstan as will provide the desirable background for a successful future. Your allotment to him is generous in the circumstances. . . . He has but to work industriously at his chosen profession, and his connection is more likely to enhance than dull our prestige as a family."

Eugenie read his letter with distaste and then in the act of folding it acknowledged her own lack of perception. Born to great wealth, she never truly assessed the value other people placed upon it. This had been to her disadvantage all her life.

XIII

EUGENIE looked out from the terrace on a sunny morning and admired her garden. Blue, feathery plumes on the bank of shrubs just below sent up a fragrance, a freshness of the dissolving dew. Perhaps the bees raised it, they were so busy about the blossoms. And the fountain, in its shallow basin, played on air over their reliable harmony.

The only discord came from her grandsons. Athel and

Willie were locked in distructive combat in the midst of the miniature parterre.

"That will do!" Eugenie's voice rang out suddenly. "You are acting very rough. Come here at once."

Tumbling bodies disengaged themselves. There was a swollen redness about Athel's right eye, and Willie limped when he walked. They stood below the terrace and looked up at their grandmother with identical challenge in their gray eyes.

"That was not a performance I cared to witness. You spoil the beauty of the morning. What have you to say for yourselves?"

There was a long pause. "I'm sorry, madam." Athel was the first to speak.

"I should think so. And you, Willie, are you not ashamed to be fighting with your brother?"

The boy hung his head and did not answer.

"He hit me first," Athel volunteered.

"You are five years old," Eugenie said. "Your brother is a year younger."

"He still hits hard."

"And you kick." Willie was defiant.

"I am ashamed of both of you. You promised your mother that you would be good. Do you think I shall allow cook to serve chocolate pudding after this behavior?"

"I meant to be good, Grandmother, ma'am. I started off today to be very good, and I thought then that you would play us your musical box."

Eugenie looked at Athel and was inclined to believe him. He had a quiet, gentle nature, which commended itself to her. Willie was different. His rages were a spectacle for the people of Clere Athel, and they had driven his father to beat him on a number of occasions, even though he was still in the nursery.

"Violence either of word or deed is to be despised. A *gentleman* might justify it on the battlefield. Nowhere else, I think."

213

Hannah stood in the doorway behind her. "They're a pair of curmudgeons."

Quick as could be, Willie said, "You hold your tongue. You're a servant!"

Unluckily, he had failed to observe that his father was directly behind Hannah.

"Willie." Athel's voice was so harsh it set Fionn up, barking, from beneath the shade of a tree. "Come and stand before me, this instant."

The child climbed the steps to the terrace slowly, and Eugenie, seeing her son coil his riding whip, pressed her hand to still the sudden thudding of her heart. "No! Athel, no. It was a shocking impertinence, but he is very young."

The boy darted her a sharp look, and Hannah was beside him. "Indeed, sir," she pleaded, "I take no offense from what an infant may say. Your lady mother and I can administer a punishment. We will lock him in the room beside the stable and he shall miss his dinner."

"A well-fed lad is not chastised because he goes without a meal."

"But perhaps it is my fault that he spoke up the way he did," Hannah persisted. "I chided him out of my place."

Eugenie said gratefully, "I do not think that is so. However, Willie can understand your generosity and wish to apologize." She grasped him firmly, urging him forward. The boy licked his lips, and the sight of his father's hands, restless on the whip, made up his mind for him.

"I . . . I am . . . sorry."

"Well, bless you, forget it," Hannah responded.

"Take the boys away, if you please, Hannah. I wish to speak with my mother." Athel's eyes followed his younger son with sullen displeasure, and the boy glanced back at him briefly. Eugenie thought: *There will be trouble between these two all their lives.*

Aloud she said, "How is Kitty?"

"The midwife says the child is dead."

214

Eugenie was shocked, not only by the news, but his delay in telling her.

"She cannot be sure. You mustn't permit Kitty to give up hope. That could be certain death for her, as well as the child. She must fight. . . . Let us go at once. . . . Why are we standing here?" She was already hurrying through the salon.

Athel, responding to her urgency, told her that he had brought the pony cart. "I hoped you might come."

"But of course! Of course!" Eugenie climbed into the trap without any assistance. "Come along." Suppose it should be a daughter. Suppose the child that Kitty was in danger of losing was the only girl child, like the one she herself had craved. She must get to Kitty in time.

She swept into the hall and ran up the stairs. There were maids in tears and two footmen supporting the housekeeper, who had chosen to "go all to pieces" on the first landing.

"Drop that woman this instant. And bring up cook and the girl who scrubs the pans."

Athel was still behind her. "The girl who scrubs the pans?" He echoed in astonishment.

"Yes. She's a strong girl, and she'll likely be clean to the elbows!"

Kitty was writhing in the silk-hung bed where Eugenie herself had lain and lost a child.

"Kitty, give me your hands. Clasp mine strongly. There . . . that tells me two things. You still have your strength, and you do not burn with the fever."

Cook and the girl from the kitchen arrived in a flutter, wiping their fingers on their aprons.

"Cook, you have had two children of your own."

"I have, my lady."

"You will remember then the value of effort. That is why I have sent for you. I want you each to grasp a wrist and the forearm . . . like this. Let her fight against you." Eugenie whipped back the bedclothes. "Now, Kitty, you have to get this child out into the light of day—dead or

215

alive. If it is weak, it can't help you. No matter the pain, thrust it out. Push, Kitty, push hard, and don't spare yourself until I tell you you can rest."

"Lady . . . Mother . . . God help me." The sweat was springing out on Kitty's face and her naked body.

Eugenie tore off the loose wrapper she herself was wearing and worked in her petticoat.

"Where's Mother Dowser?" cook asked without formality. Now there were just women working to save the life of one of their own sex and there was no station between.

"Heaven knows!" Eugenie said. "Kitty was alone when I came." She had not had time to wonder where the midwife was. "I make no doubt she's below with a tankard of barley wine."

"Very like," cook said. And then to Kitty: "Push, woman, push harder. You're not trying."

"I am."

"No, you're not."

Kitty screamed, and for an instant Athel's face appeared around the door. "Is she going? I've got Corby."

"Well, tell him he's not needed. There's no one a-dying here," the skullery maid shouted. It was the first and probably the last time she would ever utter such defiance to the Master of Clere Athel.

They worked on desperately.

"Good," Eugenie said at last. "Now very gently . . . short, strong breaths . . . several of them. . . . Two or three more . . . and again . . . there. Cook, pass the scissors, quickly . . . and the thread. . . . Bring those towels, girl."

Eugenie broke the strange birth parcel, and the baby's crumpled face was revealed to them.

"Turn it over and smack it on the back," cook said.

The baby coughed and began to wail.

"It's a girl, a fine, lusty girl."

"Kitty"—Eugenie leaned over the bed—"you have a daughter."

Kitty closed her eyes thankfully, and tears crept out

from under the lids. "Thank you, madam, Mother. Oh
. . . thank you."

"Well, then." Eugenie straightened up. "Some warm
water to bathe my daughter-in-law and swaddling for the
child."

Athel was waiting in the corridor, and she gave him the
news. "Kitty needs rest and every care."

"The child will live?"

"She seems strong enough."

"You don't say so! And Mother Dowser made sure the
heart stopped beating." He sounded detached, mildly
interested.

Eugenie stared at him, recalling that he had stayed to
chastise one of his sons for impertinence when he was
bringing her the message of Kitty's desperate situation.
Did he not care? One child more or less—was every man
indifferent once he had an heir? She remembered how
her own husband came home to the news of a lost child.
Did he ever feel the merest sting of regret? She would
never know, for he never showed it.

"I shall go back to my house, but I wish you will call me
if there is any change in Kitty's condition. She should be
kept very quiet. Hannah and I will look after the boys for
the next few days . . . with your approval."

"By all means. Thank you. That is kind."

Giles was waiting in the hall. She thought: *Poor Giles.
He is always waiting for news of someone else's birth or death*.

"There is a girl child for the Athelsons at last," she told
him, and perhaps the weariness in her tone was notice-
able.

"I am glad," he said simply. "Always compensations in
life. You will take pleasure in a granddaughter."

She assented to the truth of this and in the ensuing
years would often recall Giles' words and the way he
looked at her when he spoke them.

From that time on her relationship with Kitty
deepened into the real affection that might have existed
between mother and daughter of one blood. Long be-

fore her granddaughter, Elizabeth, was of an age to bring enjoyment with her prattle, Eugenie discovered the pleasure of receiving womanly confidences while she worked at her needlepoint. The barriers that formal manners set between them had been breached. Just occasionally, despite the reserve that was natural to her, she would offer one or two by way of exchange.

The building of the church was completed in some haste so that there might be an Easter dedication in 1745. It was not large, in fact just the size to be filled by two-thirds of the inhabitants of Clere Athel—a generous expectation at any time. There was a reluctance to give up daylight hours to worship. Women and children and old folk might go on a Sunday to matins, but their working menfolk preferred vespers, especially in summer.

The bell tower was generally thought "handsome," but held by Athel to be "a damned fancy affair." For the rest Eugenie had kept the exterior simple, as she promised. There were no finials, no gargoyles, no fussy stonework whatsoever.

Inside, Eugenie permitted herself a little recreation in the choice of paneling and carved pew ends. Perhaps the family pew, with its elaborate canopy, fretted door, and the two prie-dieus set in front of a bench for the lesser members of the family, was a trifle elaborate for a country church. Eugenie herself entertained doubts, although she liked the design. But Athel was pleased.

"Very well done. I like it, very well."

"You do not think it would be better to remove the two prie-dieus and put in a second bench?"

"Not at all. I think it quite proper that the head of our family should sit advanced from the rest of its members." He surprised her still further. "Naturally, you will occupy the place beside me."

"But surely Kitty!"

"Kitty must sit on the bench and control the children."

"Then Giles—Giles is the senior member of the family."

"He is in no way concerned with the direct line of it, and he never has been," Athel said firmly. "No. As my mother, it is fitting you should sit in the place due to you. I will have it so. When you die, then Kitty shall take your seat. But I will write it into the family records that I consider it proper for any dowager of the Athelsons to sit at the front of the pew."

His mouth set in that implacable line she had known since his childhood.

It was not for the sake of *her* dignity but for his own. Eugenie wished that he was still of an age to box his ears. She did not want to take precedence over Kitty, had never even considered such a thing, and yet there she was with a design of which she was clearly the author, apparently setting herself one step closer to heaven.

She took the first opportunity of explaining her feelings to Kitty.

"But, my dear mother, what Athel says is right."

"It does not seem so to me. He is very a tiresome boy."

Kitty laughed. "I should not like to be standing by if he heard you say so!" And then, more seriously: "I sometimes think he never knew his boyhood." It was half a question.

"If you are asking me was he always overcareful of his dignity, the answer is yes. Of course, his father took him out of my charge when he was very young, and since he never went away to school, he was never given a setdown. It is a hard thing for a man to grow up sweet and with a sense of humor when everyone calls him Master all his days."

Eugenie worked on tapestries for the seats and the kneeling stools in the pew. The altar cloth was embroidered by the women of the village, with Mistress Warrener in charge.

"Let us have wheat in it," Athel said. "Wheat and other growing things." And so that was done.

"I have invited the Mablethorpes over on Easter Monday so that they can see the church," Eugenie told Athel.

"The Mablethorpes!" He made it sound as though she had announced her intention of calling up the devil to stamp his hooves on the fresh-flagged floor.

"Certainly. Mistress Mablethorpe has been a friend of mine since I was a bride. They have taken a great interest in the design, which I showed to them on my last visit to their manor."

"But they are of the Roman faith. They won't want to cross the threshold of a Protestant church."

"Nonsense. They don't need a dispensation to look inside when there is no service being held. We are not living in the days of the Inquisition, you know."

"I won't have them here!"

"Would you shame me and rebuke the friendship your father had for them? You have never once invited the Mablethorpes here since your inheritance, and precisely on that account it has seemed necessary to me to do so."

Athel glowered at her. "Well, you must entertain them at your own house. I have never liked them."

"Yes, I remember your prejudices very well. One must at least credit you with constancy in them."

"You've a damned sharp tongue on you, Mother!"

"And you, my son, suffer from an unyielding heart and a chronic stiff neck."

It was the closest they had ever come to an outright quarrel. But he would not directly forbid her. Eugenie knew this, although she was less certain of his reasons. Did he have a filial love for her? It was so many years since he demonstrated anything beyond duty.

"Well, don't ask Corby to show them over the church. He has his principles and in my view he's entitled to 'em."

"I mind a time when Corby fancied the prettiest of the Mablethorpe girls"—Eugenie sighed—"but she married a Dorset man and died of the smallpox four years ago."

"What's that to the point?"

"Nothing. I was merely observing that Corby's principles are not inviolate."

Athel's scowl darkened. "He'd not compromise," he said staunchly. "I heard Corby talk when we were last at my Uncle Humphrey's house. I tell you a man of his faith would never be bought by a woman's smile."

"Maybe not. Your father bought him for twenty-eight pounds a year. However, enough of Corby. I do not require him to show us around the church which I have built. I have an intimate acquaintance with every stone of it."

It was sometimes Eugenie's whim to ride out to the farthest boundary of the estate. There was a track around the point, where the pine forest swept down to the very edge of the dunes, and it was possible for a careful rider to skirt the trees in summer and once beyond them to rest the eyes on nothing but sea and sky. She would go there when she wanted to be entirely alone with her thoughts.

> I'll wait for you where earth meets sky.
> I'll wait for you where sky meets sea.
> However long the time, I'll wait,
> Look for me, look for me.

That was an Italian song which had charmed her, and Matteo made a rough translation to fit the tune. She smiled and remembered.

It was, of course, a very desolate place. A wash of gray, and the pale sand. The red rocks of Elba had glowed in the evening sun above an aquamarine sea when Matteo sang to her. Such a contrast made the recollection bitter and sweet at once, as most worthwhile memories are.

Occasionally a farmboy would take the girl of his fancy to this lonely place. That was well known. But courting in Clere Athel must needs be reserved for evening when

221

work was done. At noon Eugenie could be confident of solitude, and she was startled, therefore, to round the point on a fine morning in early September and see a small boat beached just ahead of her.

It was still shining wet. She rode toward it curiously, wondering who among the villagers was so short of work that he would take out shrimping nets to feed his family. Her second thought was that the craft was larger than any belonging to Clere Athel.

An uneasy feeling tickled the nape of her neck while she sat her horse staring down into the boat. *No* nets. And the boat beached here instead of at the mouth of Little Rip where there was a channel for launching.

She was being watched, and suddenly aware and afraid, she wheeled her horse sharply to find two men standing behind her. For an instant she wondered whether to ride them down. They were strangers, and their clothes were not those of fishermen or country folk. Breeches, frogged coats—though now rimed and stiff with salt spray. The smaller of the two, a thickset fellow, had even a tricorn hat and the remnants of a pleated neckband. It was he who sprang forward and grasped her bridle.

"Not so fast, madam. We are in trouble here. Our sail was rent, and we have come ashore as the current carried us. Where are we?"

Eugenie noted his accent. A suggestion of a lilt, a full-tongued softness about certain consonants. Irish.

"You are six miles south of Upstrand on the coast of Lancashire."

"Upstrand, is it?" The tall man had the same accent, but more markedly. "Is that the nearest town?" She nodded curtly. *"You've* never ridden six miles." He looked her horse up and down, suspiciously.

"I did not say I had come from there. Our village of Clere Athel is just around the point." She gestured with her whip. "I am Eugenie Athelson."

There was a long pause. Her horse snorted in the freshening wind and sidled restlessly, but the man continued to hold the reins close to the bit.

"You'll be knowing the families hereabouts then?"

"Certainly."

"Name some of them."

"I shall do no such thing. Let go my horse this instant." She regretted her habit of riding out unattended. Usually Fionn loped beside her, but he had injured a paw which turned septic and she had left him chained up so that he could not follow her.

"Suppose I were to tell you that I had business with the Mablethorpes."

"And you came by boat?" she asked mockingly.

"How far is Mablethorpe Manor?"

No use to lie since the highway was signposted. "Four miles if you were a gull and could fly." She indicated the marshland below Clere Athel. "Eight and a half around by the road."

"Must we go by road?"

"I never heard of a man who walked that moss, even in summer. The ground is forever shifting."

"Can we hire horses in Clere Athel?"

Eugenie thought rapidly. She put together her assessment of the men and the fact of their being headed for the Mablethorpes'. Strange happenings had been reported that summer. There were those who told of riders landed from an Irish ship farther north, off Cockerham—as had been done long ago. Others said a fine bloodstock horse was ridden into Beacon Cross and abandoned in the middle of the night. An explanation occurred to her, and she would rather not have thought of it. "Strange doings," folks said. Strange thoughts voiced in the sawdust, smoke-filled inns, if Hannah's gossip was not mistaken. On market days men's talk was not only of the price of a pig. Servants' chatter—or did it really amount to rebellion? Could it possibly be true

223

that Prince Charles Edward Stuart, grandson of James II and pretender to the throne of England, was coming to recover his inheritance?

"If you look for horses anywhere on my son's estate, it will not"—she hesitated—"go unnoticed." That was as much as she could bring herself to say. Loyalties tugged her in different directions. She had no interest in the Catholic cause, yet she would have no friends suffer. The Mablethorpes were just such a family of the old faith as would rally to the flag of a Stuart. Catholic Lancashire landowners had been tried for treason in 1694. Then later, only thirty years since, there were violent demonstrations in the county when Queen Anne's crown passed to the Elector of Hanover. Jacobites were executed.

"There is a bridle path through the woods from here to the highway," she said. "You could walk." They looked at each other uncertainly. "Determined men could walk it in half a day. You might be at Mablethorpe Manor by nightfall."

"We could take the horse." It was the thickset man who spoke.

"I am very fond of this mare," Eugenie answered him directly. "And even if I were not—and even if I were more sympathetic to you than I am—it would be impossible for me to walk home without raising a hue and cry for the theft of her."

"The Mablethorpes will give us horses once we reach them," the taller man said.

"Very likely so. I will show you the path you may take." She began to walk her horse forward freely.

"You are not tricking us?" Again her reins were held.

"No. My husband, who is dead, had an old friendship for the family you seek. For the sake of that, I help you. . . . Here is the path." She gazed from one to the other. "I wish you will not lead anyone into folly. Sometimes one does better to compromise with events than to fight them by violent means."

They did not answer her but saluted with bows and

strode off along the tunnel of pines which she indicated.

Eugenie rode back to Clere Athel in a thoughtful mood, wishing with all her heart that the encounter might never have been and that, therefore, she need not fear for a family she knew to be worthy, honest and agreeable in every transaction of neighborly interest. She did not mention her adventure to anyone.

Nevertheless, long before dusk, it was known throughout the village that there had been strangers pass that way. The beached boat was discovered, which was inevitable. That proved nothing; it was merely a puzzle to the village.

Athel did not like it. "Who'd landed here, then . . . and why haven't we seen the men who rowed it?"

"Couldn't the boat have been washed up?" Eugenie suggested.

Her son was contemptuous. "Plenty of difference between the way a boat lies when it's brought in by the tide and the way it sets when its dragged up the shore. . . . Besides, there were tracks going off along the path through the wood. Don't make no sense to me, but it must have been someone who knew this part of the coast."

Eugenie watched him, concealing her anxiety. He stood with his feet planted wide apart on his own hearth, pulling at his lower lip in a worried way. His land. He hated the thought that anyone could even have brushed through a corner of it without his knowledge. His back to the firelight, it could easily have been his father. The familiar attitude. The hunched shoulders and the sunken chin. Brooding. She was just a little in awe of him, for once.

"You rode down that way today?" He darted the question at her.

"Yes—yes, I did."

"Didn't see anyone, I suppose?"

"I saw several people," Eugenie answered carefully. "Bertwold Cleper and Billy Fitch were cutting fence

225

posts in the coppice. Dolly Trapp was looking for one of her goslings, which had strayed. Mother Dowser was getting herbs on the edge of the moss."

Athel gestured irritably. "I meant strangers. . . . Well, of course you would have spoken of it if you had." He turned away, but Giles gave her an odd look, and she was uncomfortably aware of *his* scrutiny for the remainder of the evening.

It was some months since she had seen Mary Mablethorpe. Eugenie resolved to drive over and visit her within the next few days—not too soon lest she focus Athel's attention on them. Inwardly she cursed herself for having become involved, however distantly, with Jacobite activities.

XIV

CORBY was behaving in a most unusual manner. Even Athel, who never criticized him, remarked that he was "always jauntin' off somewhere these days." Still more curious, when he returned to the village between these forays, there was a sort of elation about him. He behaved in short, like a man proclaiming that he had a secret.

"What the devil's the matter with the fellow?" Giles said. "Forever taking letters into Upstrand. Last Thursday he had a package from Humphrey. I recognized the direction because it was brought up to the house, but

Corby never mentioned what was in it. What do you imagine it means?"

Eugenie could not make any sense of it either. Two weeks later she thought she had been extremely slow-witted not to guess.

Corby's triumphant announcement that he had been gathering information on various Lancashire families which might indicate where their loyalty would lie in the event of a rebellion was made in church on a Sunday.

"Good people of Clere Athel, stalwart upholders of the true and only faith! When I am not occupied with my duties among you, do you think I am idle?" His congregation had given very little thought to what he did with his spare time, but there was a mild ripple of curiosity.

Giles leaned across the pew to Eugenie. "Is he going to tell us that he has a mistress in Upstrand?"

"You may think," Corby continued, "that there is a man who sits back in his office, content to usher you in and out of the world with due forms of service. Not so. When I serve the Lord, I do so with a sword in my hand as well as a chalice."

"He has his hands full," Giles said. Athel turned to frown at his uncle disapprovingly and then leaned forward, listening intently.

"There are those—many of whom rub shoulders with you on a market day—would gladly bring in Scots and Irish, aye, and French soldiers to our beloved country. They would see you slain and see your children slain in the path toward the throne of a ne'er-do-well boy. Papists are around us. Treason abounds. In such times I have seen my duty clearly. My God calls me, and like Samuel, I have answered. . . . Good people I urge you to stand fast by your only true king, your Protestant king. Fight treachery with guile. Gather what information you can and bring it to me. In the conflict which lies ahead let it be clearly seen that Clere Athel is a stronghold of loyalty, a bastion of righteousness. In the past we have pursued a worthy ideal of tolerance, seeking only to live at peace among our neighbors, but we were deceived in them. . . ." Master Corby paused to draw a vital breath and then addressed himself pointedly to Athel. "These same people we have trusted, and who have enjoyed the hospitality of our manors, would think nothing of plunging this country into civil war to gain their own ends. . . . They would lay waste the land. . . ."

Eugenie saw Athel's face darken. Did he believe all that Corby was saying? Did she herself believe one-quarter of it? Was it likely that Mary Mablethorpe's son had involved himself in a serious plot against the king? He was a hotheaded boy, and since his father's death two years ago there was no older, cannier man to guide him. She thought of the mysterious visitors on the seashore and blamed herself for not having gone at once to Mablethorpe manor.

Violent rainstorms made the roads impassable. It was hard to find an excuse for a jaunt in such weather. Nevertheless, she should have made the effort. Perhaps her warning would come too late now. Corby was not a man to make wild accusations without proof, and there could be no doubt that his sermon was directed at their neighbors.

And why do I care? Eugenie asked herself. Corby's sermon ran on, invoking the heavens themselves to justify his arguments. *The Mablethorpes are nothing to me*, she reasoned. But if her husband were still alive, he *would* warn them. He would curse them for the trouble he was at . . . but he would warn them just the same. She felt instinctively that the Jacobite endeavor could not succeed. Gallant even in the face of certain defeat—yes, that was typical of these stubborn north-countrymen.

After the service they went back to the house for dinner, and she followed Giles to the library.

"I must speak to you."

"I wondered how long it would be. I knew you had something on your conscience."

She told him everything, of her encounter on the beach and her fears, and consulted him what should be done.

Giles did not fail her. "We should get a message to Mary Mablethorpe. That is the least we can do. It's clear Corby knows something, and we can be sure he is passing his information on to Humphrey."

"Humphrey will relate the names of those families who are disloyal?"

"Of course. Did you expect otherwise? The laying of such information will advance his political career." Giles' mouth twisted. "I do not care to be on the side of rebellion, because rebellion brings destruction. . . . But we have a duty to our friends." He stared into space for a moment. "I would see the whole country go up in one mighty conflagration if it chose and if it left Clere Athel untouched. My brother would have said the same. . . . We are at war with France now—my God, I ask you, when have we ever *not* been at war with the French . . . or with the Spanish? Still, the Mablethorpes are old friends. They have a claim on us. We must warn them."

"In this season what excuse can I make? How can I get to them?"

"There is none. We shall have to tell Athel the truth."

Eugenie stared at him. "He will stop me from going. You know how he feels about Clere Athel."

"You must try just the same. Tell him his father would have wished it."

Eugenie had a painful scene with her son. "Take no man of Athel into this enterprise," he told her sternly. "We will not be involved."

"I must have Matthew as my coachman."

"Warn him then. I wish no man of mine to go unawares betwixt two armies. . . . You know that this vagabond, Charles Edward, has entered Edinburgh. . . . I tell you this, madam, that I will dig a ditch around Clere Athel and I will fill it with fire and die in it before I allow any invader to take one foot's breadth possession here."

Eugenie warned Matthew of the danger of their journey.

"We'll go with you," he said simply. "My lad, Seth, will come up behind."

"And I will escort you," Giles added.

"You will do no such thing. The journey at this time of the year would be uncomfortable. Think of the jolts and your leg."

"I am thinking more of you," Giles remarked coolly. "There is news that Charles Edward is marching toward Lancaster."

"It is unlikely that I shall be molested at my age."

"Very unlikely. However, I shall still accompany you."

They set off at ten o'clock of the morning. As Giles could not resist remarking, he doubted Eugenie had ever had her face made up and her hair arranged at such an hour before. She agreed almost absentmindedly that he was very probably correct.

The roads were worse than she feared, and she watched his grimaces of pain as they lurched along, feeling each one of them acutely for him.

They were a scant five miles along the highroad when the coach suddenly plunged downward as though it had gone into an abyss. For an instant there was a slithering and a scrabbling and the sound of the terrified horses. Matthew's voice crying out in alarm and calling for his boy to jump clear. Then a splintering of wood—not a sharp crack—a slow tearing. For what seemed like a passage of minutes, but could only have been seconds, the coach hung and swayed and gradually subsided.

"My God," Eugenie said. "So typical of us to be on a heroic mission and to get upset in the road."

It was the last utterance she was to make before they descended in a splintering of the glass windows and a rushing in of dark, muddy water. She struck her head against the doorframe and lost consciousness.

The shaft and the traces had broken, which was probably a mercy since otherwise the horses might have tumbled backward into the mire on top of the coach. As it was, Matthew, hanging on desperately, was dragged and slightly stunned before his well-schooled animals steadied and came to a halt. Seth ran to his father first to see that he was safe, and then the two of them set about wrestling open the door of the coach, which had become its topside.

The frame was buckled, hindering their efforts, and all the while Giles struggled to hold Eugenie's head above the muddy water. It was not deep enough to drown a standing man, and once Matthew had ascertained this, and finding their attempts to free the door ineffectual, he sent his son to the next farm along the road to bring back every able-bodied man he could find.

They took four hours to get the door free. Giles supported Eugenie, cradling her head against his chest, bracing his weight against the sodden velvet seat, now perpendicular, and bearing the strain on his one good leg.

There was a frail November sunlight edging into Eugenie's room when she opened her eyes. Hannah sat in a chair mending the lace on a shift. She did not look up, and for several minutes Eugenie said nothing but lay struggling with dim thoughts. She remembered the coach . . . there had been an accident . . . yes, that was it—an accident . . . then swirling water. How did she now come to be in her own bed? It *was* her bed. She knew the pink brocade valance with its looped fringes. And it was her own room, for she recognized the swagged velvet drapes at the windows which wavered uncertainly in the distance.

"Hannah, have I been ill?" It was an effort to speak, yet the effort seemed to strengthen her, bringing back reality. The sound of her own voice was reassuring.

Hannah rose at once and came to lean over her.

"Have I been long abed?"

"Seven days," Hannah said. "Praise be you are talking

to me! We feared you might never speak again. . . . The physician was confident. Just a knock on the head, he said. Seen many cases like it before. But you lay so still you frightened me. I've scarcely dared leave you for an instant."

"I want to sit up."

"Oh, I don't think you should do that. Not yet."

"Yes, I should. My head is clearing wonderfully. I believe I even feel hungry."

"Praise be!" Hannah said again.

"Well, then don't just stand there exclaiming over me, woman. Get me some chicken broth."

When she had eaten, she slept again; then by five o'clock she was awake, feeling much stronger and insisting that Hannah fetch a bath and brush her hair.

The exertion was tiring, but her head was full of questions. She wanted to know about Giles. Was Hannah perfectly sure that he had not been injured?

Hannah replied that he had not and described how he had held Eugenie up when the coach overturned in a rain-filled rut in the road.

"They do say as how it was five feet deep if it was an inch and you'd certainly have drowned when you lost your senses if Master Giles hadn't kept your head above the water."

"Dear Giles." Eugenie smiled. "God bless him! . . . Does he know that I am recovered? I daresay he will pay me a visit this evening." She studied her reflection in the dressing-table mirror and added almost gaily, "In that case I must wear something becoming. The taffeta contouche will be the thing . . . and my prettiest muslin cap. . . ." The other woman's lack of response made her turn around. "What is the matter? Why do you look at me so?"

"It is nothing," Hannah said quickly. "Master Giles took a chill in the water, that is all. He is confined to his bed, and therefore, he cannot come to see you just at present."

"A chill—but you should have told me at once. You

232

know how dangerous it is for him. Is he fevered? Is he breathing easily?"

"I've been nursing *you*, not Master Giles." Hannah spoke tartly because she was anxious. "Now there's no need for you to put yourself in a dither. The physician said that once you began to recover you must have rest and quiet. I am sure Master Giles will be better in a day or two."

Eugenie studied her searchingly. "I will go and see him tomorrow. Tomorrow I shall be stronger."

"You will do nothing of the kind. The physician charged me to see that you did not leave your room for at least another week. I sent a message to him, and he is calling to look at you in the morning. I shall keep you here, even if I have to lock you in!"

Hannah facing her implacably, hands on hips, would be quite capable of doing such a thing.

"But I must talk to Giles. I have to find out whether he managed to get a message to the Mablethorpes." Eugenie pressed her hands to her throbbing temples. "I must know what has been happening; otherwise I shall get no rest tonight."

"Well, I don't approve of you bothering yourself with such matters at the moment, but if it will comfort you —yes, a message was taken. Matthew took it. He told me that he doubted it would do much good because young Mablethorpe has it firmly in his head that they'll win. There's word that Charles Edward has five thousand men behind him and is heading for Lancaster. No one's trying to stop him so far, and he's picking up supporters on the way."

"It seems incredible. Surely the government will send an army to meet them."

"Aye, Master Corby says they're raising the standards now, and Duke William will lead them. Anyway it's nowt to us who wins or loses since we've friends on both sides hereabouts. And one thing's certain, no army will march through Clere Athel."

That was true enough, Eugenie reflected. The moss looked after its own, as her husband had been fond of saying when she complained of its dangers to the children. Local youngsters were taught the safe paths by one of the game wardens, just as soon as they were old enough to go off on their own. And that same eerie, treacherous expanse, which looked so solid one minute and in the next, awakened by the tide, stirred with a sucking and a bubbling, had guarded Clere Athel from many unwelcome visitors. The messengers of feudal barons in long-ago days; even of kings. Together with innumerable tax collectors they were all said to have been "lost in the moss." That they were sometimes thrust there at a scythe's end or directed thither along a path which did not exist added to the enjoyment of the men of Athel when they told these tales. . . . No. An army would never choose this route, would not even forage in these parts.

The next morning saw Eugenie so much recovered that she was dressed and had taken a breakfast.

"Now send Matthew to me. I must thank him for what he did."

"Matthew is under threat of being turned off," Hannah disclosed.

"Turned off? Has Athel forgotten that the man works for me or was he anticipating my death?"

"Athel said he'd turn the family out of the cottage. You don't own the cottage. Could he do that, do you think?"

Eugenie smiled grimly. "He could. But he won't. I know precisely how to deal with my son."

So Matthew was fetched and, despite a brisk tidying by cook, brought with him sufficient evidence of his conscientious labor upon Eugenie's horses.

"Won't walk on your fine carpet," he said simply. "Stand here by the door."

"Carpets *are* for walking on," Eugenie replied, "else they would be hung on the ceiling."

Matthew grinned.

"I have to thank you," Eugenie continued simply.

234

"You saved my life. You also performed a great service to our friends, but I understand that in doing so you displeased my son and have been made to suffer for it."

"Aye, Athel Athelson was mad as Cleper's bull. He said that if I'd been seen by a government spy, it would ha' looked as if he himself sent me. Said I'd gone without authority and put Clere Athel in danger."

"You need have no fear. I will make sure that you come to no hardship for what you did. Indeed, it is my intention to reward you."

"I told my old 'ooman you'd make all right, but she's been lying awake night after night, feared for the roof over our heads. . . . I knew I done what I ought!" He hesitated. "Mind you, I'll never forgive myself over Master Giles. He said he wasn't hurt, and at the time I never thought how the wetting would harm him."

Eugenie said, "But Master Giles has merely taken a chill. He will soon make a recovery. You have nothing with which to reproach yourself."

"Is that a fact? Well, bless my soul if that isn't the best news yet! Everyone in the village given him up for dead. Said he wouldn't see another sun."

Hannah, entering two minutes later, found Eugenie still standing where Matthew had left her.

"Are you faint, my lady? . . . Let me help you back to your bed. You have tired yourself."

"Hannah! What is this about Master Giles?"

"About Master Giles?" Hannah's voice faltered.

"Matthew said he was dying." She rapped the words out relentlessly, for herself as well as for Hannah. "Is it true? Why did you keep it from me?"

"You are still weak. You mustn't be upset. What could I do?"

"How dared you?" Eugenie demanded in anguish. "How could you?"

She was across the room to her dressing closet, tearing open the door and pulling out a cloak. "Call for my chair. Why do you stand there? I must go to him at once."

235

"But you cannot go out. The physician said—"

"Devil take the physician! Do you think I care for his opinion at such a time? Call for my chair, or I shall run across the park."

Word preceded Eugenie, and by the time she reached the manor house her daughter-in-law was waiting at the door.

"Madam, you should not have left your bed so soon. This is most unwise. I was coming to see you this afternoon to assure you that everything possible was being done for Uncle Giles."

"They say he will not live." Eugenie's voice was flat and cold.

"No. I am so sorry." Kitty pressed her hand sympathetically. "I'm afraid it can only be a little while now."

"Where is Athel? Is he with his uncle?"

Kitty looked discomforted and stumbled over the explanation that he had gone to a main in Upstrand.

"He has gone to watch a *cockfight* while his uncle dies?"

"He said it might be the last chance to try his new bird for some time, the rebel army already being in Lancaster," Kitty apologized.

"Of course. And he has ever had a proper sense of what was fitting conduct for a gentleman," Eugenie said contemptuously. "Well, never mind, my child. You are not to blame. I will go to Giles. He shall have one at least of the family to watch at the side of his deathbed."

There was a maid sitting in the corner of Giles' room, but Eugenie gestured to her to leave and sank down on her knees beside the bed.

Once again she heard the same dreadful sound she heard when her husband was dying, the rasping inward breath, the choking at the end of it. Once again there was a pungent smell of the crystals being burned on the fire to help the patient.

Giles turned dilated eyes toward her. His lips moved, but no words came.

236

"My dear . . . best beloved of men . . . I only came to my senses yesterday, and no one told me you were ill."

He shaped the single word "Die."

"No, you are not going to die. What nonsense. You must fight this. You must get well." He shook his head. The awful struggle for a little air. It tortured her to watch so that she lost her composure completely and cried out, "You *cannot* die, for then how should I continue without you?"

Very tenderly she took the hand which crept toward her across the quilt and enfolded it in her own. "Now, you are going to let me look after you." She crooned the words to him, as though he were a child who must be coaxed. "I am here and I shall not leave you or allow you talk about dying."

There was a glimmer of a smile, but he shook his head again. Then seemed to signal something to her. He lifted his hand with an effort and frowned.

"What is it? What is it? . . . My cap?" Eugenie tugged at the ribbons under her chin and, casting the fragment of lace aside, released her hair.

With infinite pain Giles' fingers groped toward one long strand which tumbled over her shoulder and twined themselves within it. . . .

Eugenie knew the moment when he died. There was a sound, a terrible final agitation.

"Oh, God, dear God, carry the soul of this man very quickly to a pleasant place. He has found it hard to live his life through, here on earth. Give him rest and ease where you have taken him. Make him whole—as he has longed to be. Take ten years off my life, take twenty, take whatever you require . . . only carry him to a happier existence than he has known. . . ."

Eugenie was not aware of the passing hours. She would never know how long she knelt and prayed beside Giles, as his body stiffened beneath the sheets. It was, in any case, impossible to move. In the convulsion of death he had wound her hair so tightly about his fingers that she could not free herself even if she had wished to do so.

Kitty Hatton, understanding more than she could express and not wishing her mother-in-law to be disturbed, gave orders that no servant should enter the room until Eugenie rang the bell. They waited three hours before they went in and found her kneeling patiently beside the bed.

Nor could they open the fist which held her hair.

"We shall have to break his fingers," Heskettson said at last, reluctantly.

"No." Eugenie's tone was commanding. "Not that. Not that under any circumstances! Fetch scissors, Kitty, and cut the hair." She spoke without emotion." And then as Kitty hesitated, she added: "What is a lock of hair? I will not have Giles' corpse disturbed for the sake of it."

So they cut the hair, and when Giles was laid out, they let him take it to his grave. They arranged his hands across his chest, as was proper, and the one tightly clenched fist still held Eugenie's hair.

It was the custom—the fashionable custom—to bury people who had any social position or connection at night. This pleased Athel well, since his farmers would not feel bound to take time off work to attend.

"Your father was buried at noon," Eugenie pointed out when the arrangements were discussed. "I should have thought the same time of day fitting for your Uncle Giles. After all, he was the senior member of the family. And we are not concerned with what is modish in Clere Athel."

"It was different for my father," Athel said. "He was master here."

That was true enough, but she wanted to be sure Giles would have a good attendance at his funeral. She could not bear for him to slip away from the world without his passing duly acknowledged. The people of Clere Athel were unpredictable. Would they come to a midnight ceremony?

238

They came. Every last man and woman of the village who could walk and every child of an age to appreciate the solemnity of the occasion. They came with lanterns from the steeps of Godwin's Field and the lower edge, by the moss. They said among themselves that when one had known Master Giles, one had, indeed, known a man . . . that he was his brother's brother and his father's son . . . and though none of these tributes would have been intelligible to the outside world, they weighed a good deal in Clere Athel.

Master Corby kept his address brief. He spoke of Giles as a man of learning, a man who had "placated the deficits of the body by culturing the mind." Eugenie found no comfort in his words and even disliked his choice of them.

In procession from the church to the dank, earth-scented vault, Eugenie led the way as chief mourner, the only one of Giles' generation to be present. Her face was pale and expressionless under the fur-lined hood of her black velvet cloak.

Falling back to form a pathway of light for the family, the villagers watched Giles Athelson's coffin pass by with respect. But since death was the only drama which ever came their way, they must be forgiven a certain relish of the spectacle.

"Long coffin," Noah Tyte could be clearly heard to inform his neighbours. "Reckon that's the longest coffin I ever put a nail to." They watched it pass, pleased for Giles that he should have excelled in such a thing.

"Her ladyship, very stately." Mistress Warrener nodded approvingly. "And she don't seem to change, do she, not with all the years 'as passed since she come here."

Here came Athel Athelson. There was a wary silence as he passed, with his hand on the shoulder of his eldest son. They did not trust him in the way they had trusted his father. There was talk that he intended to enclose part of the common land and take it into the home farm. Who had ever heard of such a thing? Still, the little lad

239

was promising. In a hard time Clere Athel could always look to the future. And Kitty Hatton—"Sweet Kitty"—drew their smiles, even upon such a solemn occasion as this.

In the vault, Honesty Hawkshead, the mason, conscious of the importance of the part he had to play, tested the mix of his mortar and began to prepare an inscribed stone which would close up the cavity in the wall where the coffin was placed.

It was he who would relate to the rest of the village what happened next. He would tell his story this way —and it would be told and told again long afterward.

"I'm dressin' me stone, aren't I, and all of a sudden the Lady Eugenie steps past me, takes summat out of her muff and puts it atop of the coffin. . . . 'What's that?' says Athel, very sharp. He picks it up and looks at it under the light of his lantern. 'Pretty,' says he. 'It's gold, isn't it? . . .' My lady answers that it *is* gold, and summat called onyx.

"Well, I can see plain as the nose on your face what's goin' on in Athel Athelson's mind. . . . 'Cost a pretty penny, I should think,' he says. 'Why put it in a tomb? Uncle Giles don't need it where he's gone.' Her ladyship don't answer directly. She gives Athel a kind of stare, and you can see she's thinking plenty. Then she comes out with a very odd thing: 'Perhaps I have a need to give it to him.' She shrugs her shoulders in that Frenchified way of hers. 'Call it a whim,' and she takes the box from him and puts it back on the coffin.

" 'Deuced expensive whim,' says Athel scowling at her. For a minute I think she's going to fly into a proper rage, but she seems to change her mind and to my surprise gives the best half of a smile. 'I can afford it. I have nothing else to give now but gold . . . and after all, I am a very rich woman.' "

240

Afterword

THE outcome of the '45 rebellion is well known. In the perspective of this one tiny community in Lancashire it might almost never have been. Bonnie Prince Charlie's army passed by Clere Athel on the march south and also in retreat. A few adventurous lads, gone out specially to look for it, no doubt came back with tales to tell of the brave sight of the clans, but older folk congratulated themselves on never having seen "hair or hide" of a single soldier.

Master Corby, fancying himself as an archplotter, liked to think that he kept his flock informed of events in the outside world. But in fact there was more to be learned in Upstrand, in the taproom of the Drovers' Arms any day of the week. It was Jarrod, noted for a strong elbow when it came to raising a pint, who was able to tell Eugenie that two hundred Lancashire Catholics had joined the Stuart at Manchester, under the leadership of Colonel Francis Towneley, of Towneley Hall; Jarrod, who was the first to know young Mablethorpe was not among them, because at the last moment his mother's good sense had prevailed.

The army got as far as Derby before losing its nerve. Prince Charles was a young and untried commander. He inspired affection not confidence. His officers, unnerved by the lack of opposition to their advance and suspecting a trap, urged him to retreat. Five days before

Christmas he was back in Carlisle. There he left Towneley to try to hold the town against pursuing forces under the Duke of Cumberland. Lancashire Catholics melted away. Some of them would preserve their faith, but most of them would abandon their Jacobite loyalties forever.

Carlisle was taken, and three months after Prince Charles was finally defeated at Culloden Moor, Towneley paid for his treason with his head. Charles Edward Stuart escaped to Europe and ultimately drank himself to death in Rome.

In 1751 Athel enclosed practically all that remained of the common land. There was real hardship among the poorest villagers, and even the more prosperous farmers thought shame on him to have done such a thing. From that time forward he had written himself into the long history of his people as a greedy master.

Eugenie's decision to make the village a present of a new schoolhouse in 1752 was possibly a means to provide employment. The following year her account book shows her almost feverishly engaged in having her carriage sweep redressed, a washhouse enlarged, a window knocked out in one place and put into another. One might justifiably conclude that she did everything possible to keep money flowing.

Then, in 1757, Athel was killed by a fall from his horse. I cannot believe there is any truth in the popular legend that he brought himself to his death jumping one of his own enclosing hedges. Family records say he had a young, untried horse, which was startled by hares rising out of a cornfield. That seems more likely.

His son, succeeding to his inheritance at the age of seventeen years, called a memorable meeting of the witan. With the approval of his mother, he announced the reopening of the common land.

It seems ironic that Eugenie's eldest son should not live to inherit her vast fortune, which had been even further increased by Madeleine's death and the reversion of Carle House. To give him the benefit of the doubt, he

242

may have had excellent plans for its use. He cared for the land, if not so much for his people.

Eugenie's two remaining sons both prospered. Thurstan built himself a successful career—as much out of need, as anything, since he fathered six daughters. He visited his mother frequently, gradually assuming responsibility for her financial affairs, as well as those requiring litigation.

Dickon settled permanently in Barbados and acquired his own plantation through marriage to the daughter and heiress of a French marquis. There is one rather romantic story to tell about him: His marriage was said to have been wonderfully happy, and when his wife predeceased him, he rewrote his will, laying a peculiar condition of inheritance upon his son. The family home, he decreed, must be burned down and his son must build himself a new one. "Lest at any time in the future a bothersome marriage should defile the place where your mother and I lived, in loving companionship and true accord."

Kitty Athelson lived to the age of ninety-two. In 1765, when her eldest son brought a bride home to the manor, she retired to share the dower house with Eugenie. Kitty kept a sporadic diary, and we have a picture of the dowagers sharing two remarkable obsessions—trying to grow pineapples and attempting to get the fountain bell to work. It is a happy thought that continuing with these hobbies long after her mother-in-law's death, Kitty finally sat down to a homegrown pineapple at the supper table. She ceases to mention the fountain bell after 1790, and one must assume either that she gave up the project or that the wretched thing continued to disoblige her to the end.

There is just one final touch to this story. I write it with some misgivings, and yet I cannot resist the inclination to put it in. I am indebted to Kitty's diary.

Eugenie died in 1770 and was given an elaborate funeral. There is a welter of details and an account of the costs. And among them, briefly noted, the fact that when a cavity was being opened for her coffin, part of the wall of the vault collapsed. The only resting place to be seriously disturbed was that of Giles Athelson.

In an inventory made after Kitty's death in 1814, there is listed "a box of gold with an onyx lid (damaged)." Surely this must be the one I have been writing about. Is it too fantastic to believe that the box fell out when the wall tumbled? And did "Sweet Kitty," perhaps having heard the story of the properties of onyx from her mother-in-law, deliberately decide not to replace it? You will remember the legend: that a gift of onyx "openly given and willingly received" has the power to break a spell binding two people together. Kitty was not the kind of person to take such a trinket out of mere covetousness. It is just possible that having known them both, she reached a sentimental conclusion. Giles would never willingly accept a gift that would separate him from Eugenie. Perhaps now they are together forever.